The Far Side of the Bridge

James H. Lilley

PublishAmerica
Baltimore

First printing

ISBN: 1-59286-563-1
PUBLISHED BY PUBLISHAMERICA BOOK PUBLISHERS
www.publishamerica.com
Baltimore

Printed in the United States of America

Dedicated to
Patrolman Randolph Eugene Brightwell
of the Howard County, Maryland Police Department
who made the ultimate sacrifice
when he was shot and killed in the line of duty
May 29, 1961.

ACKNOWLEDGEMENTS

I would like to thank Lieutenant Sam Bowerman of the Baltimore County, Maryland Police Department for taking time to offer his expertise in compiling the killer's psychological profile for this book. His expert knowledge and understanding were very instrumental to the completion of this work. I would also like to thank my niece, Terry Allen, and Corporal Kevin Costello of the Howard County, Maryland Police Department for their time and skills in proof reading the manuscript. I want to recognize the following members of the Howard County Police: Mr. R. C. Bartley, Supervisor of the Forensic Services Division for his contributions to this book, Corporal Joe Baran for his expert skill in helping to create and design the cover for this book and to Al Hafner for assisting with photographs. To Dean Clark I offer my thanks for his computer magic when my skills faltered.

I owe a sincere note of gratitude to Mr. Takeshi Miyagi. In 1963 Mr. Miyagi became my karate teacher. As time passed I found him to be more than a teacher. He stood as a positive role model and taught me much more than a martial art. He taught me patience and understanding and a way to see things through the eyes of others. In that we forged a bond of friendship that has lasted for over 39 years.

As always, I can never say enough to express my love and thanks to my lovely wife, Jody, for her support and encouragement along the way. When she first came into my life I often called her the little pest who wouldn't go away. Well, she's been my loving little pest for over 15 years now. Without her love and caring none of this would be possible.

One

"Death by strangulation." The voice of Doctor Sidney Wexler rose above those of Forensic Technicians who scoured the crime scene for evidence. His diagnosis for cause of death had become all too familiar in recent months.

"Any evidence of sexual assault?" Captain Karl Thomas, Commander of the Criminal Investigations Bureau, said, his tone rather matter-of-fact.

"There appears to be traces of semen at the vaginal entrance."

"So, the Society Stalker strikes again."

"Looks that way."

Detective Jefferson Daniel Lewis stepped into the doorway of the library, nudged his trademark black Stetson back and looked around the room. Lewis shook his head, knowing the Society Stalker had claimed the life of his fourth victim, raping and then strangling her in the library of the spacious mansion. Police and the scores of reporters covering the crimes had tagged the killer with his nickname after he chose to prey upon the wives of very wealthy and extremely successful businessmen.

He committed cold, premeditated acts of violence in an area where previously crime was only talked about in whispers over cocktails at lavish parties. This killer dared to invade neighborhoods where cars with names such as Lamborghini and Ferrari were mere play toys for those living in million-dollar mansions.

"Detective Lewis," Captain Thomas said, looking in his direction, "come in. Join the party."

"Yes, sir," he said, thinking, *rape and murder sure is one hell of a party.*

"Looks just like the other cases."

"Damn," Lewis muttered. "It sure would be nice to find a motive for these killings."

"Maybe their wives were screwin' around on 'em. Maybe their husbands didn't really leave town but sneaked back later and whacked the bitches," Thomas said with no attempt to disguise his sarcasm.

Lewis ignored the comment and asked himself the same questions he'd

5

asked about the other crime scenes. How did the killer bypass the elaborate security systems in the homes of his victims? How did he know their husbands were out of town? Why were there no signs of forced entry? The answers, naturally, would seem to be the victims knew their killer. But why did he send each of them a letter telling her he was watching her? It didn't make sense.

The victims, two to six weeks prior to their deaths, received a standard white business envelope with a letter detailing their activities. The letters always concluded by telling the victim in which room of the house she would meet her demise. And in each case his prediction proved to be true.

Amanda French was discovered by her husband, lying on their bed. Cynthia Wellington was found in the kitchen and Alexandra Upchurch on the floor of the garage. Now, Kimberly McDougal was located in the library. All of their hands were bound behind their backs, clothing torn and a piece of black rope knotted tightly around their throats. And, in each case, the victim had been sexually assaulted.

"Any suspects yet?" Wexler said, looking at Lewis. And for a moment he thought the young detective would have been more comfortable in another era. Perhaps back in towns like Tombstone or Dodge, strapping on a six-gun and walking down the dusty streets at sunset.

He shook his head and said, "Hundreds, Doc. Hundreds." The suspect list, he thought, was longer than most. There were alarm and security company employees to interview. Catering services and landscaping companies. Construction and remodeling firms, all employing from five to, in some instances, over two hundred persons. Not to be forgotten were maids, cooks, butlers and chauffeurs.

"That kid has to shoulder a lot of responsibility," Wexler said to Thomas. "A boy his age and still green in the bureau assigned to investigate the stalker killings."

"Yeah. But, he'll grow up in a hurry. I have confidence in him."

"Your confidence in him won't necessarily solve these crimes. That won't win either of you a popularity contest around here."

"Hey, Doc, Lewis is like a shark when it gets the scent of blood. A little sniff of blood and he starts searching for the source. Circling. Moving in for the kill. That boy doesn't miss a thing. He's more meticulous than all the guys I have in the bureau put together. I can count on him tracking down every last clue until he solves a case."

"Sure," he said, closing the black bag. "But, so far, he hasn't got much to go on in these cases."

"I'm not worried. So far he has a damn good batting average," he said, glancing at his watch. "Look, I've gotta stop by the office. Check with Lewis if you need anything else," he muttered and headed for the door.

Lewis stood by the far wall of the library, looking over the scene in front of him. He carefully studied the details of the room, from the custom-built bookshelves to the walnut table in the center of the room. His eyes scanned left to right, back to front, and when the process ended, he began again. He knew he couldn't afford to overlook anything. If he failed to find a piece of evidence, any clue at all that would solve the case, he'd be chastised for months.

He didn't like having the stalker killings dumped in his lap. But, like any new investigator assigned to the bureau, he was saddled with the cases no one else wanted.

When the stalker murders began the cases were practically fought over, for surely the detective who solved them would reap many rewards. However, as time passed without so much of a hint as to a suspect in the grim killings, the shuffle to unload them became almost frantic. Although the reasons for passing the cases on were many, it was an unspoken fact that no detective wanted to be known as the one who failed to solve the murders of such prominent citizens.

"Detective Lewis, may I have the body removed now?" Wexler said.

He nodded. "Yes, sir."

The Deputy Medical Examiner signaled the men behind him to remove the corpse from the scene. "It certainly looks like the killer's the same as in the other three cases," he said to Lewis. "Pattern's the same."

"Yeah. It looks like a carbon copy of the others," he said as he began to walk once more around the room.

"Are you looking for anything in particular?"

He removed his Stetson and scratched his head. "Doc, I'm not sure exactly what the hell I'm lookin' for. But this whole thing bothers me."

"How's that?"

"I know you've been to more crime scenes like this than me. But doesn't this strike you as odd? I mean, doesn't this murder scene look almost too neat to you?"

Wexler put his hand to his chin. "Hmmm. You know, I've never given much thought to it. But, now that you mention it, this does seem unusually clean. And the others, they were—how do you put it? Intact?"

"Together, Doc. Together. Everything in place. No evidence of a struggle. That would seem to indicate that the victims were completely surprised by their attacker. But I can't buy that. Especially since each of them received a letter from the killer. He warned them. They sure as hell would've been more alert."

"Unless they didn't believe the letter."

"Well, I could see that happening with the first victim. She might've taken it as a joke. But when she was murdered the others should've really put their guard up."

The doctor watched as Lewis slowly circled the room, looking for any piece of evidence that would identify a suspect. He waited for a minute and then said, "Do you have any thoughts about a possible suspect?"

"Oh, I have lots of thoughts about theses cases. But not one damn hint about who's doing this. Christ, according to Grayson and Hargrove there's at least three hundred and fifty suspects."

"How many have they interviewed?"

"In the beginning, I guess they talked to a couple dozen. But when they didn't lock anybody up in the first few days they started backpedaling. Now that I have the cases, I have to start over."

Wexler was perplexed. "Don't they share information with you?"

He laughed. "You know, I'm not exactly one of their favorite people. They won't give me the time of day, let alone share information on the stalker. They said they don't wanna taint my views."

"I take it they're still pissed off about you solving a bunch of their old cases, huh?"

"Yeah. I guess so," he said, dropping to his knees to look under the table. "If I get lucky and solve these murders it won't be because of an overabundance of help."

"Well, I guess it's time for me to be going," Wexler said, reaching for his bag. "I guess I'll see you first thing in the morning."

"Yes, sir. I'll be there."

"Good luck. And, listen—if there's anything I can do to help you, please don't hesitate to call."

"Thanks. I appreciate the offer. And, believe me, if I have a question I'll call."

Lewis crossed the room and slid the black leather chair out from the highly polished walnut desk. He took off his Stetson, placed it on the desk and sat down in the large comfortable chair.

He leaned back and locked his hands behind his head as he tried to visualize the crime scenes again. From the bedroom, kitchen and garage to the library, the links were the same. An attractive, early to late forties woman, raped and murdered in her home. Killed in a place where she felt safe and secure from the crime in the outside world.

The killer was precise in his method of execution. The hands of the victims were always bound in the same fashion. The black rope knotted on the right side of the throat. The tearing of the clothes and sexual assault of the women. The baffling neatness of the crime scenes, as though he'd cleaned and straightened the rooms prior to his departure, leaving the bodies of his victims as the only immediate visible evidence of a crime. In this case, Kimberly McDougal was left on the lavish white carpet of the library floor. Her red nightgown was torn from neck to hem. An expression of shocked terror masked the face of a once beautiful and vibrant woman. A look which seemed to ask, *why?*

He got out of the chair, picked up his hat and walked toward the door. There were questions to ask, reports to write and hours to spend poring over notes and laboratory sheets, hoping to find a killer before he picked his next victim and snuffed out another innocent life. Tasks he would perform alone as usual. But, truth be known, he preferred it that way. He'd always been a loner. Even as a child.

Two

Lewis got off the elevator on the basement level of the building housing the Office of the Chief Medical Examiner. His footsteps echoed in the corridor as he passed the table where bodies about to be examined were cleaned and then photographed by the ceiling-mounted camera.

He paused in the doorway of the autopsy room and glanced at the bodies lying atop stainless steel gurneys which were situated precisely in front of bright stainless steel sinks and tables. The cutting room. A place where fortune and fame gave no status or position of priority. Rich or poor, they arrived in the cutting room atop the gurney, naked and toe tag attached.

He didn't like it here. Never had. It wasn't that he couldn't stomach the sights, sounds and smells associated with autopsies. It was the unpleasant memories the room always seemed to drag up that he disliked. For reasons he couldn't understand, this place reminded him of the hospital room where his father told him many years ago, "Mommy's very sick."

Suddenly the woman who read bedtime stories with happy endings to him was too sick to hold the small colorful books. The lovely lady with the bright smile who dried his tears, cleansed his skinned knees and assured him everything would be just fine was going away. Five-year-old Jefferson Daniel Lewis couldn't understand why the woman he called Mommy, the person who held his hand and told him how much she loved him, would want to go away. Yet, on a cloudy autumn afternoon, as a crisp breeze chased fallen brown leaves across unfamiliar ground, she was carried away by a group of people and placed in the back of a large black vehicle someone called a hearse.

A procession of cars followed the hearse out of town to a place where they passed under a red brick archway and, at last, stopped in a large meadow where white stones of various sizes and shapes dotted the grass as far as he could see. The back of the hearse was opened, and the brown and brass box was removed and carried to a spot in the meadow where it was later lowered into the ground. He then realized Mommy was gone.

Afterward his father often cried and sat alone in the dark. At family gatherings, young J.D. eavesdropped on hushed conversations where relatives talked about his father becoming close friends with somebody named Jim Beam, although he couldn't seem to recall seeing Mr. Beam around the house.

It was only two days after his seventh birthday that the policeman knocked on the door. He spoke softly as he informed the babysitter that Mr. Lewis had been involved in a very serious accident. Once again, J.D. found himself in a hospital room where his Uncle Joseph told him his father had also gone away. In the corridor he overheard Uncle Joseph mutter to Aunt Emily that his father had been driving with Jim Beam when the accident happened and that he should've listened to the warnings about keeping such fast and dangerous company.

The sudden deaths of his mother and father left him not only an orphan, but also unwanted. Uncle Joseph and Aunt Emily, with four children already, said they couldn't afford another mouth to feed. Uncle Richard and Aunt Bonnie were too busy with new and budding careers to raise a brat. Confused and alone, J.D. became a ward of the state.

The voice of Doctor Wexler snapped him back to the present. "The body is that of a well-developed and well-nourished white female. The body weighs 131 pounds, is five feet six inches in height and appears compatible with the reported age of forty-four. The body is cold and rigor is present and fixed to an equal degree...." Lewis stood in the doorway as Doctor Wexler described his ongoing examination of body cavities. Central nervous system, neck, cardiovascular system, respiratory system and biliary system. He'd heard it all before and at times the words seemed distant. But now and again certain words caught his attention. "The rope is wrapped tightly around the neck with its knot at the right side of the neck. Upon removing the rope...." Then the voice would fade again only to come back strong. "The vaginal swab shows evidence of sperm heads without tails, indicating recent sexual activity. This forty-four-year-old while female, Kimberly Ann McDougal, died of ligature strangulation. The manner of death is homicide."

Doctor Wexler stepped back from the table and turned to Lewis as he started peeling the latex gloves from his hands. "The examination confirms our suspicions. It's the same killer."

Lewis nodded. "Now all we need is a suspect to go with your confirmation."

"I can't help you there," he said, shaking his head. "I'm afraid that's something you'll have to do on your own."

"Thanks, Doc," he said as he turned toward the door. "I guess it's time to go face the powers that be."

Lewis had barely crossed the threshold of the Criminal Investigations Bureau when his name blared from the Public Address System summoning him to the CIB conference room.

Lieutenant Leonard Adams, whose red complexion and sharp facial features earned him the nickname of The Buzzard, sat at the head of the table gulping black coffee. His only acknowledgment of Lewis' entry was a weak wave of his hand.

J.D. took his Stetson off, sat down in a straight backed wooden chair and waited for Adams to speak. The Buzzard sat, eyes fixed on the dark metal door, and sipped his coffee. A moment later, as though Adams had willed it, the door swung open and Sergeant Bill Wallace, along with Detectives Don Grayson and Frank Hargrove, walked into the room.

Lewis suppressed his sudden urge to laugh at the Suck-Ass Triplets as they were so often called, as they jockeyed for positions of favor beside Adams. They were seen now and then walking behind Adams and sometimes even mimicking a few of his gestures. Now seated, they fixed their eyes on the man at the head of the table, probably expecting that at any moment he would, with a mere wave of his hand, change his coffee into wine.

Adams nervously traced small circles with his blue coffee mug on the table top.

"Well, Lewis, what's the verdict from the medical examiner?"

"Doctor Wexler says it's the same killer as in the other cases."

"Who's your prime suspect?"

He shifted in his chair. "Right now there's no prime suspect. In fact, there's no suspect at all."

Grayson smirked. "You mean you haven't developed a suspect yet?"

"I've only had the cases for a week. Or don't...."

Adams raised a hand and pointed a finger at him. "I wanna know what you've been doing for the past week."

"Reading the case files. Trying to sort out the information in Grayson's and Hargrove's reports."

"What're you saying about their reports, Lewis?" Wallace said, placing the palms of his hands on the table and leaning forward. "Are you criticizing the work or report writing of veteran detectives?"

"No, I'm not. I'm trying to tell you it takes time to read through those reports and sift out the pertinent information. Remember, I'm beginning at square one and I'm looking for facts I can use in my investigation. And, last night was the first time I'd been to one of the crime scenes."

"Lewis, I'd suggest you get your ass in gear," Adams said, rapping his knuckles on the table. "All of us are gonna be watching you closely. So don't screw up. Understand?"

He fully understood the point that Adams was making. He'd be under the microscope daily. The prying eyes of those who loathed him would be lying in wait for him to stumble and fall. Failure on his part would certainly cause him to be held up for public ridicule and the blame for a murderer being permitted to freely roam among society's elite would rest squarely on his shoulders. He was even more aware of the fact that should he develop a strong suspect in the stalker cases, in all likelihood they would be taken and given back to those who wouldn't mind basking in the glory of someone else's deeds.

He reached for his hat. "Lieutenant, I'll make every effort possible to identify and arrest a suspect in these murders."

Adams smiled as he removed a slip of paper from his shirt pocket and shoved it toward him. "You can begin by taking a drive out to the Barrows mansion on Huntley Manor Road. Here's the address. Contact Zachary Barrows."

"Does he have information on the stalker cases?"

"Well, yes and no."

"Christ, why didn't you say something sooner?"

"There were other matters to discuss first," Adams said.

J.D. gritted his teeth knowing Adams purposely held the information back. "Okay. What information does he have?"

"His wife received a letter from the killer this morning. It looks like he's chosen his next victim."

"Already?" Lewis said, shaking his head.

"Yeah, already. Oh and one more thing," Adams said, getting to his feet. "The chief's appointed you the personal guardian of Mrs. Barrows."

"Just what does that mean?"

"You're gonna be her bodyguard."

"Jesus," he muttered. "How the hell am I supposed to play nursemaid to Mrs. Barrows and investigate these homicides at the same time?"

Wallace laughed. "You're a hotshot detective, you figure it out."

Lewis watched the trio rise and fall in line behind Adams as he marched to the door. He couldn't hide his grin as he thought how pathetic they looked chasing him.

Hargrove caught his smile from the corner of his eye and spun quickly, glaring at him. "What's so fuckin' funny, Lewis?"

"Oh, nothin' much, Frank," he replied, leaning across the table. "I was just thinking that an abrupt halt by Adams would require a major surgical procedure to remove certain whiffers from front running anal canals."

"What? What's that mean?"

"You're a big shot—I believe that's a hotshot detective," he whispered to him. "You figure it out."

Alone in the room, Lewis dropped back into his chair and thought about his situation. He knew that Chief Sam Greenberg didn't assign him to be the guardian of Mrs. Barrows. The chief maintained a strict hands off policy when it came to the day to day running of the department. And that would include the assigning of an officer to act as a bodyguard for a citizen. So that put it squarely on Adams and friends.

The next question he faced was, why did the Society Stalker suddenly change his pattern? He usually waited six months before selecting his next victim and sending his letter of intent. This was a drastic alteration of behavior or a copycat looking for a few minutes of fame.

He glanced at his watch and saw the lunch hour was near. He decided to grab a sandwich and eat on the way to Huntley Manor Road and his meeting with Mr. Zachary Barrows.

He laughed as he figured his streak of bad luck would continue with the meeting of Mrs. Barrows. Until now, the victims of the stalker were very attractive. For reasons he couldn't explain, he imagined her to be of very rotund dimensions and that she ate handfuls of chocolate candy and scoops of ice cream for breakfast.

Three

Number 21 Huntley Manor Road looked more like a posh country club than a house. A wall, constructed of beige bricks, rose and fell with the flow of the land on both sides of an electrically operated black iron gate. The gate could be opened from inside the estate, after the party requesting entry properly identified themselves via the entrance telephone or by knowing the coded entry numbers.

The gate swung slowly open for Lewis and he drove along an asphalt driveway that was lined with neatly pruned and evenly spaced white pine trees. The driveway wound its way up a gradual incline until at the top it divided into a circular pathway. The left fork led to a large garage with closed doors, leaving him to wonder what luxury and expense was housed there. The right fork led to the house, or as he saw it, the Barrows family castle.

Halfway around the drive he stopped his car and stared at the beige brick marvel.

The bricks perfectly matched those of the wall surrounding the estate. He didn't dare venture a guess as to the number of rooms in the house, but knew his modest apartment would probably occupy a corner of one of the rooms.

He stopped the car under the passage at the entrance to the house and looked over the carefully constructed brick pillars that supported the roof of the archway. He glanced to his right and looked at the dark oak double doors with highly polished brass fixtures, the gateway to the world of the Barrows family.

As he reached to open the door a tall, slender, silver-haired black man, attired in an impeccably pressed and creased steward's uniform, appeared and opened it for him. As he got out of the car, J.D. extended his hand to the man. "Thank you, sir. I'm Detective Lewis. I'm here to see Mr. Barrows."

The old man was momentarily taken aback by the action and stood looking blankly at the hand offered to him. He was unaccustomed to anyone offering to shake his hand and even more shocked over being addressed as sir by someone calling on Mr. Barrows. But the jolt ebbed and he firmly clasped the hand of the young detective. "It sure is a pleasure to meet you, sir," he said, his accent sounding as if he'd come straight from a plantation in the old South. "If you'll follow me, I'll take you to Mr. Barrows."

"Thank you. And by the way, what's your name?"

"Uh—Ezra. Ezra Dawkins."

"Well, Mr. Dawkins," he said, "I guess I'll be seein' a lot of you for the next couple of weeks."

"Uh, sir, most folks just call me Ezra."

When they reached the entrance, Lewis opened the door and gestured for Ezra to enter ahead of him. The old man smiled, displaying a row of sparkling white teeth. "Sir, it sure is gonna take time gettin' used to you bein' 'round here."

In a room Ezra called the office study, Lewis was introduced to Zachary Barrows, who after giving a cordial handshake sat down behind his highly buffed mahogany desk. As Lewis glanced around the room it was evident the decorative theme was mahogany. The table in the center of the room, the chairs, the bookshelves and cabinets were all constructed of the shiny, reddish-brown wood.

"I assume you know why you're here," Barrows said, leaning back in his chair.

"Yes, sir, I was told," he said, deciding he wasn't going to like this man. "But before we get into that I'd like to see the letter your wife received."

"What?"

"I'd like to see the letter."

"Sure," Barrows said, seemingly stunned by the detective's audacity. He paused for a second and then opened the center drawer of his desk. He pulled an envelope out and passed it across the desk to Lewis. "My wife and I have both handled the letter, Detective."

Lewis nodded as he opened the envelope and carefully removed a single sheet of white paper. He clasped one corner between the nails of his thumb and index finger and shook it open. Even if Barrows and his wife had handled the letter, he'd still have the lab go over it for prints. Maybe the killer was careless this time, he thought, as he began to read the letter.

> *Dearest Tiffany,*
> *I've been watching you for some time and I find you truly irresistible. I so admire your taut body, especially those long tanned legs and firm, round breasts. I am looking forward to feeling your*

body pressed against mine when I choke the life out of you in the library. It will be such a thrill giving you the ultimate orgasm, that of death. Until then, my darling, I will see you at the country club and health spa and dream of our final meeting.

Lewis said nothing after finishing the letter. He cautiously tucked it and its envelope into a larger brown envelope labeled evidence and slipped it under his clipboard.

"You do understand why you're here, Detective Lewis?" Barrows said, rocking back and forth.

"I know why I was assigned here. What I don't understand is why you just didn't go out and hire someone for the job."

"I don't want some Five and Dime Rent-a-Cop protecting my wife."

"Well, it sure as hell looks like you could afford to hire the very best in the business," he said.

"I did just that, son. My companies funneled over two hundred thousand dollars into the governor's re-election campaign. With that little token of my appreciation I bought and paid for the very best. You." Smug arrogance showed all over the face of Zachary Barrows as he rocked back once more in his chair and smiled at him. "The moment you walked through that door I became your boss. Oh, you might answer to your superiors in the police department, but I'm your boss. And, you're to be available to go with my wife anywhere, anytime, day or night." Barrows tossed a gold pen onto the desk, crossed his arms and looked at him.

"What the hell do you want me to do? Move in with you?"

Barrows sat silent staring at him for a few moments. He rocked forward in his chair and said, "Hell, I like the way you think. You'd be an artful competitor in the business world. Sure. You do that."

"Do what?"

"Move in here."

"What? Jesus, I can't do that."

"Sure you can. You can have a room in the east wing and I'll see to it you have another room you can use as office space—with the latest equipment, of course. I'll have a telephone installed for your use and naturally I'll pick up the expenses."

"You're joking, right?"

"No, I'm not. I'm dead serious. You tell me what you want and it's yours. I intend to see that nothing happens to my wife, no matter what it costs."

Lewis shook his head. "You really want me to stay here?"

"Absolutely."

"Damn, I'll have to think about that."

"Christ, man, what the hell's there to think about?" Barrows said, springing to his feet. "You'll have a private office to work out of. Your own computer terminal and telephone. Besides that, you'll have opportunities the likes of which you never dreamed of. You'll attend parties and fund raisers with my wife. You'll meet influential people. Very influential people. You know, people who could do things for your career."

He appreciated what he was saying; however, J.D. didn't give a damn about prominent people tendering a boost to his career. The private office, computer and telephone on the other hand did have an appealing sound. In the CIB office he always had to wait, sometimes for hours, before he could complete his reports because of the endless line for a computer terminal. It was like taking a number and waiting at a restaurant and learning number 17 is being served while you're holding number 49.

"Come on. What's your answer?"

"Mr. Barrows, were you made aware of the fact that I'm also responsible for investigating the deaths of the other four women?"

Barrows paced quickly back and forth behind his desk. "Yes," he replied with a wave of his hand. "Yes, I know all about that."

"I hope you realize your wife might have to alter her plans so I can follow up on leads as they develop. I can't spend 24 hours a day acting only as her bodyguard."

Barrows nodded. "Okay. Okay. Under the circumstances we'll concede that plans may have to be altered to suit your duties."

Lewis fixed his eyes on Zachary Barrows. "In that case I guess you can call me your employee." He wasn't especially fond of the answer, but for now he could live with it.

A smile showed on Barrows' face as he sat down again in the plush leather chair. "Good. Now, tonight my wife's attending a fund raiser at the Huntley Manor Country Club. I'm leaving town this afternoon on business. So, I'll expect you to accompany Tiffany to the event. It's black tie, naturally. I'll phone Pierre at French's Men's Night and Day Fashions on Bentley Drive. He'll outfit you with the proper attire. Any questions?"

"What time should I pick Mrs. Barrows up?"

His smile broadened. "She'd like to leave promptly at seven. Jason will drive you to the club."

"Yes, sir," he said, putting on his hat.

"By the way, I'll need a list of things you want in your office." He pushed a pad across the desk toward him and tapped his fingers on the desk.

Lewis jotted down a number of items and slid it back to Barrows. "I'll be back well before seven. I'd like to look around and get familiar with the place."

"That's fine. I'll have Ezra show you around. And, I'll see to it that you're supplied with the proper alarm and entry codes for the home and grounds."

When the door closed Barrows thought about the youthful detective who'd just departed. He couldn't put his finger on it, but he could sense that the boyish cop was mature beyond his years. Something told him this policeman was relentless. Maybe it was the look in his eyes. He had the eyes of a hunter. A faint smile creased his lips. He felt that in certain ways they possessed the very same qualities.

Four

Lewis left the estate thinking he'd never compare himself to Zachary Barrows. As he drove along Huntley Manor Road he thought that Barrows was a pompous ass. A man who believed his money could buy him the world, or the loyalty of those who walked its winding roads. He was in a no-win situation with Mr. Barrows on one side and the Buzzard and Suck-Ass Triplets on the other. One side assuming it owned him body and soul, while the other sat waiting for him to fall.

The afternoon passed quickly as he dropped off the letter to crime lab technicians for processing, gathered clothes from his apartment and picked up a tuxedo from Pierre. By the time he returned to 21 Huntley Manor Road, it was five o'clock.

Ezra took him first to the library on the ground floor of the house near the east wing. Barrows had designated the library as his office. He was amazed when he saw a computer and a telephone already installed on a desk that sat in a cozy corner of the room.

The library was more to his liking, with a rustic décor and feeling of warmth. He liked the dark wood furnishings which were complemented by light oak walls and thick gold carpet on the floor. This was a room where a person could settle in and really feel welcome.

Ezra next escorted him to a bedroom on the second floor of the mansion. He immediately approved of the room, wondering if Barrows somehow sensed his taste in comfort. The interior design was Early American and again gave a feeling of warmth. He'd also enjoy the pleasure of his own bath, complete with sauna and hot tub.

He took a tour of the grounds, returned to the second floor and casually walked down the long corridor toward his room. Abruptly, he recalled a time in the past when he walked down another hallway.

The lights in the hallway of the foster home were dim and it led to a damp, musty room at the end of the hall. The door seemed to give an ominous thud as it was closed behind him and the key clicked, locking him in the room until morning. He soon found this would be the daily routine after the evening meal, which never seemed to be enough. He hated the room and its filthy furniture along with its mildewed smell and vile odor it left on his clothes.

It took a few weeks for him to open the window, which had remained stuck because of poor care and too much paint. He made a passage to freedom and started using it every night after he finished his homework. He studied diligently because he didn't want to draw unwanted attention to himself and God knows what consequences if he did poorly in school.

Initially, the nightly excursions were merely his way of avoiding confinement in the shabby room. He wandered around exploring the neighborhood, being careful to avoid detection and returning home in plenty of time to rest for school the following day.

It was on one of his nighttime outings that he found a place that held him spellbound. While tiptoeing along a side street, he peeked through an open door and saw a group of barefooted men dressed in spotless white uniforms with belts of white, green, brown and black going through a strange ritual. A small Asian man with a black belt spoke foreign words and the others performed crisp punches or sharp kicks following his commands.

The nights now held purpose for him as he completed his homework and sneaked out to watch the men carry on the routine that fascinated him so much. By his fourth visit he was invited inside to watch and asked if he cared to join the class. He desperately wanted to be a part of their cult, but he had no money for dues. He was about to leave in despair when a black man who looked like he'd been chiseled from granite whispered to the Asian man. Seconds later Jefferson Lewis was shaking hands with Takayoshi Higa and John Henry Johnson.

Before leaving that night he found out that Mr. Higa was from Okinawa and a sixth degree black belt. Mr. Johnson, a third degree black belt was a sergeant with the local police department and lived not far from the karate school. He sneaked home with a new outlook on life. He'd found a place where he was wanted and two men he was sure would be his friends.

After showering and dressing in the tuxedo he looked at his reflection in the mirror and mumbled, "Man, I hope I don't have to get duded up like this every day."

He left his room and took his time walking to the main entrance to await his much anticipated introduction to Mrs. Barrows. He strolled across the marble floor without making a sound and inspected the paintings that hung on the walls.

The slight rustling of fabric some distance away alerted him that someone was approaching from his right. Instinctively he turned toward the noise that caught his attention, pivoting smoothly on his feet as he'd been trained to do. His breath caught at the sight of the woman as she drew nearer to him. Damn, he thought, what a beautiful woman.

The woman stepped to the center of the foyer and smiled. She was a picture of sheer elegant beauty; tall, darkly tanned, deep sea blue eyes and shoulder length blonde hair that seemed to glisten in the twinkling lights of the entrance hall. She wore a black full-length dress which accented every line and curve of her body and didn't reveal a single flaw. To add to her aristocratic air, her attire was completed by a short diamond necklace, teardrop diamond earrings and a diamond tennis bracelet.

She paused several feet from him. "You must be Detective Lewis," she said in a soft voice, looking at the dark-haired, handsome young man.

"Yes, ma'am."

"I'm Tiffany Barrows." Her smile widened as she held out her hand to him. "I'm pleased to meet you." She looked him over, guessing that he was 6 feet tall and about 210 pounds. And none of that 210 pounds looked as though it was fat. She liked that. And a look into his deep brown eyes showed a certain caring and warmth.

He took her hand and was immediately impressed by the strength of her handshake. "Pleased to meet you, ma'am."

She took his arm and guided him toward the door. "Well, are you ready to mingle with the snobbery?"

"Yes, ma'am. At least as best as I know how, which isn't much." He realized she was trying to put him at ease and somehow he felt she wasn't the look down her nose type of person. And certainly she was a far cry from her husband.

"Don't worry," she said. "You'll be okay."

Jason opened the door to the Rolls Royce and Lewis felt his first real twinge of discomfort. He was accustomed to driving himself wherever he wanted to go, not being chauffeured there; however, this was the other world he was pretending to be a part of and, like it or not, he was a passenger in the back seat of a car he'd only walked by in the past.

As he suspected, the Huntley Manor Country Club was for members and invited guests only. The men in tuxedos at the gate who were making a pretense of checking membership passes even looked a bit stiff-necked. Inside there were small pockets of highbrows, some engaged in boastful jousting matches while others simply laughed and chatted over champagne.

They were greeted at the door and informed they would be seated at table number one. As they walked into the ballroom Tiffany slipped her arm around his and strolled casually across the floor as though she and Lewis had been lifelong friends. Suddenly conversations stopped and heads turned to look at the couple as they made their way to their table.

"We'll be the talk of the town by tomorrow morning," she muttered softly to him. "God, how some of these people love to gossip."

Sure enough the parade of the curious began almost immediately to form in front of and beside them. Men and women alike appeared one after another to get an eye and ear full. Loaded questions and comments flowed like the waters in the fountain in the lobby.

While Tiffany answered the questions and lightly passed off the lewdly veiled comments, most of which were made by women, Lewis looked over the crowd searching for a hint of anything out of the ordinary. He looked at the faces and eyes, hoping to see a clue as to who sent the letter. But nothing was obvious.

He was pleased when Tiffany decided to end the evening earlier then anticipated, although this would probably add fuel to the already raging fires of the gossip mill. He was certain that by noon tomorrow telephone lines would be dripping with the hot news of how passions must be aflame in the Barrows Mansion.

They parted cordially in the foyer and he went quickly to his room to change. He slipped on a pair of sweat pants and tee shirt and went downstairs to his office. In the center of the desk he found an envelope and a note from Zachary Barrows. Indeed the man was making a gallant effort at buying his undying loyalty. The envelope contained two thousand dollars in cash and a credit card for his personal use.

He opened the file folder he'd brought down with him and removed the copy he'd made of the letter. He hoped the lab techs had found fingerprints on the original, but he knew the stalker was a shrewd individual who'd left no evidence of prints in the past. He turned on the desk lamp and read the letter again.

It was short and to the point as the others had been, but here he noted something different. The letter began with "Dearest" instead of "Dear." He wondered, is this a copycat or is this guy smart enough to change his method just to throw us off?

"You know, I'm supposed to die in this room."

He glanced up from the letter and saw Tiffany standing in the doorway dressed in navy blue shorts and tee shirt. "Uh—yes. Yes, ma'am. Well, I wasn't sure if there was another library in the house or not."

"No. This is it."

"Can I ask you a question?" he said, leaning back and looking at her.

"Sure?"

"Why don't you just get out of the house? I mean, why stay here after you've been threatened? You know he's carried out his other threats."

"Detective Lewis, I won't be chased out of my house by some demented pervert. I refuse to run away and hide. Besides, how long would I be running?"

"I just wanted to know," he said and decided that she was a brave woman.

"May I come in?"

"Yes, ma'am."

She moved a chair beside the desk and sat down. "I noticed you didn't have a drink at the country club. Don't you drink?"

"Yes, ma'am, I drink. At the country club I was on duty and I don't drink alcohol when I'm working."

"Are you off duty now?"

"Yes, ma'am."

"Would you care for a drink?"

"I don't suppose you'd have a bottle or can of Coors in the house."

She smiled. "We have several imported beers for those with expensive tastes and we have Coors and Coors Light for those who just enjoy a beer."

He nodded and laughed. "Coors is just fine."

She was out of the chair and headed for the door before he could say another word. He watched until she vanished from sight and muttered to himself, "Damn, what a gorgeous woman."

She returned with a champagne bucket that contained four bottles of Coors packed in ice. She placed the bucket on the floor beside the desk and passed a bottle to him. "May I join you?"

"Yes, ma'am. Please."

"I wish you'd stop calling me ma'am. You're making me feel like I'm an old woman."

"Sorry. What should I call you?"

"How about Tiffany?"

"You sure that's okay?"

"Yes. It's fine. And what should I call you? I don't want to go around calling you Detective Lewis all the time."

"Well, most of my friends call me J.D. or Cowboy. Either one would be okay."

"How'd you get a nickname like Cowboy?"

"I guess it's 'cause I wear a Stetson and cowboy boots most of the time."

"I bet you've been called a lot worse."

"I sure have," he said and they both laughed. "Most of which I wouldn't repeat here in front of you."

They chatted for almost an hour before she left him to his work. It was mostly idle conversation concerning the next day's schedule which included a trip to the health club in the morning. She seemed quite pleased to learn he was a fitness buff and enjoyed weight lifting, running and biking. He neglected to tell her of his background in the martial arts, but figured it wasn't really necessary.

During their conversation he detected something behind the glimmer in her blue eyes. Although her eyes held a certain sparkle when she spoke to him, he was sure he could see a touch of sadness, even loneliness there; however, understanding it would be another matter.

Then he thought, *if Tiffany was a lonely woman would she send the letter just to get attention?* It didn't seem likely. But because of his position he had to look at every single possibility. *Are there troubles in the Barrows Household? Did Zachary Barrows piss somebody off and they sent the letter as a way of gaining some measure of revenge? Or did Zachary Barrows send the letter to test his clout in the governor's office? I guess anything's possible.*

He stood up and began to pace slowly around the room, thinking, *God, I hate being stuck with these cases. I wish there was someone I could turn to for advice. Oh, what the hell? I've had to make tough decisions before and they turned out okay. But this time a woman's life is on the line. It's not like back in the Corps when I knew I could depend on the guy beside me to take care of me and himself when the shit hit the fan. I looked out for him. He looked out for me. But this is different.*

While he struggled to find answers to his questions, Tiffany stretched out on her king-sized bed and stared up into the darkness for a long time. Finally she buried her face in the pillow and cried herself to sleep.

Five

By 9:00 a.m. Tiffany and J.D., as she preferred to call him, were getting ready to leave for the Huntley Manor Health and Fitness Spa. When they went outside though, he balked at the idea of being taken to workout in a chauffeur driven Rolls Royce. He said he'd rather take the police car, but she offered him the choice of taking any car from the garage as long as he was willing to drive. He nodded and walked to the garage.

When the doors opened his eyes immediately went to the black Lamborghini and she knew he was in love with the sleek, dark machine. He walked around the car a full three times, stopping twice to touch the brightly waxed finish. She smiled, thinking he looked like a little boy in a toy store at Christmas. She handed him the keys and he opened the gull-winged door on the driver's side and dropped into the seat. She laughed as he just shook his head and looked over the interior.

It was a few minutes before he inserted the key into the ignition, turned it and brought the engine to life. The growl of the engine brought a wide grin to his face and he gushed, "Wow."

She opened the passenger's door and tossed their gym bags to the floor. She slid into the seat beside him and gently nudged his arm. "Put it in gear and let's go."

"With pleasure, ma'am."

She was thrilled over having the opportunity to watch a child with a new toy. He eased the car out of the garage, immediately revved the engine and took off for one lap around the driveway. With the preliminary lap finished, he headed into the straightaway and worked through the gears like a racecar driver. She soon realized she was enjoying this as much as him. It had been a very long time since she'd ridden in the Lamborghini.

When they arrived at the health spa he was still beaming over his new driving adventure. "What a machine. I've gotta sneak this baby out on the interstate late one night and just blow it out."

"Only if you take me with you," she said.

"You got it."

"What happens if the state police stop you?"

"I'll plead insanity. Tell them my lust for speed got the best of me."

They walked into the spa and, as was the case the evening before, eyebrows shot up and hushed voices started asking the same spicy questions. "Are they an item? Does Zachary know? Is she favoring him with the pleasure of her body, a body many men seemed to long for?"

He found the men's locker room quite different from the places to which he was normally accustomed. Sparkling white tile floors, mirrors free of cracks and grimy film, sinks and toilets that worked and were void of dirt, hair and other disgustingly gross deposits. The air here was scented with fresheners instead of stale perspiration and urine. Also missing was the lone sock or athletic supporter stuck in a corner or hanging from an open locker door.

Rose Anna Guilford, Tiffany's best friend, followed her into the ladies' dressing room. "God, Tiffany, who is that darling piece of flesh you brought in with you?"

Tiffany hadn't taken a lot of time thinking about how to explain a bodyguard. "Oh. Uh—well, Zachary's worried about the killings and—and said he'd feel better knowing someone was around to, uh, sort of watch out for me when he's out of town on business."

Rose Anna gave her a curious glance. "You mean Zachary knows all about this hunk?"

"Yes."

"Wherever did he find him?"

"J.D. works for the police department and…."

"He's a cop! Oh, God, that means he has handcuffs. Brrrr," she said, giving her body an exaggerated shake. "I get chills just thinking about him cuffing me and taking advantage of me."

"You would, Rose Anna."

"Tiffany, tell me the thought hasn't crossed your mind."

Tiffany threw her bag into her locker. "My, God, he's just a child."

Rose Anna laughed. "Not that young, my dear. Not that young. Besides, you're only 41. There can't be too many years separating you."

"What're you saying?"

"Oh, come on. Admit it. You'd love to wrap your arms around him and feel that hard young flesh pressed against you."

Tiffany felt the blood surge up along her neck and the warmth flooding her face.

"That's absurd," she said, trying to hide her reddening face from her friend.

Again Rose Ann laughed. "Not from where I'm standing it's not. Remember, I'm your friend. I know your dark, innermost secrets. I know what goes on in your house and what doesn't. If I were in your shoes, I'd tumble this guy on the sheets at the first available opportunity."

"I'm ready to workout," she said, turning and walking for the door.

"Avoiding the issue won't make it go away," Rose Anna said, following closely on her heels.

The weight lifting room of the Huntley Manor Health and Fitness Spa was larger and certainly better equipped than any Lewis had been in before. There were free weights and Nautilus and Universal machines. There were stair climbers, ski tracks, stationary bicycles and the most modern of treadmills.

He noticed that there were a lot of men and women in the room. There were a number of them who used the equipment and were in excellent condition. But for the most part he saw that the majority of those in the room simply found this to be just another arm of their social clubs. They stood around in expensive warm-up suits, using only their jaw and voice muscles to discuss business deals or share the latest in juicy gossip. These people he classified in sizes as medium, large, portly, rotund and holy fuckin' wow, which meant they were too large to describe.

He had no trouble using the free weights and keeping an eye on Tiffany as she worked out on the Nautilus equipment. As he pushed onward and upward with the bench press, he was unaware of Rose Anna's leering. When he lowered 350 pounds to his chest, pushed it straight up and eased it back into its cradle, she walked over to him.

"Anytime you want to lift me and lower me to your body I won't object," she said, licking her lips. "Just keep me there for awhile."

He lowered his head and blushed slightly. When he raised his eyes he saw the man and instantly the warning bell sounded. Although his apparel matched that of the others, the man was out of place. The way he carried himself and his glances in Tiffany's direction made him all wrong. In Lewis' mind, he belonged in a smoke filled room in the back of some sleazy pool hall or waterfront saloon.

Lewis' senses went up a notch as the man walked toward the Nautilus equipment, his eyes roaming up and down Tiffany's body. He walked around the equipment, continuing to gawk at Tiffany and showing no intention of working out.

Lewis casually walked over and stood in front of Rose Anna. "Do you know the guy in the black and gray warm-up suit?"

She smiled. "No," she purred. "He must be a new member."

"You never saw him in here before?"

"No, sugar. Never."

He moved back to the free weight bench and beckoned one of the many personal trainers to him. "Are you familiar with the man in the black and gray warm-up suit over there at the Nautilus equipment?"

The trainer studied the man for a few seconds and shook his head. "No, I'm not. But then again he could be a new member. I've been away on vacation for the past two weeks."

Lewis wasn't in the habit of name dropping, but in this case he thought it might be appropriate in order to get by the sure to come mile long list of questions when he asked for information. "Look, I'm a police officer working for Zachary Barrows. He hired me to keep an eye on his wife. Since nobody here seems to know who the guy is, could you check the desk register and tell me his name?"

"Hey, if you're working for Mr. Barrows it won't be any problem at all." He turned and walked toward a small corner office. "I'll call the desk and see who he is."

Lewis walked slowly toward the office, all the while keeping his eyes on the stranger. He formed a picture of the man in his mind. Something of a Hollywood Heavy type who looked to be in pretty fair physical condition; however, it did look like he'd blocked one too many punches with his nose, as it was pushed back into his face with a slight twist to the left.

He turned his attention to the office when the young man called to him. "The last person to register at the desk signed in as Z. Barrows."

"Christ," he spat. "Doesn't anybody check the fuckin' names to be sure they match the faces?"

"Uh—signing in is just a formality."

"Bullshit formalities could get somebody killed." He spun around and noticed the man was no longer at the Nautilus equipment. He took two quick steps and saw Rose Anna and Tiffany still working together at their stations. He looked around the room for the man, but didn't see him. He walked toward the locker room, his eyes darting back and forth over the crowd. A hasty check of the dressing area didn't find the stranger either.

Lewis trotted across the weight room and sprinted down the stairs to the door. He ran out to the parking lot in time to see the fictitious Mr. Barrows speed away from the spa in a blue Mustang. "Damn it," he growled when he couldn't read the registration plate of the fleeing car.

Tiffany and Rose Anna were waiting at the top of the stairs when he came back. "What's wrong?" Tiffany said.

"I need to ask the staff and club members a few questions before I can answer that."

He spoke first with the employees, asking about the man who impersonated Mr. Barrows. All agreed that they hadn't seen him in the spa before today. Two employees who were at the desk when he came in agreed that he was pleasant, even going so far as to joke with them while signing the register.

Next he went to club members and asked, "Has this man been a visitor to the Huntley Manor Country Club?" A logical question, as those present at the spa were also members of the country club. Polling club members was one thing; however, getting a reasonable answer was far and away another matter. Several men swore they'd played golf with him at the club on at least a dozen occasions. Others said that the man had never set foot in the club. A rather large woman insisted they'd danced the night away only a week ago and he'd made sexual advances toward her. Other women denied ever seeing the man at any of their almost nightly soirees. Of course, their physical description of the stranger ranged from flattering to grotesque.

He wasn't amazed by their tales of knowing the man in some fashion or another, nor their description of him. After all, he knew no two people would give the same account of socializing with or knowledge of the stranger. From the information he'd gathered from spa employees and club members, he figured that today was the first time any of them saw the man. The stories of those who claimed they knew the man were probably fantasy.

He took Tiffany aside to explain the problem and immediately offended Rose Anna. "You'll have to smooth things over with your friend later. I think that anything she overheard would be repeated and spiced up."

"You're right. I mean, she's my best friend and I love her like a sister, but she does tend to exaggerate things."

"Anyway, did you notice the guy in the black and gray warm-up suit?"

"Ummmm, yes. But, I didn't really pay much attention to him?" she said, noticing the concern on his face.

"Well, today's the first time he's been in here. And he signed the register as Z. Barrows."

"You're joking."

"No, I'm not. And he took a great interest in you. When I asked the trainer about him, the guy pulled a disappearing act and made tracks for his car."

"You think he sent the letter?"

"I really don't know. Sorry. Right now I have more questions than answers."

"What should we do next?"

"Well, I've gotta go to the police station to pick up some reports and check on the lab results from the last case."

"Okay. I'll shower and get dressed."

He caught her by the arm as she tried to walk away. "Wait until you get home to shower."

"What?" she said, staring at him. "Why should I wait till I get home to shower?"

"Look, I'm responsible for your safety. Since I obviously can't shower with you, that means I can't be sure no harm comes to you. So, it's in your best interest to wait until you get home."

She blinked, knowing from his stern tone that he was absolutely serious. "Sure. Okay. I'll wait." She would've continued to argue with him, but she sensed that it would've proved futile.

She gathered her clothes from the locker room while he stood just inside the doorway. Of course, he'd gallantly made sure the room was clear before he went in. As she turned to leave she felt a sudden surge of comfort as she watched him looking around for anything out of the ordinary.

Six

They made the drive to the police station in silence as Lewis struggled to make sense of the latest development. But no matter what logic he used to try and make sense of it, he only ended up with more questions. And for the time being there didn't seem to be any answers. Where were the answers he desperately sought?

He parked the car and saw Captain Thomas leaving the building. Thomas cut a quick detour through the maze of parked cars when he saw him and walked to the back of the shiny black car. "Nice wheels, Lewis. How'd you manage this on a cop's salary?" he said, shaking his head.

"Uh, it's not mine, sir. It belongs to Mrs. Barrows. She let me drive it."

"Actually I insisted he drive it," Tiffany said, getting out of the car.

"Mrs. Barrows. What a pleasure to see you," Thomas said, walking around to greet her. He extended his hand, saying, "We met a few months back. At the fund raiser for the Police Athletic League."

"Oh, yes," she said, nodding and taking his hand. "Captain Karl Thomas, right?"

"I'm flattered that you'd remembered me."

She smiled. "It's easy to associate faces with the worthy causes they represent."

He turned back to Lewis. "Anything new in your investigation?"

"Still plodding along, sir. A million questions and no answers."

"Don't give up. You'll find what you're looking for."

"God, I hope it's soon," he said, adjusting his hat. "I just wish I had some help with this. This is a helluva thing for a rookie investigator to handle."

"Look at the job you did on those cold cases that were dumped in your lap. Outstanding work. The way you took things in hand and solved them made people stop and take notice of your abilities. Pissed a few off too. But, what the hell, it goes with the territory. Listen, you can solve these murders. Just keep diggin'."

"Yes, sir. I'll do my best."

"I know. That's why I wanted you in the Bureau."

As Thomas walked away, Lewis took Tiffany to his desk in the CIB Office and left to collect lab reports and case files on the stalker killings. He was nearly back to his desk when the voice crackled over the PA system, "Detective Lewis, contact Lieutenant Adams in the conference room."

He walked into the room and was immediately overjoyed to find his favorite people assembled and waiting. He guessed from the "I've got you by the balls" look on their faces that they were anticipating his lynching or at least his transfer to a traffic post in Antarctica.

"You were assigned to protect the wife of Zachary Barrows, correct?" Adams said, glaring at him.

"Yes, sir."

"Can you tell me why you dragged some slut in here and parked her ass at your desk?"

"Slut? Uh, Lieutenant...."

"Yeah," Grayson cut in. "You got a lotta nerve bringin' some sweaty whore in here when you're supposed to be protectin' Mrs. Barrows' life."

Lewis suddenly realized that the door hadn't closed tightly behind him when he came into the room. And since they were making a point of raising their voices to dramatize their comments, Tiffany in all probability could hear every word.

"What did you pay for that whore, Lewis?" Wallace laughed. "A buck ninety-eight?"

Without a word he left the room and walked to his desk. He gently took Tiffany by the arm and led her back into the conference area. He raised his hand and pointed to each of them as he called their names. "Lieutenant Adams. Sergeant Wallace. Detective Hargrove. Detective Grayson."

He then turned and eased her closer beside him. "This slut standing to my left, the one you referred to as a buck ninety-eight sweaty whore, is Tiffany Barrows, wife of Zachary Barrows." With that he calmly turned and walked from the room with Tiffany in tow.

His words echoed like gunshots. He'd dropped a bomb in their laps, leaving them wide-eyed and with mouths agape.

When they reached the sidewalk she stopped, looked at him, threw her head back and laughed. "You're one in a million. That was magnificent. God, the look on their faces was priceless. My husband couldn't have handled that situation as well."

"Yeah. Well, I'll probably be up to my ass in alligators before long."

"Why?"

"Because of my introduction."

"Wait just a minute," she said, a hint of irritation in her tone. "They made the remarks first. You just turned them around and kicked those idiots in the ba—in…in…oh, you know what I mean."

He grinned. "I know exactly what you mean."

Later in the evening he felt awkward sitting in the dinning room with her and being waited on by Ezra and a woman who worked in the kitchen. Although he wasn't as uncomfortable as he was the evening before at the country club, he knew that he was far out of his familiar element.

When the table had been cleared, she asked Ezra to bring them each a Cognac.

She took a sip from the glass and stared over the rim at the young man seated across from her. "I've been thinking—I know someone you'd be a perfect match for."

He raised his hands. "Whoa. Hold on a second. If you're referrin' to fixin' me up with somebody, I don't think you should do that."

"Why not?"

"Well, let me see if I can explain," he said, looking into her eyes. "I come from a different world. I belong where blue jeans, tee shirts, country music, cowboy boots and hats are everyday dress. Where fried chicken and mashed potatoes go well on a paper plate. My country club plays western music. It has lots of pictures of cowboys on the walls. There, you throw peanut shells on the floor. But the beer's cold, the company's good and the Friday night special is a T-bone steak cooked the way you like it. Now, your world's not like that. You have servants to wait on you and clean your house. You have chauffeurs to drive you where you wanna go. You walk in the circles of only the rich and I don't think you know a whole lot about the real world. Now, I'm not tryin' to offend you. Hell, you're not a snob like a lot of the others I've run into so far. But, you still live over here on the far side of the bridge."

"That's the first time I've heard it referred to in that way," she said, raising the glass again to her lips as she continued to gaze into his eyes. "I didn't know a bridge separated our lives."

"What I'm sayin' is, even if there's no real bridge, there's still a gap that divides us. The rich on one side and the rest of us on the other."

She put the glass down on the table and stared at the golden liquid, his words still echoing in her ears. "I guess you've given me a view of the world

I've never seen."

He pushed his chair back from the table. "Ma'am, if you'll excuse me, I've got to go over those case files and try and figure out who's responsible for killing those women and sending you the letter."

"Oh," she whispered. "Please forgive me. I seemed to have forgotten that you have other responsibilities."

"Believe me, sometimes I'd like to forget it."

When he reached the door she called to him, "Would you take me there sometime?"

"Where's that?"

"Your country club."

"Uh—sure. If you really wanna go."

"I'd love to."

"Just pick a night," he said, a smile brightening his face.

"By the way, what's the name of your club?"

"One Step West."

He sat at the desk looking over the files. French. Upchurch. Wellington and McDougal. All dead. The file to his right labeled Barrows, with the word "pending" printed in red ink like some morbid prediction from the Grim Reaper.

While he went over his notes and looked through laboratory and incident reports searching for even the smallest of clues to guide him to a suspect, Tiffany walked slowly to her bedroom.

She changed into a comfortable gown, chose a book from the stand under the night table and piled several pillows behind her. After reading for only a few minutes the tears began to trickle from her eyes, rolling slowly along her cheeks until they fell silently to the front of her pale blue gown. The book slipped from her hands onto the bed beside her as she clutched a pillow to her and wept.

Seven

The steaming water running from the showerhead rolled over his shoulders and back while he continued to try and find a solution to the murders. He knew the killer could learn a lot about his intended victims by taking the time to research public records. If he spent a few dollars and made trips to the Department of Motor Vehicles, Tax Assessor's Office, Census Bureau, or browsing marriage records, voter registers and military records he could learn a lot about the victim and her family. It was surprising how easy it was for someone to learn another party's date and place of birth, driving record, vehicle ownership, salary, marital or divorce status and address.

On the lighter side though, was the thought of yesterday's run-in with The Buzzard and Suck-Ass Triplets. They jumped to a conclusion before taking a close look at the woman who was with him. But they were notorious for jumping to conclusions long before they had all of the facts.

Adams, Wallace, Grayson and Hargrove were huddled in a booth at the back of the Pine Tree Diner, gulping coffee and belching from churning stomach acid.

Adams emptied his third cup and tapped the mug on the faded, pale green tabletop. "That son-of-a-bitch made us look like complete fools."

"Yeah," Wallace muttered with a loud burp. "He should've introduced her to us the minute he brought her into the station."

"You think he's layin' the wood to her already?" Hargrove said, unable to control his perverted sense of curiosity.

"Maybe," Adams said, signaling the waitress to bring more coffee. "It sure would be great for us if he was and we could prove it." He gave a low whistle. "Man, can you imagine the shit hittin' the fan on that? The media'd castrate the prick. The department would hafta fire his ass after old man Barrows got through screamin'."

"Yeah. But we gotta catch him first," Hargrove said. "And, let's face it, that ain't gonna be easy."

"Well, before we start thinkin' about that, we outta discuss what we're gonna do about yesterday," Wallace said, opening a packet of sugar.

Adams smiled. "If we play our cards right we might have the fucker by the short hairs. He dragged the wife of Zachary Barrows into the conference room and called her a slut and cheap sweaty whore in front of us. At least that's what we could say. We all heard him, right? Hell, I can file charges against him. The old catch all. Conduct Unbecoming. Shit, we might even have an ace—her. He embarrassed that woman in front of us. We bring her in as a witness and the department has no choice but to take action."

"Sounds good to me," Wallace said, slapping the table and chuckling.

"I think you're jumpin' the gun," Grayson said. "It won't fly."

"What?" Adams shot back, staring at him.

"It won't fly."

"And why not?"

"First of all, you gotta get her to testify against Lewis. I don't think she's gonna do that."

"Why?"

"Call it a gut reaction. I think she likes him. Something about the way she acted when she was standing beside him. And personally I think the Conduct Unbecoming is pretty chicken shit. That's always been the favorite catch all when nothing else would work. If we try it, we could all end up with our dick in our hand and lookin' like even bigger fools."

"Christ, Don, whose side're you on?" Wallace said, pushing his mug toward him. "It sounds like you're takin' up for Lewis."

"Hey, let's face it. We've had a hard-on for him since the day he first transferred into the Bureau. The guy worked his ass off on the street, that's why he got the job in the first place. He was damn good."

"Shit, I don't believe this. I don't believe you're taking his side."

"I'm just sayin' maybe we should lighten up on him."

"Fuck him," Hargrove blurted. "He ain't exactly done anything to endear himself to us since he came in."

"You mean you're pissed off 'cause he solved a bunch of our old cases, don't you, Frank? Yeah, maybe he did make us look bad. But it sure as shit wasn't his fault. He dug up evidence we missed. He tracked down witnesses we didn't. That wasn't his doing, it was ours. We fucked up. Not Lewis."

"Holy shit," Wallace said. "I really don't fuckin' believe this. I guess we can't count on you to testify against him if we file charges."

"No thanks. I want no parts of a railroad job. Something legit, yeah. But he didn't call Mrs. Barrows a slut. He didn't call her a sweaty whore. It was you guys. I won't lie just to get a piece of his ass."

Lewis sat at the table with Tiffany in the kitchen and enjoyed a delicious breakfast prepared by Lolita Jenkins. After clearing his plate of sausage and blueberry pancakes for the second time he pushed his chair back a few inches from the table as if to signal his surrender, turned and complimented Miss Jenkins on the tasty meal.

He waited for Tiffany to finish her orange juice and said, "Would you mind telling me what Mr. Barrows does for a living?"

She tilted her head slightly and for a fleeting moment he again thought he saw a hint of sadness in her eyes. "Well, he works at rebuilding failing companies into very successful enterprises. He's a very intelligent businessman and knows how to get an organization back on its feet. Sometimes he asks a consulting fee of the company for providing them with practical advice on improving production, or sales and cutting costs. Then there are times when he'll just buy the business outright, put it back on track and sell it—for a sizeable profit, of course."

"Does he limit his work to a specific area?"

"Oh, no. He travels coast to coast. Florida. Maine. California. Texas. Georgia. Colorado. Even Canada."

"It sounds like he spends a lot of time traveling."

She poured another cup of coffee from the silver pot and sighed. "Sometimes he's gone two and three weeks at a time. Once he was out of town for a month trying to close a deal."

"You must get pretty lonely," he said.

She lifted her head and closed her eyes. He knew he'd made a mistake. He'd asked about her personal life and he should've kept their relationship on a professional level. "I'm sorry. I had no right to say that."

"That's okay." She took a deep breath, sipped her coffee and looked out the window. She gathered her thoughts together before looking at him again. "The truth is, I get very lonely. I have lots of things to keep me occupied. My husband sees to that. I stay busy with fund-raisers, club parties and working out. But that's not the same as sharing your time with someone you love and care about. Sleeping alone in a king-sized bed is even less enjoyable. Don't get me wrong. My husband cares for me very much. When he's away on business a day doesn't go by that I don't receive some token of his affection. Flowers. Candy. Cards. Telegrams. Phone calls. But his business deals have taken up too much of his time over the past few years, even when he's home."

He detected a note of bitterness in her voice and he noticed that she seldom referred to her husband by name. So again those nagging little suspicions crept into his mind. Could she be so resentful of her husband's activities that she'd resort to desperate means to get his attention? He didn't want to believe she'd resort to such tactics.

Unexpectedly, she laughed. "I can't believe I just said those things to you. But, you know, I feel better. I feel good."

"Maybe you just needed to blow off a little steam."

"I guess as long as I'm blowing off steam, I might as well get the rest of it off my chest." She stood up and said, "Let's go outside."

They went outside and began casually walking around the grounds. At first she was silent as she paced beside him, but at last said, "I'm sure my husband has strayed from the straight and narrow. Certainly while he's out of town he's dallied in more than one indiscretion. He's a handsome man. And I'm sure many women would be more than pleased to share their bed with him. Then, knowing him as I do, I think I can safely say he's bounced on the box springs with more than one of them. As odd as it might seem, I forgive him for those follies. I'm sure there must be a feeling of power over a rival or some hotshot CEO when you bed his wife or girlfriend. On the other hand, there's me."

She fell silent again and stared at the ground as they continued their casual walk.

Suddenly, in a rapid fire burst, she spouted, "What about me? What about my needs? Damn it, I need it too. I want it. I miss those—" She stopped abruptly and started to cry.

He put his hand on her shoulder and felt a sudden impulse to take her in his arms. To hold her. To comfort her. But he resisted the temptation. He had a job to do and one step over the line might cloud his judgement and possibly compromise his investigation.

She regained her composure and whispered, "Sorry. I didn't mean to burden you with my troubles."

"There's nothing to be sorry for," he said, ever so gently squeezing her shoulder.

She wiped at her eyes and forced a smile. "Let's go to the spa. I need a good workout."

Once again he put the Lamborghini through its paces as he drove to the spa. His mind was in overdrive as he drove through the curves and slight valleys and crests of the road. Not more than thirty minutes ago Tiffany had told him that she knew her husband was unfaithful and her needs weren't being fulfilled. He wondered what surprise might be lurking just around the next corner.

Rose Anna was close behind Tiffany when she walked into the dressing room. "Well, did you take my advice and roll him in the hay?"

"No, I didn't," she said. "And I have no intention of rolling him in the hay."

"At least admit to me that you'd like to."

She dropped to the bench as if she was exhausted and lowered her head. Seconds ticked by in cold silence until she finally looked up at her friend. "Are we alone?"

Rose Anna quickly looked around. "Yes. We have the room to ourselves."

"Rose Anna, you've always kept things in confidence when I've asked you to. I'm asking you now, please, for God's sake, don't repeat a word of what I'm about to tell you. Not to a living soul."

"You have my promise that I won't now or ever repeat what you're about to tell me."

Tiffany looked her friend squarely in the eyes. "The very moment I saw him standing in the foyer I wanted him to tear my clothes off and make love to me. I wanted him to take me right there on the marble floor. On the staircase. It didn't matter. Just seeing him lit a fire in me like I haven't felt in years."

"My God, why didn't you just haul him to your room and screw your frustrations away?"

"I just couldn't—and I can't. I've been faithful to Zachary every day of our marriage and I just can't stray now."

Rose Anna's response was blunt. "Tiffany, when was the last time you were laid?"

She could feel the tears burning again in her eyes and she fought to control her urge to break down and sob. "He—he hasn't made love to me in almost seven years."

"Seven years! Sweet mother. How have you survived all that time? A vibrator? A cucumber? Damn, I'm humping the bedpost after just a few days. How could you make it for seven years without a good hard fuck now and then?"

"At times I really don't know. Maybe I'm strong-willed."

Rose Anna sat down beside her. "Tiffany, how much longer do you think you can can hold out around this young stud?"

"I don't know. You have no idea what it's been like at night having him under the same roof. Knowing that by just walking down the hallway I could be in his room. Naked in his arms. His body pressed against mine." She shook her head. "I've cried myself to sleep at night, partly because I'm ashamed of what I'm feeling and because of my desire to be satisfied."

"Well, if our roles were reversed, he'd already be taking care of my needs. Even if I had to rape him."

"To be honest, I think I've added to my problem."

"How?"

"I asked him to take me out."

"What? You asked him for a date?"

"No. Not exactly." She took a deep breath. "We were having a talk about…about…some things and he told me about a place where he goes. The next thing I knew I was asking him to take me there."

"Tell me this," she said. "Do you really want to go?"

"Yes," she whispered.

"Uh oh," Rose Anna chuckled. "Like it or not, you and your young stud are going for a tumble in the sheets."

"I can't. I can't do that."

"You're more than halfway there. You just don't realize it yet."

"I can't give in for the sake of lust. I can't cheat on my husband."

"Honey, he hasn't exactly worn a chastity belt. Not since the day you married him. So you don't have any reason to feel guilty if you decide to quench your thirst. I don't care how much you protest. The longer you're around this hard bodied stud, the more attractive you're going to find him. Sooner or later you'll end up in his arms."

"I've got to be strong. I've been loyal for all these years and I know my husband has to be aware of that. I can't help but think that any day now things will be like they were before and we'll be a happy couple again."

Rose Anna stood. "If you say so. But, don't be too disappointed if that dream doesn't come true. On the other hand, if it doesn't, you can always screw J.D. until you're just a puddle on the mattress."

Tiffany stood up. "Let's work out."

"Okay. But it really won't change anything."

Eight

Dusk was settling over the Barrows estate when J.D. told Tiffany that he wanted to go to the police station to do more research on the stalker killings.

Once again he drove the sleek, black Lamborghini. He was beginning to like the feeling of being behind the wheel of this car. Maybe tonight he'd take a run down the interstate and, if it wasn't too crowded, just blow the carbon out. The mere thought of opening up the growling beast and letting it run sent a surge of excitement through him.

They'd just left the mansion grounds when she noticed him anxiously looking back and forth to the rearview mirrors. "Is something wrong?"

"I thought I saw headlights behind us, but they just seemed to disappear."

She laughed. "We don't own exclusive rights to the road. At least I don't believe its been purchased in the Barrows name. So, it's okay for other cars to drive on it."

"Maybe it was nothing," he said. But he thought the lights appeared too suddenly on a straightaway as if the car had been driven in the dark for some time.

At the station he went to the Records Division where he gathered information on the four murder victims. He checked the files under their names, their husbands' names and by the listed street address. He looked for reports of suspicious persons, telephone calls, accidental burglar alarms and suspicious cars or trucks in the vicinity of their homes. He didn't find anything to indicate unusual activity prior to their deaths. But this didn't bother him. Something out of the norm could've happened and they chose to ignore it, or simply didn't report it.

He went back to get Tiffany. "Care to try a shot at the interstate?"

"Why not?" she laughed. "You won't rest until you've tried to break the sound barrier."

"I'd better put some gas in first. I'd hate to be halfway there and run outta fuel."

He stopped beside the fuel islands and got out to whistles and nods from

42

an audience of gawking admirers. No doubt, wherever this engineering masterpiece stopped it would attract a crowd of worshipers.

He turned on the pump and glanced up just in time to see the outline of the Mustang go by. He walked briskly to the edge of the lot and looked over the darkened street for the car, but it had vanished.

With the gas tank topped off he drove back onto the street with another purpose, finding the Mustang. He drove slowly along the boulevard, glancing down side streets and looking over store front lots for the car, but didn't see it. Either he was dealing with a slick individual, or the car that passed by them at the gas station was not the same one from the health spa.

He was shifting into third gear when he glanced in the rearview mirror and saw the silhouette moving up rapidly behind them. Even in the dim light he could see the contour lines which distinctly set the car apart from other models. The Mustang was closing the distance between them.

It was time to be certain the car without its lights on and gaining ground was there to follow them. He checked the mirrors for traffic to his right. The lane was clear. He cut the wheel sharply to the right and accelerated. The Mustang veered from the center lane and followed.

Tiffany shifted her position, saying, "What's wrong?"

"We have company."

"Where?" she said, looking over her shoulder and straining her eyes in the darkness. "I don't see anything."

"He's there. He's runnin' without lights." He wanted to stop the car on the narrow street and confront the person following them; however, training and common sense told him not to. He wasn't wearing his soft body armor and he couldn't be sure there was only one person in the car. But foremost in his mind was the safety of the woman in the seat beside him. Therefore, the confrontation he wanted would have to wait.

At the next intersection he turned left, raced ahead and took another left while checking the mirror to be sure he hadn't outrun the Mustang. When he reached the main road he came to a complete stop and waited for the car to pull up behind them. He smiled as he put the Lamborghini in first gear. "Hold on to your seat." He gunned the engine and popped the clutch. The sound of screeching tires and the smell of burning rubber filled the night air as the powerful machine rocketed back onto the highway. He worked through the gears and headed for the freeway ramp that was just ahead.

When he reached the on-ramp of the highway he purposely slowed to let the Mustang catch up. As the car drew near he braked and dropped back into second gear. With a gleam of anticipation in his eyes he punched the accelerator and roared onto the interstate highway.

"Damn, what a beast," he laughed, as the distance opened between them and the other car. His timing was precise as he shifted gears, watching the speedometer needle shoot beyond the 120 mile per hour mark. He glanced in the mirror and saw the Mustang fading from view, but he continued to hold the accelerator to the floor.

"How fast are we going?" she called to him.

"Right now we're just hitting 145." With that he started to release the pressure on the accelerator and watched the red speedometer needle drift from his fantasy of warp speed back toward reality. When it dropped to 70 miles per hour he crossed the traffic lanes and left the freeway. "Now that was a ride," he said, stopping on the bridge and cutting the lights off.

"That's the fastest I've ever traveled in a car," she said, her voice filled with excitement. "I probably won't sleep for a week."

"Well, this baby still had plenty left."

"Do you think he saw us get off the interstate?"

"Nah," he chuckled, pointing to the Mustang in the fast lane. "We dusted him."

"Are you going to chase him?"

"Not tonight. Besides, I have a feeling we'll be seeing him again real soon."

He was in the library two hours later, racking his brain to piece the stranger into the puzzle. He tapped his fingers on the brim of his Stetson and worked the pieces around. But no matter what fashion he arranged them in, a persistent little itch kept bugging him.

Ezra's knock broke his train of thought. "Miss Tiffany said I should bring you some cold beer."

"Thanks, Ezra. Come in."

Lewis twisted the cap off a cold bottle of Coors and after a sip motioned for Ezra to sit down. "Why don't you have one with me?"

"Oh no, sir," the old man said, his face showing his surprise. "I couldn't do that. Mr. Barrows wouldn't like it."

"Fuck Mr. Barrows," he said, taking a beer from the bucket and handing it to Ezra. "The Almighty Lord and Master isn't here now. Besides, I'd like you to have a beer with me."

The old man smiled as he took the bottle from him. "Sir, I sure do like the way you think."

"Well, it's not usually the way I think that gets me in deep shit. It's sayin' what's on my mind that makes people wanna piss on my parade."

Ezra laughed and soon J.D. was laughing with him. In many ways Ezra's laugh reminded him of John Henry Johnson's. Only John Henry could shake the walls when he gave his best howl. But like John Henry's, Ezra's guffaw was infectious.

Tiffany soaked in a tub of steaming water scented with lilac bath oil. She recalled her conversation with Rose Anna and the scene that played in her mind was much like volleys in a tennis match. But in this game there were two men in front of her. The man she married some twenty years ago and J.D. Lewis who appeared like a bolt of lightning from a sky filled with storm clouds.

Rose Anna's words, like them or not, were beginning to make sense as she tried to relax in the steamy water. The disturbing truth became clear. She and the handsome young detective were on a collision course unless she found some way to prevent such a clash.

Her vision cleared a little as the steam from the hot water rose around her. There was only one course of action. When Zachary returned from his latest business trip she'd overwhelm him with her passion. She'd become the temptress of old and seduce him as she had when they were first married. Her body was still firm and curvaceous and she remembered how he'd lustfully leer at her during their lovemaking sessions. She'd regain his physical affection by using her body to distract him from his too many newfound interests.

Later, as she clutched the pillow, she had no desire to cry. She had a plan and now while drifting off to dreamland she was confident her plan would succeed. Floating on misty clouds to another land, the picture grew clearer.

The warm night air carried a gentle breeze that seemed to whisper vows of yesterday and gave her hope for a new beginning. The white sands still glowing from the days of sunshine brushed over her feet as she walked to the water's edge to be with Zachary. He greeted her with a deeply passionate kiss that told her the fires of years gone by were being rekindled. The searing flames of desire within her roared to life once again as the moon above cast the shadows of the lovers over the waves of the inviting cool waters.

Hand in hand they walked out to meet the calling voice of the sea and clung to each other as the water climbed higher and higher around them. They dipped beneath the surface where their lips met in a salty, fiery kiss that told of bodies that would soon be wrapped in love's embrace. They broke through the water's surface, gasping for air and clinging to each other. She pressed her body to him and looked lovingly into the haunting, stormy deep brown eyes of Jefferson Daniel Lewis.

Nine

Ten days after his latest business outing, The Lord and Master, Zachary Barrows, returned home triumphant again in his bid to take over a failing company. Although his arrival was not greeted with blaring trumpets and red carpets, he made every effort to see that it was a production.

Lewis looked at Ezra and smiled as he watched Barrows strut from the Rolls Royce, reminding him of a rooster who'd stand in the middle of the hen house beating his wings and crowing to call attention to himself. Indeed, the King of the Rhode Island Reds had come home to roost.

Barrows embraced Tiffany with a flowery show of affection, making sure that everybody, especially Lewis, could see his love for her. After the display he summoned Lewis to his office.

"Bring me up to date on what's been happening," he said, seeming impatient. "Last night when I called, Tiffany told me there's been some trouble."

"There were two incidents while you were away. First, someone signed in at the health club using your name. When I saw him around Mrs. Barrows I checked on him and he took off. Then we were followed by someone I assume was the same man one evening when we went to the police station."

"Why'd you take my wife to the police station?"

"Well, I couldn't leave her here and still keep an eye on her. I had work to do on the killings, so I took her along."

"I don't like it. Not at all. I don't want my wife exposed to the riffraff around the police station."

"I sure as hell didn't take her into the cell block if that's what you mean. If not, the only riffraff she was exposed to was me and the other cops."

"What's the status on your investigation into the murders?" Barrows said. "What?"

"What's the status of your investigation? I expect to be kept up to date on your progress. I want a written report on your progress in—"

"Just a damn minute," Lewis said. "I'm here to act as a guardian for your wife. Nothing more. You're not a law enforcement officer and that means you're not gonna get that information. Whatever happens that in any way concerns your wife, I'll report to you. But don't expect me to open the case files just to satisfy your curiosity."

"By God," Barrows yelled, springing from his chair and slamming his fist on the desktop. "You'll give me any damn information I want."

"Bullshit. It won't happen. And, if you don't like it, you can relieve me of the job of protecting your wife and I'll get back to work full-time."

Barrows was angered by the brash young man in the Stetson standing across the desk from him. No one under his roof spoke to him with such disrespect. People spoke to him in reverent tones or approached on bended knee. "Well, we'll see about that. I'll call the chief of police and the governor if necessary."

"I don't give a rat's ass if you call His Holiness, the Pope. You're not getting my reports."

"Get out," Barrows said, pointing a trembling finger toward the door. "Get out of my office, you arrogant son-of-a-bitch."

Lewis took his time walking across the room, knowing his deliberate act was causing Barrows' blood pressure to soar. And now one more person wanted to piss on his parade.

In the hallway, Ezra's smile told him he'd heard the argument. "You sure got Mr. Barrows riled up. I ain't never heard him scream like that, but I like it. It's 'bout time somebody put him in his place."

"He needs his dick stepped on now and then," J.D. said with a grin and gave Ezra a friendly pat on the back.

"And you're just the man to do it too."

He walked outside thinking how the Barrows household, in many ways, stirred up memories of the foster home. There were many similarities. John and Mary Smith were a mirrored image of Zachary Barrows, but without his riches. Everything had to be done their way or they'd punish him for breaking their rules. But their children rarely seemed to get any of the same treatment.

He could still see them standing on the worn, blue carpet in the living room, hands on hips, jabbering away about house rules and him obeying them. As time passed he began to think of them as The Bitch and The Bastard.

He hated the house and spent as much time as possible away from John and Mary Smith and their four children. The days, which turned to weeks and eventually months, were made less bearable at meal time. Being a young boy he had a very hearty appetite, but when food on the table became sparse the Smith children helped themselves to his meager share. If he complained about their thievery he was struck with the back of Mary's hand across his face or she took the towel she always carried and knotted it around his throat.

It was the kindness of Mr. Higa and John Henry Johnson that gave him the will to go on under such horrible conditions. It was years before he knew that they were aware of his problem not long after their first meeting. But their calls to the proper agencies were lost in the bureaucracy.

In those early days of learning and practicing with the two men he didn't ask why classes ended with a meal. He eagerly ate whatever was put in front of him. As time passed he found out what they'd been doing for him and with that he learned the true meaning of friendship.

His Saturday mornings were spent working out at the karate school and it was soon a custom to fill the afternoons at the home of John Henry Johnson. Within minutes of his first visit he was in awe when he was led into the den. That's where he saw the picture of John Henry in his dress blues shaking hands with the President of the United States and another of him gripping the hand of the governor. It was then that he vowed to follow in the footsteps of the man he'd grown to idolize.

Although his trust in Takayoshi Higa and John Henry Johnson was implicit, years passed before he told them about the goings on in the Smith home. His confidence in them was so complete he even confessed that sometimes he wanted to turn the table on Mary and knot the towel around her throat.

"Are you ready to go to the spa?"

"Huh?" he muttered, turning to see Tiffany with her gym bag. "Uh, sure. Yeah. Let's go."

She waited until they were outside the gate and said, "You really managed to upset my husband."

"You heard?"

"Oh, yes," she replied, with a bit of a smile. "I haven't heard him yell like that in years. What in the world did you do?"

"Refused to give him the police reports on the murders."

"Why did he want your police reports?"

"He said he wanted to be kept up to date on everything. When I told him that wasn't gonna happen, he got pissed off."

"That sounds like him."

"Well, he'd better get used to it. I have no intention of giving him the reports."

She figured it was better to change the subject. "When we're at the spa why will you let me change clothes in the locker room, but not shower?"

"Well, when we get there almost everybody's dressed and working out or talking. That means the locker room's quiet. And your friend Rose Anna always follows you into the room. I stand close enough to the room so I can hear any loud voices or struggle. But if the shower's running, it'll mask or drown out the sounds of a struggle."

"Do you think I'm safe with Rose Anna along?"

He smiled. "I don't really look at her as a bodyguard. But the killer isn't likely to attack you as long as someone's with you. Remember, all of the victims were alone when they were murdered. This guy doesn't want to leave a witness who could identify him later on. But I still don't wanna take any chances."

"Uh, when you're standing outside the locker room, can you hear what's being said inside?"

"No. The walls are pretty well insulated and the door's heavy. I can hear people talkin', but I can't understand what they're saying. I'd have to open the door to do that. Why do you ask?"

"Oh, just curious." Her sense of relief was overwhelming. Thank God he hadn't overheard her intimate confession. But she wondered what his reaction would've been. Then she recalled the dream with the shared embrace and passions flaming around them in the bubbling surf. Suddenly the warmth raced through her and her face darkened from the swift surge of heated blood. She clutched tightly to the bag in her lap, trying to force the thought from her mind.

"Tiffany. Tiffany, you can open the door now," he said, touching her arm.

"What?" she said, jumping at his touch. "Oh—we're here."

"Are you okay?"

"Yes. Fine."

As they worked out he sensed that Tiffany was preoccupied. She wasn't herself today. Her workout seemed forced and not that of her normal fluid routine; however, he didn't ask what was wrong. He stayed away, believing it was better to leave her alone.

Ten

By early afternoon Lewis was working in his office, looking for that link he'd yet to discover that would tie one person to the murders. He ran through his notes again and made computer entries, stopping now and then to cross check his references and listings. He was about to stop when he saw it. There, lost in the hundreds of other data entries, the name Gary Wilson sprang out and went to the top of the list.

Well, Gary, he thought, *let's see what brings you to the top of the heap.* A search of the files showed Gary Wilson to be white, 34-years-old and employed by the Weldon Landscape Corporation. A brief check of police files showed two prior arrests, one for indecent exposure and the other for sexual assault. *Gary, if your name shows up on the work orders for the Wellington, Upchruch, French or McDougal residences, you and me will definitely have to sit down for a little one on one chat.*

He couldn't understand how the Suck-Ass Triplets missed Wilson's name when they were compiling their list of suspects. Surely they would've jumped at such an obvious clue, or had they already done so and were concealing the information in the hopes he'd fail to find it. But it was possible that they'd just overlooked it.

With Zachary Barrows home for a few days he hoped he'd have a little more freedom to pursue the investigation. With Gary Wilson's name popping up he needed to do some old-fashioned leg work and do a background check as soon as possible, but he didn't want to do it so fast that his actions warned Gary Wilson that he'd become a suspect in the Society Stalker killings.

He was ready for opposition to his request to leave the grounds, only to be stunned when Barrows waved his hand in the air and muttered, "Go do what you want."

His first stop was at the Weldon Landscape Corporation where he used a bit of charm and a little sweet talk to coax the secretary into letting him access the company's files. A smile and a little white lie managed to get him a copy of specific work orders.

He next visited the court house and researched trial records. While thumbing through the documents he found that Gary Wilson was tried and convicted of indecent exposure when he was 23 years old. More interesting was the fact that, at the time, Wilson was working for Brentmore Security Systems installing burglar alarms in homes and businesses. This offense occurred while he was working when he exposed himself to a secretary of a legal firm. Shortly after his arrest he was fired from Brentmore Security Systems.

He was 27 years old when he was arrested for sexual assault. According to court records, he was employed by Weldon Landscape Corporation at the time and again the offense took place while he was working. He was taken into custody after a woman, who admitted sunbathing in the buff, accused him of fondling her breasts. After a trial, marked by heated arguments from both the prosecution and defense, Wilson was found guilty and given a six-month suspended sentence; however, Gordon Weldon refused to fire him.

Lewis thought about the information gathered so far as he left the courthouse and drove to the police station. Wilson had more than just a little knowledge of burglar alarm systems and would certainly be aware of both their strengths and weaknesses. With that background he could probably bypass or even shut down a "foolproof" system. Later on, according to work orders, Wilson performed landscaping chores at the homes of all of the victims. And he'd been arrested twice for sex crimes. Had he graduated from exposing himself and coping a feel to murder?

At the police station he picked up the arrest photograph of Gary Wilson. *Well, Gary, you aren't the guy from the spa. But you sure could've made my life simpler if you had been.* Now he had two men in the puzzle, but only one of them had a name.

He was turning to leave when he bumped into Lieutenant Adams. "Ah, Lewis, just the man I'm looking for. Come to my office."

Lewis followed him to his office and was about to close the door when the Suck-Ass Triplets came in and plopped their asses in three chairs arranged side by side. He forced a cough, hoping it would hide his sudden urge to laugh.

He stood in front of the desk and watched as Adams produced a number of official documents from a large manila envelope. With a curious smirk on his face he handed the papers to him. "You can read the charges against you."

Lewis began reading the papers that were Internal Affairs Division forms charging him with Conduct Unbecoming an Officer based on accusations sworn to by Adams. "You can't be serious," he said, shaking his head.

"Oh, yes I am," Adams said, clasping his hands behind his head and rocking back in his chair, the smirk growing larger.

"You guys called Mrs. Barrows a slut and a sweaty whore, not me."

"That's not the way we see it, Detective Lewis."

"Well, she sure as hell took what I said as a joke."

"Bullshit," Wallace said. "She was upset. It was written all over her face."

"Mrs. Barrows laughed about it outside. You were the ones who looked like idiots. You tried to jam me and stepped on your dicks. So, now you're pissed off and think you can charge me with some bullshit offense. No fuckin' way."

"Lewis," Adams said, sitting up in his chair, "if you have the nerve to ask for a trial board over this...."

"Don't worry about that. I intend to. I'm not gonna take this shit."

"You'd better get a good lawyer."

To argue further would've been useless. Instead, he signed the paper to acknowledge receipt of the documents and left the room. As the door closed behind him, Grayson said, "I think this is a big mistake."

"For God's sake, Don, settle down," Adams said. "He'll never request a trial board. He'll jump at the first bargain offered."

"I don't think so. That guy's a fighter. He won't take this shit layin' down. You just wait and see."

"It's four of us against him. We can't lose. And we got old lady Barrows."

"You'd better make that three. I sure as hell ain't puttin' my career on the line by lying under oath about this. Besides, you'll never get Mrs. Barrows to testify against him."

"You might wanna reconsider your position, Don. There might just be another opening in the Bureau," Adams said, pointing a finger at him. "Get my drift."

"Oh, yeah. I get it."

Eleven

The sun was beginning to fade in the distance and, as it did, it gave everybody its daily light show. The shades of brilliant red, orange and yellow reflected against a backdrop of sky blue and fluffy white clouds that seemed to be predicting a comfortable evening for anyone who wished to stop and enjoy its beauty.

Lewis planned to print up his report on today's findings and map out tomorrow's strategy. He knew his best approach was to dig further into Wilson's background before questioning him. He wanted to learn as much as possible about Gary Wilson to avoid the investigative pitfalls that could seriously damage his case. In a strategic sense, knowing the enemy beforehand passed the advantage to the antagonist.

Tiffany's seduction scheme was in motion when she sat down at the dinner table with Zachary. She'd carefully calculated every move, beginning with the meal. She'd ordered his favorite meal prepared: prime rib, cooked to perfection and served with wild rice and mixed vegetables with fresh garden salad on the side. A special red wine from their cellar was to be served. Phase one of her plan to draw him back into her arms was on schedule.

Zachary sat across from her and, after sipping the wine and nodding, realigned the forks so they were precisely in line one with the other. He placed the white linen napkin in his lap, adjusting the edge to fit snugly just below his waist line.

"I missed you," Tiffany said, gazing over the rim of her wineglass.

"I missed you too, darling," he said, though his tone was without passion.

"I get so lonely when you're out of town on business. The nights seem especially long and empty."

"But you have so much to keep you busy. How can you possibly be lonely?"

She wet her lips and smiled seductively. "I'm talking about another kind of lonely."

"Oh. I see," he said and immediately turned his attention to cutting the meat on his plate.

When the dessert plates were removed from the table, she got up and took him by the arm. She wasted little time guiding him to the bedroom where a bottle of exquisite red wine awaited them. She poured a glass of wine for him and waited for him to sip the crimson nectar.

The scenario moved to its next stage as she began to undress him. He offered no resistance to her advances and he seemed to be enjoying her every move. She could feel her excitement mounting and her hands trembled as she peeled away the last of his clothing.

Her mouth suddenly felt very dry as she whispered, "I'll be right back." She moved away on unsteady legs, feeling her heart pound with expectancy. She was aflame with desire as she slipped off her dress and reached for the intimate, sexy apparel he once loved seeing her wear. The sexy clothing and a hint of perfume in just the right spots would be the perfect rebuilding block for their love.

As she crossed the room she could see his eyes drinking in her body, exploring her as he once had from head to toe. She stood for a moment, allowing him to continue feeling her up with his gaze. She desperately wanted him, yet she wished to prolong this very special moment.

She moved onto the bed and beside him, where she began to gently kiss his neck and run her fingers through his thick mat of hair. Her hands and fingers played softly over his muscular shoulders and chest as she continued to kiss him on the neck. When she moved the kisses from his neck to his face and lips, she felt him abruptly tense.

She let it pass, working down over his throat to his chest, only to find his body had become like a coiled roll of icy steel. Still, she refused to give up, letting her hand slide down between his legs where she caressed and massaged his manhood, praying for a sign of life. When he failed to respond to her touch, she lowered her head and took him in her mouth. This she knew never failed to arouse him, but this time there was nothing.

She pulled away and looked up at him, seeing his head buried in the pillow, eyes closed. "Zachary." He didn't answer. But she was sure he was awake. "Zachary." Again there was no response.

Tiffany stumbled from the bed, fighting to hold back the tears that welled up in her eyes. She walked quickly to the bathroom, closed the door and turned on the shower as the tears burned and blurred her vision. She ripped away the flimsy clothing and hurled it to the floor, cursing the makers of intimate garments. She then stepped into the waves of steaming water, sank to the floor and sobbed uncontrollably.

It was almost midnight when she pulled on the terrycloth robe and walked barefoot down the darkened hallway. She stopped at the end of the corridor and stared out the window, hoping to find solace in the darkness outside. She found instead the young man who recently dared to make a habit of invading her dreams and her heart jumped into her throat.

In the shimmering light of the full moon she watched him, clad in only black sweat pants, performing a ritual she knew from her school days was connected to the martial arts. She felt the slight twitch in her stomach as she watched the fluid motions of his muscular body as he moved gracefully through the routine. She tried to turn away, but her eyes stayed glued to the man who continued to glide through the dance of death in the moonlight on the lawn below.

Whether it was the magnetism of his boyish charm or simply her need to be with someone she was uncertain. But she found herself carrying the bucket of ice cold beer through the kitchen door and over the cool grass to where he stood. "I thought you might enjoy a cold beer. That is, if you're finished your workout."

"Yes, I would," he said, picking his sweatshirt up from the ground and wiping the sweat from his brow. "I just finished. But you're the last person I expected to see."

"I couldn't sleep."

"Yeah. I know what you mean," he said, reaching for a beer. "I have nights like that myself."

Is it because you're so goddamned horny you're tied in knots, she thought, momentarily wishing that she had the nerve to ask. "How long have you been practicing the martial arts?" she said.

"How'd you know I practiced a martial art?"

"I saw you from the window," she said, pointing to the house.

"Oh." He sipped his beer and noticed her red swollen eyes. "A little over twenty years."

"My God! Did you start as an infant?"

"Not quite," he laughed. "I was eight years old."

"Still, that's pretty young."

"Yes and no. Some kids start even younger." He wanted to ask why she'd been crying, but let it pass.

She stood beside him in the moonlight and watched the beads of sweat trickle slowly along his face and drip one by one to the shirt he had draped over his shoulders. Broad, muscular shoulders. Shoulders that would be so nice to touch and caress. For a fleeting instant she thought of stripping off her robe and crushing her body against his. To feel his strong, young body pressed to hers and, then and there, under the light of the full moon satisfy her lustful yearnings.

Zachary Barrows stared down at the couple standing side by side, so close their bodies almost touched, and he wondered why they were together. He felt the jealous knot tighten in his chest and vowed that he'd assert himself and his rules come morning.

Twelve

When Tiffany sat down at the breakfast table there were already four dozen long-stemmed red roses in the center of it. To the left of her coffee cup there was a beautiful card with expressions of love imprinted in gold over a red rose floral design.

Zachary stood behind her chair, cupped her shoulders, leaned down and softly kissed her cheek. "I love you, my darling. You mean more to me than words can ever express. I hope you know that."

Still feeling the frustration of last night's failed attempt at lovemaking, she wasn't overpowered by his show of affection. In recent years, material things had become his way of making love when she would've preferred a display of caveman animalism.

"After breakfast we'll take a drive into town. I'm sure a diamond bracelet will be the appropriate topping for the flowers."

"A diamond bracelet isn't really necessary," she replied while thinking, *I don't want it.*

"Nothing's too good for you, darling. And you know what they say, diamonds are a girl's best friend."

She closed her eyes as she raised her coffee cup and thought, *right now my best friend would be a hard throbbing cock shoved so far into me I'd scream. But, around here lately, the only thing hard in this house is a diamond.* Almost immediately she felt a pang of remorse and quickly sought to rationalize his impotence. It had to be something with the business. But business had been her rationalization for the past seven years.

Zachary downed his breakfast in near record time and excused himself. His second priority of the day was to put young Detective Lewis in his place, and he was building up a head of steam to do just that. He was disappointed when he learned that the detective had gotten up early and left without even having a cup of coffee. Naturally he saw Lewis' leaving without his approval as another act of contemptuous behavior.

~~~

By nine o'clock J.D. was seated in the principal's office of Dominion High School and, over coffee, discussing the scholastic achievements and personal conduct of Gary Wilson.

Mary Ellen Jarvis was in her twenty-second year as principal of the school and, as always, managed to astonish anyone asking about those who had long since left the hallowed halls of learning, with her keen memory. "Gary was certainly above average. He was more than capable of maintaining an A average in all subjects. But he never fully applied himself and seemed satisfied when a B or two showed up on his report card."

"So, he didn't really apply himself?"

"He was scholarship material if he wanted to be," she said, after a sip of her coffee. "I was very disappointed when he chose not to attend college. He could've done well at any number of top learning institutions."

"What was his behavior in general?" he said, waving away her offer to refill his cup. "Did he disrupt classes or cause other problems?"

"There were several incidents, but nothing positive to link Gary to them." Mrs. Jarvis tapped the desk top with the eraser of her pencil and went on. "But I just had this feeling that he was the person responsible. You know the feeling, I'm sure."

"Yes, ma'am, I do," he said, smiling. "Do you recall the incidents?"

"As I remember, the first one took place during a biology class when the lights were turned off prior to the showing of a film. The instant the lights were switched off someone grabbed a female student by the breasts and ran a hand up her dress and squeezed her crotch. She screamed and by the time the lights were turned on, Gary, who'd been standing right beside her, was several seats away laughing. Of course, he was the prime target of a school inquiry, but we couldn't prove a thing."

"What about the other incidents?"

"Two very attractive girls, both cheerleaders, received sexually explicit letters and notes."

"How'd they get them?" he said, leaning forward in his chair.

"Some were left in their lockers. Some placed in their purses. Others were put in their books."

"How explicit were the letters?"

"Oh, my," she replied, shuffling nervously in her chair. "They were vivid indeed. The letters described in great detail how he wanted to take them to specific places, such as rooms in a house and one or two locations here in the school and perform various sex acts with them. And, I must say, the letters left absolutely nothing to the imagination."

"And I take it Gary Wilson was the prime suspect?"

"Yes, he was."

"What made him the prime suspect?"

"He seemed almost obsessed with these two girls. He attended every football and basketball game and managed to stay as close as possible to them throughout the games. He would show up at parties uninvited and follow them around. He stared at them during classes, especially on game days because they wore their cheerleading outfits to school."

He nodded. "Do you know if he ever asked them for dates, or asked them to spend time with him working on a school project or anything?"

"No. Not that I'm aware of."

"Are the letters still filed away someplace?"

"That's another strange thing, Detective Lewis. The night before the police were to be called in to investigate the incidents, there was a break-in here at the school and those letters were stolen along with some petty cash, a radio and a watch."

"Yeah. That sure is strange. Do you remember if Gary was questioned about that?"

"The police questioned him several times, but they were never able to connect him to the crime. And in this particular instance his name didn't surface in the school grapevine in connection with the break in."

"What about the other incidents? Did his name come up in the grapevine connecting him with them?" he said, knowing the rumor mill often had a way of holding the truth.

"You could say he received top billing in regards to the biology class fondling and as the writer of the letters. But, as I said before, nothing was ever proved."

"Since leaving school, has he returned for any reason? Class reunion? Football games?"

"I personally haven't seen him at a school function since he graduated, and no other teacher has mentioned seeing him on the grounds or in the building."

"Do the victims of these incidents still live in the area?"

"The girls who received the letters are married and are residing out of state. Betty Haskins, the girl from the biology class, was killed in a traffic accident shortly after her graduation."

He thanked Mrs. Jarvis for her help and went back to the mansion to add the latest information to his report. He'd barely started tapping at the computer keys when Ezra came in and told him that Mr. Barrows wanted to see him.

He found Barrows seated at his desk methodically stacking papers in wooden trays labeled Immediate Attention, In and File. Barrows ignored him and continued to sort the papers in precisely arranged stacks in the trays, leaving Lewis to wonder when the master would get around to acknowledging his presence.

When he was satisfied that the papers were sorted to his liking, Barrows stood and faced him. "I want to remind you of just what your duties are around here," he said, leaning down and tapping a finger on his desk. "You're here to ensure my wife's safety. Nothing more. Do you understand?"

"Yes, sir. I thought that's what I've been doing."

"I damn sure expect everything to remain on a strictly professional level. There's to be no contact with my wife other than as required in the performance of your duty. Do I make myself clear?"

"Yes, sir. But I hope you understand that my duties demand daily contact with your wife while you're away on business. You can't expect me to allow her to leave the house and go and come as she pleases and still hold me responsible for her safety."

"That's what you're here for, to protect her," Barrows yelled, his face reddening. "But that's where it's to end. I don't want any socializing between you after hours. Is that a littler clearer?"

Lewis suddenly realized he was being lectured by a man who was in the midst of a jealous rage; however, he guessed that this show of anger was due to Barrows looking at Tiffany more as his personal possession than his wife. "Oh, it's absolutely clear. But I think you're trying to read more into this than—"

"I'm not interested in your opinion. I just want to be certain you understand your position. You're here merely as an employee I've bought and paid for. Not one damn thing more."

Lewis' first inclination was to reach across the desk, take Barrows by the throat and say, "Fuck you, asshole." But with a great deal of self discipline he managed to control his urge and not choke him until he turned a deathly shade of blue. "Well, I think I know what you're trying to say."

Barrows glared at him. "Just remember your place, Mr. Lewis."

"Shit. How could I ever forget with you here to remind me every fuckin' day?" he muttered.

"What?"

"I said, don't worry, I won't forget."

Thirteen

Lewis went back to the library and was getting ready to enter data into the computer when he was interrupted again. This time by his pager. He glanced down and saw the now familiar number for Captain Thomas' office. He called and the telephone was answered almost immediately.

"Captain, this is Lewis."

"Hope I'm not bothering you. I just wanted to see how you were doing with your investigation."

"Well, sir, I've developed a possible suspect," he said, flipping over a page in his notebook.

"Really?"

"Yes, sir. But, I've just started really lookin' at him. I'd rather do a background work up before I confront him."

"Smart thinking. What's his name?"

"Gary Wilson."

"Hummm. Doesn't ring a bell. When do you think you'll be interviewing him?"

"Soon. Maybe tomorrow. But I don't wanna rush in like an idiot and screw things up."

"Take your time," Thomas said, suddenly sounding distant. "Keep me posted."

"Yes, sir."

When the call ended Lewis stared at the phone for moment and wondered about Thomas. He wasn't a happy man and hadn't been for some time. Not since the breakup of his marriage. Although he didn't know all of the details about the failure of his marriage, he'd heard the usual ugly talk going around the police station. He scratched his head and thought that maybe he should do a background work up on Captain Thomas.

He shrugged his shoulders and added the latest details to his report. Later in the evening he'd drop the reports off and hoped that would keep Wallace and Adams off his back. Then he'd give Gary Wilson's neighborhood a once over.

He figured he'd take a little more time to review his facts and plan his approach before speaking with Wilson face to face. Caution was the key to success in this case and moving too quickly might scare Wilson into a corner with an attorney hanging onto his arm.

After showering, he picked his police report up and walked out to his car. As he was opening the door he saw Ezra, very casually dressed and leisurely strolling around the yard. "Where's the uniform?"

"I have the evenin' off."

"Wanna ride into town with me while I drop off some paperwork?"

Ezra smiled. "Yes, sir. I'd sure like that."

Lewis stepped around to the passenger's side of the pale blue Ford and opened the door for him. "Maybe we could grab some dinner while we're in town."

"I'd be happy to have dinner with you," he said, pleased to be asked to share dinner with a man he admired from the moment they met. He was grinning from ear to ear as he slid into the passenger's seat and buckled his safety belt. "This is the first time I've ever been in a police car."

"Well, Ezra, you were invited. Most people usually ride in the backseat in leg irons and handcuffs."

The atmosphere was relaxed and filled with good natured chatter as they drove to the police station. The two men talked as though they'd been lifelong friends. After dropping his reports on Wallace's desk, Lewis took Ezra on a tour of the police station.

As they rounded a corner near the Communications Division they came upon the Suck-Ass Triplets laughing over something.

The laughter stopped abruptly when they saw Lewis nearing their huddle and Frank Hargrove pointed a finger at him. "Hey, hotshot. Solve the murders yet?"

"Not yet, Frank. Then again, I haven't reached your level of expertise."

"Keep that in mind."

Ezra, a very wise man, could read people easily. He immediately sensed the hostility from the trio. He was tempted to fire a barb back at Hargrove, but figured it was better to keep his thoughts to himself.

Lewis guided Ezra down the hallway toward the main lobby. He knew that staying in contact with the triplets would probably cause trouble and at the present he had more than enough problems.

He and Ezra drove to the Spring Meadows Apartments and cruised slowly along the freshly paved road until they located 3006 Spring Valley Drive. In front of the building Gary Wilson was applying a coat of wax to a spotless red Camaro while talking with an attractive brunette.

He circled the neighborhood, noting that it was well-kept with neatly trimmed shrubs lining the sidewalks and apartment fronts. The walkways and streets were clean to the point of being void of discarded cigarettes and chewing gum. Junked cars that were occasionally left on the parking lots of many apartment complexes were conspicuously absent here at Spring Meadows.

Satisfied with everything, J.D. drove to a restaurant on the outskirts of town where they dined on fried chicken, mashed potatoes with gravy, black-eyed peas and corn bread fresh from the oven. They topped off their meal with home baked apple pie and hot coffee.

"That's what I call good eatin'," Ezra said, leaning back and patting his stomach.

"You can't beat this place for fried chicken and ribs," Lewis replied. "They have the best around."

"Mr. Lewis, you got a little Soul Brother in you?"

"Nah. Just grew up around a family who knew how to eat right."

They talked for awhile about families and friends over a cold beer. Lewis told him about John Henry Johnson and how John Henry's wife eventually became Mama Johnson to him and about spending much of his time growing up around the Johnson Family.

Halfway through his second beer, Ezra said, "You know, I think Miss Tiffany's a very lonely woman."

"Why do you say that?"

"Well, you can see it in her eyes. I've been around Miss Tiffany since they were married 20 years ago. A few years back things changed. She started actin' different."

"What do you mean?" Lewis said, leaning back in his chair. How did she start actin' different?"

"Well, Mr. Barrows started spendin' a lot more time outta town. The next thing you know Miss Tiffany had all these things to do around the country club. But she kinda reminded me of a robot. You know, just goin' through the motions. Then I noticed she looked like she'd been cryin' a lot. Her eyes were red and puffed up. She looked sad. And I got the feelin' Mr. Barrows wasn't payin' her the proper kind of attention. You know—like he wasn't takin' care of business."

He nodded. "Yeah, Ezra. I think I know what you mean."

"Then Miss Tiffany started worryin' because of the murders. Those women who were killed were friends of Miss Tiffany and she was afraid when Mr. Barrows left to go outta town."

"Why was she afraid? She had you and Jason around. And Jason looks like he's more than capable of takin' care of himself."

"Jason wasn't around all the time when Mr. Barrows left town. Sometimes he went with Mr. Barrows, especially if he was gonna be outta town longer than usual."

Lewis shook his head. "Was Mr. Barrows out of town when the murders were committed?"

Ezra rolled his head back and looked up at the ceiling for a moment. "You know, come to think about it, he was outta town when they were killed."

"All of 'em?"

"Yes, sir."

"Do you know if Jason went with Mr. Barrows on those trips? When the women were killed?"

"You got me there, Mr. Lewis," he said, raising his beer mug. "I don't really recall. Why? You don't suspect Jason, do you?"

"Sorry. I start askin' questions and sometimes I just forget where to stop."

"That's okay. But, I sure wish things would go better for Miss Tiffany. She's a good person."

"Yeah. She sure is."

"She deserves to be happy."

At the Huntley Manor Country Club, Tiffany was anything but happy. Zachary had promised her a private, candle-lit table for two in a quiet corner of the club. She immediately saw the proposal as a prelude to him whispering of pent-up passion and promises of future lust-filled evenings.

Zachary hurried her through dinner while gulping Johnnie Walker Blue Label as if he was drinking fresh spring water. He then insisted they delay dessert in order to greet a few acquaintances he felt they'd recently snubbed; however, this was just an excuse to parade her from table to table and brag about his buying a $20,000 trinket of affection for the wife he so dearly loved.

Tiffany became increasingly uncomfortable as he continued to speak of his love for her. He even insisted that their friends compliment her beauty. Her embarrassment grew as they bowed to his demands. Finally she said,

"Zachary, I think we should leave."

"It's still early," he answered, his speech slurred from the scotch.

"Uh—I'm not feeling very well."

Her request touched a nerve. "What brought on this sudden illness?" he said.

"I'm...I'm not sure. Maybe something I ate didn't agree with me."

"Are you sure you're ill?" he said, reaching out and tightly clutching her forearm.

"Or could it be you're just in a hurry to get home?"

"You're hurting me."

He didn't seem to notice her pain as he forcefully pushed her to the foyer. "Are you going to be late for a parley with your detective friend? Is that why you're in such a hurry to get home? Has his interest in guarding your body gone from professional to personal? Or are you giving him some motherly guidance on the joys of sex?"

She spun around to face him, her right hand rising and landing a stinging slap to his left cheek. "How dare you talk to me that way." She glared at him and pulled her arm away. "I'm not some cheap whore you picked up in a bar and I won't be treated like one."

She turned and walked away, leaving him dazed and touching his face where she'd struck him. Never in their relationship had she even raised her voice to him in anger. Now in a brief span of hazy moments she not only raised her voice to him, but also slapped him across the jaw. He recovered too late to overtake her. He reached the door in time to see the taillights of the Rolls disappear in the dark.

Jason dropped her off at the mansion and she walked to the east wing. Her heart beat a little faster as she made her way down the darkened hall and saw the light from under the library door. J.D. was there.

He glanced up from the computer screen as the door opened and nearly blurted, "God, you're beautiful" to the woman in the doorway. His eyes remained fixed on her as she walked over and stood beside the desk.

"May I sit down?"

"Yes. Please."

She wasted no time with small talk, but began telling him of the argument with Zachary. She was very careful to omit certain parts of the heated fight, but she sensed that J.D. knew some details were left out.

"I'm sorry your evening was a disaster."

"I guess he had too much too drink. That doesn't happen often, but sometimes he gets a little carried away when he's drinking scotch."

"It can happen to anybody," he said. "I'm sure he'll be sorry for what happened when he wakes up in the morning."

She managed to laugh. "For what? The argument or having too much to drink?"

He smiled. "Probably both."

She reached out and touched his hand, saying, "Thanks for listening to my problems." Her voice was barely a whisper as her hand covered his and her heart started to race when he didn't try to move away from her touch.

"That's okay. Anytime," he said, feeling his mouth suddenly go dry.

The knowledge that Zachary would soon be home snapped her back to reality and she stood. "Thanks again." She squeezed his hand as she got ready to go and fought to conquer her desire to kiss him. She turned away before she hurled caution to the wind.

He watched her cross the room and felt the strange flutter in his stomach and asked himself what was happening. *Man, this is crazy*, he thought. *I can't feel like this. I've got a job to do and gettin' all hung up on her is sure as shit gonna complicate things*. He closed his eyes and wondered what it would be like to make love to her.

Fourteen

J.D. Lewis' prophecy started to come true at the breakfast table. Zachary stood with his head bowed and offered an apology for his outrageous behavior. It was, to be sure, a first for him. Begging for forgiveness was something he believed belonged to others. But on this misty morning he'd become one of the meek. "Tiffany, please forgive me for last night. I know I had too much to drink, but that's no excuse for what I did."

"You said some very cruel things."

"I know. How can I make it up to you? Another bracelet? A necklace?"

For a few moments he'd seemed to be humbled by what had happened. But just as quickly he returned to the man he'd always been. "Please, Zachary," she said. "No. No bracelet. No necklace. Nothing like that. Your answer to every problem is buy it or pay it off. Necklaces and bracelets aren't the solution here. A heartfelt apology would mean more than material things."

He continued looking at the woman who, in their 20 plus years of marriage, had never questioned his decisions. Now, in a matter of hours she was standing up to him for a second time. And he could see from the look on her face that she wasn't going to give in. "I…I'm sorry," he said. "I didn't know you felt that way." His mind was spinning in search of something that would allow him a graceful escape, but the dull throb left by the scotch numbed him.

She saw that he was very uncomfortable and said, "Why don't we spend some time together after breakfast? We could discuss this further if you'd like." She couldn't understand why she allowed him a way out. But, then again, maybe it was because she wasn't used to seeing him on the defensive. Or was it because she suddenly felt sorry for him?

"What about your morning workout?"

"I can skip today. Go ahead and start breakfast. I'll tell Detective Lewis he can go without me."

She left the room and found J.D. already at work in his office. "Good morning," she said, walking into the room. "I'm not going to the spa this morning. Why don't you go without me?"

"Okay," he said, trying to hide his disappointment.

"Tomorrow for sure."

"That's fine," he said, then laughed. "Maybe Rose Anna will keep me company today."

"You stay away from her," she said. "I mean, you watch out for her. She…she might try—she…."

"Might try and seduce me?"

"Well, she does have a bit of a reputation."

"I'll keep her at arm's length," he laughed. As she turned to leave he said, "Oh, by the way, I think you might be interested in reading this." He held the charging document up he'd been given by Adams.

She crossed the room, took the papers and began reading. Within seconds the slight smile faded and her jaw tightened. "This is a damn lie. I can't believe this trash. May I take this with me?"

"Well, yeah. But—"

"Let me take care of this. We'll see how Mr. Adams and his friends like dealing with Bob Courtney."

"You mean Big Bob Courtney? The attorney?"

"Yes."

He threw his head back and laughed. "Jesus. He'll tie those idiots up in so many knots they'll develop ulcers for sure."

"Well, Bob, my husband and I are very close friends. In fact, his wife and I co-chair a lot of charity events. I'm sure, as a favor to us, he'll be very happy to deal with this." She turned and left the room.

"Jesus Christ! I can't believe you went ahead and filed those charges," Grayson snapped, as he paced back and forth in the conference room. "They'll never stick."

"Will you calm down, Don?" Adams muttered. "We don't have a thing to worry about."

"Damn it. I told you before, this kid Lewis isn't gonna take this layin' back on his ass. He's gonna fight it and we're all gonna end up eatin' shit."

Wallace laughed. "The only one who'll be eatin' shit is Lewis. With old lady Barrows testifying against him, we can't lose."

"If you think she'll testify against him you're wrong. We've been through this once already. I'm tellin' you she's on his side, not ours. The smart move right now would be to drop the charges, forget everything and move on. Leave Lewis alone."

"We'll see," Adams said. "When this is all over and Lewis is crucified in the papers and maybe even television, then we'll see how handsome and muscular my daughter thinks he is."

"Wait a minute," Grayson said, shaking his finger. "That's what this is all about. It has nothing to do with what he's done on the job. It's not because he got his shield when he was only 28. Or that he solved a shit load of cold cases. This is some personal bullshit because your 13-year-old daughter has a crush on him. Holy shit. What a fuckin' joke."

Adams stared down into his coffee mug as Wallace said, "That's a goddamn crock, Grayson, and you know it."

"No. No, you wait too. I remember all of it now. It was last year at the F.O.P. picnic. Even your wife got a little wet in the pants over him."

"That's a lie," Wallace shouted, jumping to his feet.

"No. No, I don't think so. I was right there when she called him a gorgeous hunk and you about shit. And when she went out of her way to talk to him later on, I thought we'd have to put you in irons to keep you from pickin' a fight with him. Now, I see the whole picture. This thing's over him personally, not professionally. You're just jealous because your wife and your daughter had a little flutter over him."

"My daughter still talks about him," Adams blurted. "Always on the phone to her friends. He's so cute. He's so muscular. I'm sick of it."

"What about your wife?" he said, looking at Wallace. "She still talking about him?"

"No," he mumbled. "But it wouldn't surprise me if she was fantasy fuckin' him while I'm ballin' her."

"Well, I'm puttin' my cards on the table right now. I said it before and I'm sayin' it again, I want no part of this. I'm not gonna lie and especially now that I know it's some personal vendetta."

"What about you, Frank?" Adams said, looking over at Hargrove. "Are you still with us?"

"Yeah. I'll testify. I'll back you."

"I think you're outta your mind, Frank," Grayson said, walking for the door.

"Yeah. Well, I'm lookin' out for my future. I'd like to make sergeant."

Grayson laughed. "If this blows up in everybody's face, which it probably will, I think you can kiss your sergeant's stripes goodbye. If I ever make sergeant, I hope and pray to God that it's because I earned it with hard work and not by sticking a knife in somebody's back." He walked out and slammed the door behind him.

"We'd better keep a close eye on him," Adams said, taking a sip of his now-cold coffee. "I don't like his new attitude."

Wallace pointed to Hargrove. "Go see if you can talk some sense into him."

"Yeah. Okay."

Hargrove found Grayson refilling his coffee cup. "Don, let's have a little talk. I mean, just you and me."

"You're not gonna change my mind."

"At least listen to what I have to say," he said, leading him into one of the interview rooms. "Look, man, Lenny's always taken good care of us. And Wallace has been a standup guy when it comes to us. Why don't you stick with them now and help bag Lewis' ass?"

"Not for some chicken shit charge. If Lewis did something wrong, yeah, I'd stick with them. But he's done nothing wrong. The kid's a hard worker who's out there every day bustin' his balls to do a good job. I won't screw him for that."

"I think you're makin' a big mistake."

"No, Frank. You're the one who's makin' the mistake. Adams and Wallace are just pissed over a little tizzy their daughter and wife had a year ago. So what if they think he's a muscular hunk. Hell, let's face it, the guy's built like a brick shithouse and he's got the looks to go with it. Some chicks cat that up. But, some passing comments at a picnic or a teenage girl's crush aren't reason enough to go after the guy. Now, if he was bangin' Wallace's old lady or puttin' the moves on Adams' little girl, then go after him. What they're doing is bullshit and you know it."

"And you don't think Mrs. Barrows'll testify against him."

"Hell no," he replied, shaking his head. "Jesus, just look at it from your side. You wondered if he was layin' the wood to her. Just for the sake of argument, let's suppose he is. Do you think she'd admit it in a hearing? Do you really think she'd give up everything she's got just because she's gettin' some cock on the side? Besides, maybe her old man doesn't give a shit. And if Lewis is treatin' her right, she sure as hell won't turn on him."

"Damn," Hargrove muttered. "Now I'm not sure what to do."

"Think about it, Frank," he said, turning to leave. "Think long and hard about it."

Fifteen

Lewis changed clothes and left for the Huntley Manor Spa with a smug grin on his face. Knowing that Robert "Big Bob" Courtney would be in his corner was reason to feel somewhat complacent. After all, Courtney was hailed by his colleagues as the best attorney in the business.

He'd barely stepped into the weight room when Rose Anna saw that he was alone. Before he knew it she had him by the arm and was leading him toward the free weights. "Where's Tiffany this morning?"

"She decided to take the day off."

The glint in her deep green eyes flashed a hint of mischief. "In that case, I guess I'll have to give you a little extra special attention." She rolled her tongue over her lips and ran her fingers lightly down and over his chest. "Umm. What firm muscles you have."

"I know there's some smart reply to that," he said, "but I think I'll pass."

She forced a frown and he realized that she was a very attractive woman. He judged her to be in her mid to late thirties, with somewhat of an hourglass figure. She was well-blessed in the bosom area, but he thought she was a little heavier than she should be. Yet, he had to admit she was a lovely woman.

She remained close as he worked out, showering him with bits of flattery and calmly slipping in several comments about erotic body massage, bathing together and strolling naked in the moonlight by a secluded lake. Stories ran wild around the spa and country club that Rose Anna Guilford had entertained a number of much younger men in past years, one of those on his eighteenth birthday. But, as is the case with a lot of gossip, most of the tales were never proven. On the other hand, she did little to dispel the tales that got her the fame and she actually seemed to bask in the rumors.

When his workout ended he tried to leave as quickly as possible, but she wasn't giving him up without a fight. "Let me treat you to lunch. I promise I won't molest you, at least while we're eating."

"I really have a lotta work to do."

"I think you're afraid of me. Do I look like the Big Bad Wolf in Little Red

Riding Hood's cape?"

"Not really," he replied. He chuckled as he tried to picture her wearing nothing but a red cape and carrying a basket filled with exotic bath oils.

"Then have lunch with me."

"Oh, hell, why not? Come on, Red Riding Hood."

She reached out and patted his buttocks. "Oh, if you only knew what Little Red would like to do with you."

"I can only imagine," he muttered, feeling the blood rush to his face as he moved away from her roving hand.

He followed her to a restaurant not far from the spa and, at her request, they were seated at an out of the way, dimly-lit table. They ate salad, sesame seed bread and drank herbal tea, which she insisted was really an aphrodisiac.

When the last dish was cleared from the table she slid her chair closer to his. "So, tell me, how'd you get to be a bodyguard?"

"I was assigned the job."

"You've never been a bodyguard before?"

"No, I haven't."

"But I bet you've defended the honor of many young women," she said, reaching for his hand. "You have, haven't you?"

He was a little embarrassed. "Well, uh—I...."

"Oh, come on. Admit it," she teased. "You've fought for the honor of at least one woman in your life."

"Well, yeah," he said, glancing down at the tablecloth.

"I knew it," she gushed, clasping her hands together. "When? What happened?"

"It was a long time ago." He was silent for a moment, collecting his thoughts.

He started telling her a story from another time, another town. Days of books, school lunches, a bashful smile and the search for enough courage to ask a special someone for a date. The weeks of clanging bells, slamming book lockers, the sounds of running footsteps in hallways to reach a class before the door closed and forced you to the office to explain your tardiness.

The first day of his sophomore year the name Jefferson Lewis was relatively unknown in high school circles. But he was destined for stardom and the reason for his star rising would happen minutes after setting foot on campus on opening day.

Rachel Magliano, a tall, raven-haired Italian beauty and a new student, found herself the object of unwanted attention by Billy Woods and his friends.

They walked around her in a tight circle, tugging at her long hair, poking at her well-developed breasts and trying to pull her skirt up. She was on the verge of tears when the voice called out, "Leave her alone."

Rachel's early childhood dream of a knight in shining armor riding to her rescue was beginning to take shape in the form of a young man in well-worn black jeans and black tee shirt. His thick dark hair curled slightly at the nape of his neck and the fire in his brown eyes held a warning she could see, even if the others couldn't.

Woods and his friends turned their attention to the young man who dared challenge their opening day fun and games. With odds favoring them four to one, they felt more than cocky when facing someone who probably hadn't heard of their standing on the ladder of famed bad asses. They laughed as they stepped toward him and he dropped his books to the ground.

Billy's first punch never reached its intended target. It was parried aside in a flash of blinding speed and followed by a quick one-two combination to his sternum and face. The air rushed from his lungs at almost the same instant his nose changed direction and sprayed blood over his friends. The thug to Billy's left opened his mouth to protest just as a foot hit him squarely in the chest, sending him to the ground. The two remaining tough guys decided to begin track try outs early and abandoned their friends.

Suddenly a new hero was in town, but everyone was sure he'd soon fall from his pedestal when Jesse Woods came to defend the wounded pride of his younger brother. That's the way things always happened. Billy would pick a fight with a student and, with the help of his friends, push him around. But if he failed while pretending to be one of the tougher boys in school, his brother was there with his own band of hoodlums to save him.

So day number two of the school year began with Lewis being escorted to the boy's room at the back of the school by the older Woods. Crowds of students already were lined five and six deep at the windows, hoping to get a first hand peek at what they were sure would be the demise of "The Black Knight" as Lewis had been tagged.

Billy, with his nose bandaged and two black eyes, stood to one side with his friends while Jesse and his hoods pushed J.D. against a wall. Two of Jesse's friends held a tearful Rachel Magliano by the arms so she'd be forced to witness the downfall of her hero. They'd promised her a little fun after they finished with Lewis.

Jesse struck a match and touched it to the end of a Marlboro cigarette, and then blew a cloud of smoke into Lewis' face. He sucked and puffed on the cigarette, the fireball growing along with the tip of gray ashes. Jesse raised the cigarette and began flicking the ashes into Lewis' hair and over his black tee shirt, laughing and taunting the younger boy. "Not so tough now, are ya?"

J.D. remained calm, taking stock of his situation and eyeing his tormentor. Jesse Woods was at least three inches taller and easily held a twenty-pound weight advantage. But the paunch that hung over his wide leather belt said that his physical condition was inferior to the younger boy's.

Jesse puffed hard on the cigarette until the fireball at the end met his approval. He held the butt in front of his face and used his foul-smelling breath to fan the glow of the burning tobacco. He guided the cigarette toward Jefferson Lewis' face, smiling and saying, "I'm gonna brand you good, boy."

Lewis' hands were a blur as they shot up to knock the cigarette away from his face. He grabbed the hand that held the Marlboro and twisted it back and up. What happened next was a topic of conversation for weeks. By accident the cigarette was jammed into the right nostril of Jesse Woods, although everyone who saw the struggle swore on the graves of their mothers and grandmothers that it was intentional.

In the blink of an eye, Jesse Woods was transformed from tough guy, hooligan king, to a dancing fool. He screamed and leaped around the room, slapping at his face with open hands, furiously fighting to get the hot coals of tobacco out of his nose. What made it worse was his friends laughed at him.

While the fire dance continued, J.D. dropped the two laughing hoods who still held Rachel, with kicks between their legs. He pushed her toward the door, while looking over his shoulder to be sure nobody was going to get a cheap shot in while they made their escape.

The legend of "The Black Knight," Mr. Jefferson Daniel Lewis, was talked about in hallways, classrooms, bathrooms and the cafeteria. The tale grew each time it was told as did the number of persons who swore they witnessed the incident.

The reputations and egos of the Woods brothers and their close friends were badly damaged by the beating they took from their previously unknown classmate. Although they loudly swore to avenge their humiliation, they kept a safe distance from J.D.

Through it all, J.D. remained the soft-spoken loner who wanted to stay out of the limelight and avoid the backslaps of those who suddenly wanted to be his friend. But he didn't object to the company of Rachel Marie Magliano and she became an intricate part of his remaining high school years.

Rose Anna had moved closer to him while he told her of his first defense of a woman. She was almost breathless when she said, "What happened to Rachel? Did you become lovers?"

"Well, this story doesn't have a happily ever after ending."

"Oh, I'm sorry." And truly she was. "I didn't mean to open an old wound."

"That's okay," he said, looking away for a moment. "I've never really talked about it."

"Care to go on?" she said, touching his arm and he felt a caring person behind the lustful talker, a woman who could be trusted with his secret.

"Why not?" he said, shrugging his shoulders.

Rose Anna painted a picture in her mind of the events he spoke of in such vivid detail. Rachel developed an immediate affection for J.D. because he took charge where others stood by and did nothing to help her. Dozens of other boys, freshmen to seniors, watched as she was physically and verbally abused by Billy Woods and friends. Only J.D. had the courage to stand and defend her.

When it was over, despite the objections of her parents, Rachel became his constant sidekick. In the eyes of her family he was the boy from the wrong side of the tracks. His clothes were not of the finest quality and his hair was a little too long for their taste. He came from a foster home, which surely indicated an unstable family background, though they didn't bother to ask why he'd been placed in foster care.

They remained only friends for a little more than a year and half. They talked every day and managed to go to school plays and dances and often found time to sneak away to the museum on weekends. Midway through the spring semester of their junior year, on a very warm afternoon, they decided to cut classes and go to the country.

They walked along a path to a stream deep in the woods, sat on the bank and watched the signs of the season. Birds chirped and carried twigs and grass for building their nests, while chipmunks chattered and played tag over a fallen tree.

It was while wading in the cold waters of the stream that Rachel slipped and fell into his arms. He hoisted her up and when their eyes met, the hot smoldering fires that had been hidden for so long roared to life. A first nervous kiss led to a trembling embrace and the flames burned hotter. There in the forest on a bed constructed of pine needles, leaves and hastily removed clothing, Rachel and J.D. fell together and made love.

The following morning as they stood in the principal's office to explain their absence, the secretary noted the glow in their eyes and smiled. She recalled a spring day that now didn't seem so long ago when she too missed an afternoon class and returned with a gleam in her eyes and a radiance in her heart.

"This sounds so good," Rose Anna said, her eyes sparkling. "How could this possibly have a tragic ending?"

"We were best friends and lovers right through graduation. We spent our graduation night together and when I tried to sneak her home in the morning, her parents were waiting. There was yelling and screaming and accusations of rape. Her father said we'd never see each other again."

"What happened?"

"Well, we went on seeing each other, but then the bad news came. Her father's company was transferring him. They moved away about a month later and went out to the west coast. Seattle. She was still only seventeen and had no choice. She had to go with her family."

"Didn't you stay in touch?"

"Yeah. Letters. Phone calls. But we never got together again. Not that I didn't want to."

"God, what happened?"

"About four months after she left I enlisted in the Marine Corps. We still wrote to each other while I was in boot camp and even for a time after. I was in scout/sniper school when I got the letter. I guess you know how they begin. 'This is the hardest letter I've ever had to write. I feel so bad. It really hurts me to have to say this, but there's someone else. He's here and you're not. Forgive me. Be happy for me. I hope you find someone new.' And that's the way it ended."

"I guess that hurt pretty bad."

"Yeah. It hurt like hell. But in time I got over it."

She smiled. "I bet you've had a string of women since then. In fact, I'll bet you've left a trail of broken hearts a mile long."

He shook his head. "I'm not really lucky in love. Not at all."

"Maybe all that'll change. Anyway, I see a bright future for you," she said, the gleam showing again in her eyes.

"Oh. Are you a fortune teller?"

"Maybe. But first tell me if you're looking favorably on another woman." Rose Anna hoped he'd admit he felt something for Tiffany, but he wasn't one who was easily caught off guard.

"Could be." Indeed he wouldn't tell her he was beginning to feel this burning desire to sweep Tiffany into his arms and make love to her.

She turned his hand palm up and ran a fingernail across it. "I see a hot love affair on the horizon, possibly with an older woman. A woman you're very close to."

It was time to go. "I've got work to do," he said, pulling his hand away from her.

"If you say so," she said, squeezing his hand.

She paid for lunch and they parted, but not before she kissed him on the cheek and ran her hand across his buttocks again.

He drove back to the mansion, suddenly feeling out of his element and trying to force the distraction out of his mind. He needed a clear head. In a matter of a few hours he'd be contacting Gary Wilson and he couldn't afford to make a mistake when he talked with him.

Sixteen

Robert Courtney, Attorney at Law, presented his case, but not in front of a packed courtroom. In this case there was only one witness, Chief of Police Samuel Greenberg. While Courtney calmly presented the facts, Greenberg's temperature went up. When the closed-door session ended, and Courtney was leaving, Greenberg screamed into the telephone for Captain Karl Thomas to report to his office.

The old saying about dung rolling down hill would soon have a new meaning, and Captain Thomas was the first to find out that the shit storm had hit. Greenberg took the ball and dropped it in Thomas' lap. "Karl, I don't know what those brainless wonders are trying to do, but one or all of them had better eat this charging document before the day's over."

Thomas was stunned when Greenberg slapped the papers on the desk in front of him. He scanned the pages and looked back at the chief. "Sir, I can assure you I didn't know a thing about this."

"Well, now that you're aware of it, I expect you to deal with it in the appropriate manner," he growled through clenched teeth. "I don't want Bob Courtney in my office again unless it's to invite me to play golf."

Thomas burned a path from the chief's office to the CIB conference room as the snowball picked up speed. He screamed for Adams to round up the triplets and join him as he read the Internal Affairs forms again.

The door opened and they marched into the room in single file, three of them smiling as though the grins had been glued to their faces. When they stopped, Thomas bellowed, "Do you fuckers think you're in a goddamn parade?"

Adams opened his mouth, but Thomas cut him off. "I sure hope to God one of you assholes can explain this to me." He hurled the papers at Adams who tried to catch them, but failed.

Adams picked the papers up and broke into a smile. "Oh, yes, sir. We got Lewis by the balls. He…."

"Bullshit. You couldn't get a piss ant by the balls. What you did was step on your dick."

"But Captain, Mrs. Barrows...."

"Mrs. Barrows would like to see you fuckers castrated. But I don't think they could find anything to cut off. Do you know Bob Courtney just raked Chief Greenberg over the coals? Then Greenberg ripped me a new ass. Well, boys, the shit's comin' downhill fast and it's gonna be on your heads."

They stared at Thomas and waited. Then the giant shit ball dropped. "Patrol's gonna be a little shorthanded because of in-service training for the next couple of weeks. So you turds are gonna work the night shift out of the Southern District—except for you, Grayson. You were smart enough to have your name removed from the witness list. You'll stay here and work. The rest of you get your uniforms ready."

"Sir, I don't think you can do that without preferring some type of charge against us," Adams said.

"Asshole, as your commander I can do it. It's my duty to assist the Patrol Bureau when necessary. Besides, if I file charges against you idiots and a trial board convenes, Mrs. Barrows would probably testify against you. That would mean you'd end up down on the docks walkin' a foot beat with the rats. So, it's the night shift out of Southern District, or share your dinner with a few thousand rodents."

"But we're working the stalker murders."

"That won't fly. You must think you've really pulled the best snow job ever on the captain here. Well, think again. You made sure those cases were dumped on that new kid, Lewis. Now, that just might backfire on you. He's at least developed a possible suspect. That's far more than you did. So start packin'." He turned and stormed out of the room, leaving them staring at each other.

"Wallace, you didn't tell me Lewis had a suspect in the murders," Adams said.

"I put the reports on your desk."

"Shit. I don't have time to read everything that's dropped on my desk," he said. "Something that important should've been brought to my attention right away. Christ, suppose he solves the cases?"

"Lenny, Thomas said it was only a possible suspect. And the way I read the reports, Lewis hasn't got a thing but circumstantial evidence right now."

"Bill, wake up. We stuck him with those cases, remember? We thought he'd fall on his ass. If he makes an arrest and the charges stick, we'll be laughed right outta the fuckin' bureau."

"Look, we can't fight amongst ourselves. We've gotta work together. We gotta think of something."

Adams paced back and forth for a few moments. "We can't let Lewis bring us down. Even if we do end up in the Southern District for a few weeks, we've gotta keep on top of his investigation. If things start to look too good for him, we'll have to find a way to cut him off at the knees."

"What're you sayin'?"

"That we should short circuit the prick—and take the credit."

Wallace grinned. "Let him do the work and we take the bows. I like it."

"That's right," Adams said and then turned to Grayson. "You," he said, jabbing a finger in his direction. "I won't forget what you did. That was a goddamn underhanded thing you did, going behind our backs and takin' your name off the witness list. Now we know where your loyalty lies."

"Hey, I told all of you those charges wouldn't stand, and I told you I wanted no part of what you were doing. Don't blame me for your fuck-up."

"We'll be thinkin' about you every night while we're poundin' a fuckin' beat in the damn Southern District."

While their discussion continued, Lewis was getting out of his car in front of 3006 Spring Valley Drive. Casually dressed in jeans, black tee shirt, Stetson and cowboy boots, he tucked his Sig Sauer, Model P226 under his belt behind his back and walked toward the entrance.

He paused outside the door to apartment 1-A and listed for signs of anything out of the ordinary. Hearing only music, he knocked. After getting no response to his first knock, he rapped his knuckles a little heavier on the metal door. Inside a voice called out, "Hold on. I'll be right there."

When the door opened it was obvious Wilson had just stepped out of the shower. He was dressed only in blue jeans, his hair disheveled and wet and beads of water still dotting his chest and shoulders. "Can I help you?"

"I'm Detective Lewis," he said, displaying his badge and ID Card. "I'd like to talk to you for a few minutes."

"Ah, Jesus, man," Wilson muttered, moving back two steps. "I've been clean for a long time. I swear."

"I know that. You're just one on a list of hundreds of people I've gotta talk to."

"Oh. Okay. Come in."

"Sorry I rousted you outta the shower."

"That's okay," he said, stepping aside to let Lewis in. "Can you give me a minute or two to get dressed?"

"Sure. Take your time."

As Wilson crossed the floor, Lewis began looking over the apartment. The apartment was clean and everything was in its place to the point where it appeared that the unit was a display model instead of an occupied module. Not even a minute speck of dust was visible on the furniture.

In the dining area he noticed an envelope on the table with the name Ginny written on the front in blue ink. Beside the card was a small tan and gold box bearing the name Night Heat in bold letters. Looking closer at the label he saw that the box held a bottle of perfume distributed by ELSBETH, LTD., a company owned by Elizabeth Ames.

"So, what do you need to talk to me about?" Wilson said as he returned to the room.

"I'm investigating the stalker killings and I've gotta talk to everybody who had any type of contact with the victims."

"Man, I hope you're not sayin' you think I had anything to do with them."

"No, not at all. But you did landscaping or lawn care for them and maybe you saw or heard something that might help me."

"Yeah. Well, I don't know about that. All I did was cut the grass, put mulch around the plants and trim the shrubs. I mean, I didn't see anybody sneakin' around the houses or anything like that."

"I wouldn't expect you to, unless you were there at night."

"Nah. All of my work was done early in the day. When we did a job for the rich, we started first thing and were outta there by mid-afternoon. They didn't really want us around after four o'clock. Parties and other high-class social shit. You know what I mean."

Lewis saw that Wilson didn't exhibit any outward signs of nervousness. There was no pausing, stammering or rolling of the eyes as if he was searching for the right answer. His answers were straightforward and he made eye contact when he gave them. He decided to take a few steps back in his line of questioning. "You say you've been clean for awhile."

"Yeah. Since my last arrest I've been tryin' to get my life back on track."

"How's that?"

"I've been goin' to counseling and dating this really super woman. Ginny's been a big help to me."

"How long have you been dating Ginny?"

"Almost six years. We're gonna get married in September."

Lewis nodded. "Congratulations."

"Thanks."

"So, I take it she knows all about your past troubles with the law?"

"Oh, yeah. She talked me into goin' to counseling and even went with me at first. You know, kinda stuck around till I felt comfortable and talked about the things I did."

The tiny opening was there and Lewis moved like the shark in deep waters a great distance from its prey and gliding casually closer and then swimming in an ever tightening circle. "You had more than your share for a time, didn't you?"

"Yeah," Wilson said with a slight laugh that seemed more like a sigh of relief.

"Kinda like me when I was in high school," Lewis said, laughing with him. "I spent a little time on the carpet in the principal's office."

"You too, huh? Yeah, I sure did some dumb ass things back when I was in high school."

Lewis leaned forward and kept his voice low. "You're not the guy who groped the girl during biology class, are you?"

"Man, how'd you know about that?"

The shark had the scent of blood. "Christ. That was the talk of the school. Man, everybody knew. You grabbed a handful of tit from Betty Haskins and pinched her box at the same time. Things like that make people legends."

"Everybody did talk about it for a long time," he said.

The fin of the shark broke the surface. "Then there were the letters you sent to the cheerleaders."

Wilson cupped his hands behind his head and sat back on the sofa. "Yeah. That too." He realized too late that the shark had closed his jaws firmly around him. His face paled as he looked at the detective sitting across from him. "Nobody knew that for sure—until now."

"Don't worry. Nobody's gonna know. I'm not gonna go back and tell Mrs. Jarvis that you wrote the letters. But there are a few things I need to know and I want you to be straight with me."

"Why should I answer anymore fuckin' questions?"

Circumstantially, Wilson was becoming a stronger suspect in the stalker slayings. "Gary, just as sure as I'm sittin' here with you right now, somebody's gonna eventually point the finger in your direction and say you're the guy who killed the rich broads."

"No fuckin' way," he shouted, jumping to his feet. "I didn't kill those women."

"Okay," he said, getting to his feet. "If that's the truth, let's work together to prove you're not the man."

"Just how the fuck are we gonna do that?" he said.

"Will you answer my questions?"

"Yeah. Sure. I guess so."

"Do you own a computer?"

"No, I don't."

"Do you have access to a computer at work? Or does Ginny own one?"

"I use the computer at work sometimes and Ginny just bought one a few months back."

"I'll need some printed samples from both," he said, jotting down a few notes.

"Why?"

"If you've kept up with the facts on the murders, you know the killer sent letters to his victims before he murdered them. Those letters were printed on a computer. The FBI can at least tell me what type of printer was used."

All of a sudden Wilson seemed more relaxed. "They didn't come from Ginny's or the one at work. I can swear to that. And those are the only ones I have access to."

"Let's go a step further. Would you be willing to give a blood sample?"

"Yeah. I guess so. But why would you need that?"

"DNA fingerprinting. All the victims were sexually assaulted and by comparing known blood samples with semen obtained from the women, we can identify or eliminate a suspect."

"In that case, you can have a gallon if you want it. 'Cause I know I didn't kill them."

"I'll make arrangements to have blood taken," Lewis said, jotting a few notes in his book again. "Then I'll call and let you know where and when."

"That's fine. But could Ginny come along?"

"I don't have a problem with it."

"I'd really feel better if she was there."

"I understand."

"How long does it take for them to do the tests? I mean, after I give blood, can they do it right there?" he said.

"You've gotta remember this is a scientific process and it takes time to complete. They can't rush it. And we don't do the testing ourselves. We have to send the blood and other samples to an outside lab for testing. So it might take anywhere from six to twelve weeks to get the results back."

"Damn, that's a long time."

"You wouldn't want them to rush through the tests and make a mistake, would you?"

"Hell, no. I just hate waitin' like that."

"I know what you mean. But if it takes six weeks or six months and proves you're innocent, it's worth the wait, right?"

"Yeah. I guess so."

The predator backed off. He didn't want to destroy the confidence he felt he'd built between them. The other questions could wait. Wilson had completed a job at the Barrows Mansion just days before the letter arrived in the mail for Tiffany. Therefore, it wouldn't serve any purpose to ask a question that might chase a man away who seemed to trust him. He figured it was best to end the interview and leave looking like Wilson's savior instead of his hangman. "Gary, I'll be in touch in a day or two."

The two shook hands and Lewis left the apartment with a nagging feeling. He knew that on paper Gary Wilson would stand out as a man who should be taken away, interrogated and his blood taken by force, if necessary, via a search warrant. But he was still uncertain about Wilson.

He sat in his car and thought about the mysterious Mr. Mustang who'd vanished just as quickly as he'd appeared. Where was he and what kind of game was he playing? It was the same as always. Questions without answers.

Tiffany and Zachary spent the day together, but she still felt as gloomy as the sky outside. Her efforts to reach him seemed as though they were repelled by some unseen force. He remained distant, his efforts to communicate with her strained.

In the gloominess that surrounded her, an evil witch stirred her cauldron and pulled up sinister images of other women standing in front of her awaiting Zachary's favors. She closed her eyes and wondered how many women had taken her place in Zachary's arms. Rose Anna's words came back like a scream. "Honey, if he isn't taking care of business at home, he's sure as hell taking care of it elsewhere."

Seventeen

The crime scene photographs were spread over the library table, their splotches of varying colors making an odd cover. Lewis paced a slow circle around the table carefully studying each picture, as he had on so many occasions, looking for the killer's flaw.

He walked slowly from Wellington, to McDougal, to Upchurch and French, back and forth, his eyes moving carefully over each photograph. For reasons he couldn't understand he continually returned to the crime scene pictures of the first victim, Amanda French.

He sat down and picked up the picture of Amanda French lying face up on her bed, blue robe open, exposing her body and the black rope knotted around her throat. *Damn, what a waste*, he thought, as he put the picture of the once vibrant, lovely brunette back on the table.

The crime scene technicians had photographed the room from every angle, taking in each and every piece of furniture and fixture. But one photograph in particular attracted his attention. He held the picture of the mirrored vanity table at arm's length, turning it to look at it from different angles. He noticed the assortment of bottles, tubes and dispensers of creams, lotions and powders.

His eyes started to water from staring at it for so long, but through the mist one of the bottles caught his attention. He took a magnifying glass out of his briefcase and looked at the dispenser. The name Night Heat came into focus. "That's the same kind of perfume I saw on Wilson's dining room table," he muttered.

He was about to start pacing again when Ezra knocked lightly on the door. "Could I interest you in a cold beer?"

"You sure could, but only if you'll have one with me."

"Uh—I don't know 'bout that. Mr. Barrows bein' home and all."

Lewis raised his hand in front of him. "One of these fingers is for Mr. Barrows."

"I bet I know which one," Ezra chuckled. "Now you just have to hope he can read sign language."

Lewis walked to the desk and picked up a mug shot of Gary Wilson. "Do you remember seeing this guy around here?" he said, handing the picture to Ezra.

"Yes, sir," he said, shaking his head. "He was here not too long ago workin' around the yard."

"Did you notice anything unusual about him? The way he acted or anything?"

"No, sir. 'Cept he seemed to have a rovin' eye for Miss Tiffany."

"You mean like lookin' her over from head to toe."

"Yes, sir. That's exactly it."

He nodded and opened a bottle of beer. "Did he say anything to her?"

"Hummmm," he said, scratching his chin. "No. I don't actually recall him sayin' a word to her."

"Did he try to touch her in any way? Even shake hands with her?"

"No. He just kept a real close eye on her every time she came outta the house."

"Damn," Lewis said, slapping the mug shot back on the desk.

"What's wrong, Mr. Lewis?"

Ezra was a man he was certain could be trusted with any secret and probably had many stored in his memory. Surely, at some of the parties hosted by the Barrows family he'd been a witness to a few follies. "It seems everything I've dug up so far points to this guy Wilson as the Society Stalker."

"But your heart keeps tellin' you otherwise."

He nodded. "My gut keeps saying I might be knockin' on the wrong door, but cold, hard facts point to him."

"You know, Mr. Lewis, for as long as I can remember, I've always believed a man should trust what he feels. 'Cause sometimes what he sees right there in front of him just ain't so."

"It's good to meet a man who thinks like that," he said, raising his beer bottle to Ezra.

"But if what you're feelin' is true, then who's the killer?"

Lewis sat down in the chair behind the desk. "For a long time I've had an idea about the killer, but it's almost too spooky to talk about."

"You don't have to say anything to me if you don't want to. But whatever you tell me won't leave this room. I swear that to be the truth."

"I know," he said, getting to his feet and walking to the window where he stared out into the darkness. "Either the guy I'm lookin' for is one shrewd individual or he's a cop. And if he's a cop, he's gotta be one I work with. One who has access to the case files. But, hell, a lotta cops have access to the reports."

"Why do you think it might be a policeman?"

"Pattern changes. Like sendin' a letter to Mrs. Barrows immediately after the last murder. Usually the guy waits for a few months before he picks his next victim."

"You think he coulda just slipped up?"

"Nah. He made the change on purpose. The more confusing this guy makes it, the more difficult it's gonna be to nab him."

"Why's that?"

"After a while you don't know if it's the real killer or some copycat trying to make a name for himself. And even worse is the one who kills somebody and tries to cover it up by using the other killer's MO. Then there's the headline seeker. He strolls in and confesses to a crime or a series of crimes just to get his name in the paper or his face on television. While the cops are wastin' time with that asshole, the real killer just sits back and waits for his next opportunity."

"I never knew your job got so tough," Ezra said, hoisting his beer and tipping it slightly toward Lewis. "Here's to you, sir. May the Good Lord always keep you safe and grant you the wisdom to do what's right."

"Thank you, Ezra." The young detective was deeply touched by his expression of friendship. "I appreciate your blessing."

Ezra drained his bottle and smiled. "Well, sir, I'd better leave here before King Zachary comes down and sees me socializin' with the other hired help."

Ezra left, leaving J.D. to think about his strange theory and dig through the endless pile of evidence again. A stack of clues that he was sure held an answer he'd so far failed to uncover.

He walked back to the table and looked over the photographs and recalled the basic teachings regarding crime scenes. "Remember, when you're called to investigate a crime, the perpetrator either leaves something behind, or takes something with him." In the stalker cases the killer had left a strand of black rope knotted around the victim's throat and his body fluids. But it was still unknown whether or not he'd taken anything with him.

He went back to the computer to add the latest data to his report, while known facts from the murders and his so many unanswered questions clashed. Ifs, maybes and whys became a jumbled mess as he struggled to sift through them and draw a single conclusion.

However, with evidence leaving Wilson alone at the top of the list and his senses trying to tell him otherwise, he had a lot of work to do. If his feelings were leading him in the right direction he had to do everything possible to eliminate Wilson as a suspect. If he failed to clear him, there'd be some who were willing to take their chances with him just to clear the cases and gain public favor. *God, I wish I had some help with this*, he thought. *It would sure take a lot off my mind.*

He wasn't sure what time it was when he finally crawled into bed. But even then he was restless. Tossing and turning while visions of murder victims flashed before him. Suddenly he hurled the sheets back and leaped out of bed. He stumbled around the room, his heart thumping like a bass drum. At last he found the lamp and turned it on.

He sank back to the edge of the bed trying to remember what the nightmare was about, but the horrifying image was gone. He got up and began to pace. He was too shaken to sit still and wanted to move around to clear his head. *What was it? What the hell was the dream?* he asked himself over and over.

When his heartbeat finally returned to normal, he knew it would be useless to lie down and try to sleep again. The terrifying dream rattled him and he didn't want to close his eyes and have it come back again. One bad dream for the night was enough.

He dressed, left his room and walked quietly to the front door. He paused for a moment and then slipped outside. He felt the thickness of the air and looked up. Dark, ominous clouds rolled and swirled above as if they were sending a warning that a violent storm was just over the horizon. He ignored the signs and walked slowly around in the wet grass as the winds lashed out and pushed against him. He looked up at the clouds again and the fury of two storms clashed in the night.

Eighteen

Zachary Barrows would even defy the weather, which pelted the driveway and lawn with torrents of water, to reach the hastily called business meeting. The telephone call came early in the morning, summoning him to travel a few hundred miles and rake in millions. And neither pleas nor fierce, wind driven rains would delay him.

He left and with him went the rains. The clouds raced across the sky with rays of sunshine breaking through from time to time, teasing sun worshipers with the promise of warmth in the sand and surf.

Shortly after breakfast Lewis was behind the wheel of the Lamborghini again, taking Tiffany to the spa. His thoughts as he drove over the rain-soaked road were haunted by questions about last night's dream.

"A penny for your thoughts."

"Huh?" he stammered, hearing the voice that sounded far away.

"You're a million miles away, Cowboy."

"Sorry. I just had something on my mind."

"Well, come back to earth and talk to me."

He forced a smile. "That's the first time you've called me Cowboy."

"Yes," she said. "You're right."

"Why the change?"

"I'm not sure. Maybe it seems more appropriate for you. With the hat and boots you wear most of the time, I guess it suits you a little better."

"Should I get a horse?"

"You know, I can picture you on a horse. I bet you would've made a great cattle rancher in the old west."

"Cattle rancher! Not me. I would've been more the U. S. Marshal or Texas Ranger type."

She turned her head and looked at him, feeling a long-forgotten flutter in her heart. "So you were a lawman in your previous life as well."

"Yes, ma'am," he answered in a deep drawl. "Used to chase outlaws across the badlands."

"And what did you do after you corralled those desperados and brought them to justice?"

"Stopped by the saloon and had a beer with my woman."

The lighthearted talk of the old west stopped when they arrived at the spa. But they seemed as though they would've been happier if it had continued.

Rose Anna skipped the preliminary chitchat and went to the heart of the subject she couldn't wait to tell. She spoke softly, but her gestures were quite animated as she told Tiffany of her luncheon date with J.D., wanting it to sound as intimate as possible.

J.D. went through his weightlifting routine being careful not to eavesdrop on their conversation, but he kept a wary eye on anyone coming into the room. The dream, whatever it was, managed to grind a sharper edge to his senses and his eyes darted around the room like lasers searching for a target.

He was so caught up in his lift and scan cycle he didn't see Tiffany's increasing level of annoyance. The depth of Rose Anna's titillating tale was matched by Tiffany's rising anger and she was rapidly becoming a powder keg with a hot burning fuse. Rose Anna teased and taunted her friend with the tale until the fire reached its destination and the keg exploded.

Tiffany balled her hands tightly into fists and stormed across the floor to J.D. Her face was flushed and her eyes blazed. "We have to talk—now."

"What?" he said.

"You heard me. We have to talk." Her hands rested squarely on her hips and she glared at him with a fury he'd never before imagined could lie hidden within such a lovely woman.

"Yeah. Sure."

She turned and walked toward the stairs and he followed, seeing that she was a woman with an obvious purpose in mind. But he didn't understand what caused her to become so enraged. He'd barely set foot on the parking lot when she spun around. "I hope you enjoyed your lunch."

"What?"

"You just had to take her up on her offer, didn't you? I even warned you about her and you still went."

"You mean this is about me havin' lunch with Rose Anna?" he said.

"You know damn well it is. Why did you go out with that—that bitch?"

He was beginning a slow burn of his own. "Well, it wasn't exactly a date. Besides, she would've pestered me until I gave in. Rather than create a scene, I accepted."

"According to her, you two had quite a good time together."

"And what the hell's that supposed to mean?"

"Would you like me to draw you a picture?" she said, brushing her hair back.

"Christ," he snapped, "you make it sound like we were fuckin' on the table in the restaurant. We talked. Nothing more."

"I guess that's why she can describe what a tight ass you have. I suppose she found that out by just talking."

"I had lunch with her," he said, stepping close enough to grasp her arms at the elbows. "I talked with her. I didn't indulge in some wild sexual fantasy with her. But, yes, she grabbed my ass. That's Rose Anna."

"What?" she sputtered.

"That's Rose Anna. She enjoys her reputation. In fact, I'd bet her escapades are more talk and innuendo than anything else. Sure, she might've had a fling here and there, but I seriously doubt that she's jumpin' in the sack with every guy who looks her way."

"Oh, so you spend a little time with her and you know all about her. Well, I—"

"You're her friend, for God's sake. And you know damn well she's not screwin' every guy who walks in the spa or country club. She's a flirt and she just loves all the attention. She enjoys the hell outta being in the center of the gossip mill. Why, I don't know. Maybe it's because it makes her the envy of most of those Flute Snoot Bitches. Now, am I right or wrong?"

She dropped her head and bit her lower lip. "You're right," she whispered.

Rose Anna watched from the second story window as the verbal duel on the lot below began to subside. *It worked,* she thought. *I wouldn't mention what he told me to another soul but you, Tiffany. And I must say I'm rather pleased with the results. A little jealous tizzy can go a long way toward getting you two together and I'm damn good at planting the seeds of possessive desire.*

Outside, J.D. went on. "And you have no right to jump my ass about what I do on my time."

"You're right," she said, looking at the ground between them. "I'm sorry." She looked back at him, tears forming in the corners of her eyes.

When he saw the pained expression his first impulse was to take her in his arms and kiss her, but again logic prevailed. Instead, he reached out and gently brushed away the tear that trickled along her left cheek.

"How can I make up for being such a fool?" she said, touching his hand.

"Today's Friday," he said, shrugging his shoulders. "It's steak night at

One Step West."

"My treat," she said, feeling her heart racing like a motor.

"Okay."

"But what'll I wear? Do I need western clothes? Jeans? Boots? Hat? What?"

"That's up to you," he said. "Western clothes aren't mandatory."

He still held her arms and she inched a little closer to him. "I want the clothes. I want the right look. But I don't know where to go to buy them."

"Well, I do," he said, smiling and letting go of her.

"Let's get our clothes and go shopping."

"Sure enough, ma'am," he said, his drawl returning. His serious side surfaced again as they walked side by side to the door. "I think I owe you an apology too. I'm sorry I growled at you."

"That's okay. I had it coming."

It didn't take long for him to whisk her away to The Wild West Rodeo, a store noted for its fine western wearing apparel and exquisite leather goods for the horse lover. The shelves and racks were filled with hundreds of hats, boots, jeans and shirts of every cut and size.

She seemed momentarily lost, but soon found her direction and walked up to the hat counter. After trying on more than a dozen, she settled on a tan Stetson and moved to the shirt rack. She chose several in varying colors and naturally had to model each one for J.D. before selecting one that suited her taste. He was relieved when it took her only fifteen minutes to pick out blue jeans and a pair of tan boots.

While she stood talking with the clerk and paying for the items she'd selected, a cold chill raced along the back of Lewis' neck. It felt as if someone had touched him with an icy hand. He turned quickly, his eyes narrowing as his defense system went to full alert. Every fiber of his body told him someone was watching them.

He moved without a sound and stood behind Tiffany, his back to hers, as he continued to look for the person with the prying eyes. Some distance away a large rack holding Drover or Long Rider Coats swayed slightly and then a figure darted for the side door. His glimpse of the fleeing party was brief, but good enough for him to recognize the man he called Mr. Mustang.

He took several steps in pursuit of the man, but stopped, remembering that his first obligation was to Tiffany and her personal safety. *I hope we meet soon, my friend*, he thought. *Very soon.*

Tiffany was brimming with excitement as they walked to the car, lugging bags and boxes. She tried to recall the last time she felt this almost electric surge of nervous energy racing through her and thought it must've been the evening of her high school senior prom.

She laughed to herself as she dropped into the seat and remembered an evening that now seemed so long ago. She was more anxious about planned events after the prom than the dance itself. This was the night. After all, she and Robby Morris had been dating for eleven months and they'd been building themselves up for the big moment by bumping and grinding against each other for weeks.

It was in the backseat of Robby's Chrysler that he, after some very awkward fumbling, managed to pull his erect and throbbing penis from his pants. She was breathing heavily and her mouth was dry as her heart tried to push through her chest. She nervously reached out and took him in her hand. At that moment he exploded and showered the front of her blue gown with months worth of pent-up emotions. It was their last date.

She closed her eyes and eased her head back, knowing she wasn't going to the prom this evening and there wouldn't be any backseat groping. But she was breathing a little faster, her mouth was getting dry and her heart was indeed trying to send a message. *Still*, she thought, *I can't let it happen*.

He drove through the mid-day traffic while looking over the endless mass of the lunch hour rush for the blue Mustang. He was sure it was out there somewhere in the jumble of metal and rubber, but he couldn't see it.

Nineteen

Tiffany was too distracted to notice Lewis anxiously turning his head and looking in the mirror as they left the estate and drove along the tree-lined road. She also didn't notice the light rain that once again began to fall. Her thoughts were filled with what she was doing right now, which by all definitions was going on a dinner date.

They'd traveled about a mile when he saw the car some distance behind them. He intentionally dropped the speed of the car by downshifting to a lower gear, but the car pacing them kept its distance. The driver of the chase car certainly seemed to be well-schooled in surveillance techniques and wouldn't be taken in by a tactic that would fool the inexperienced.

He eased his foot down on the accelerator and pulled away from the car, hoping to put enough distance between them so he could lose their pursuer in the evening traffic. He looked in the rearview mirror again and was satisfied, for the time being, that his escape attempt was successful.

The dinner crowd was just beginning to arrive at One Step West when they got out of the car. He took her by the arm and walked to the entrance where the hostess warmly greeted him. "Long time no see, Cowboy," she purred. "I sure hope you haven't been tryin' to avoid me."

"Never, Holly. You know you're my favorite hostess."

"Oh, J.D., I've always known that," she said, winking at him. "Table for two in a cozy corner?"

"That'll be just fine."

Tiffany's ears went deaf to the flirting almost as soon as it began. She was captured by the surroundings of One Step West. Its décor flowed with open-armed hospitality. It was truly a page of western history. Pictures of heroes on horseback from Tom Mix to Hopalong Cassidy, Roy Rogers, Gene Autry, The Lone Ranger, John Wayne and Clint Eastwood hung from the walls. Posters touting *High Noon*, *Gunfight at the O.K. Corral*, *True Grit*, *The Alamo* and *A Fistful of Dollars* covered walls and hung above the doorways.

Horseshoes for Quarter Horses and Clydesdales were nailed to heavy wooden posts, while bridles, harnesses and dusty saddles were hung about as decorative ornaments and a reminder of the days of stagecoaches and cattle roundups.

The rough-hewn wooden floors echoed with the footsteps of those wearing leather-heeled cowboy boots, while Willie Nelson's voice came from speakers hidden in the timber rafters high above and crooned "My Heroes Have Always Been Cowboys."

Replicas of Six Shooters, Winchester Carbines and Henry Rifles rested on pegs of wood above and beside the mirror on the wall behind the bar—a bar, which could've come from Kansas, Arizona, New Mexico or Texas of old, complete with brass foot rail and evenly spaced spittoons.

The waiters and waitresses dressed to blend with the era, moving from table to table as gunfighters, dancehall girls, cattle barons and ladies of the evening. They took orders for steaks, pit beef and chicken cooked over hot coals. This restaurant didn't serve dishes with foreign names, nor fancy filled pastries for dessert.

"Well, what do you think?" he said after they'd been seated for a few minutes and her eyes stopped roaming.

"I…I've never been in a place like this in my life. It's—I just don't even know how to describe it."

"Don't you like it?"

"I love it," she said almost breathless.

"You must have costume parties over there on the far side of the bridge."

"Yes, but nothing there could compare to this. Everybody here seems so real. So down to earth. Friendly. There's too much starch in the underwear at some of the parties held at Huntley Manor."

"Ouch," he laughed. "Starched shorts."

"I'm upset," she said, forcing a frown and looking him in the eyes. "You didn't say a thing about my outfit."

"You look great," he replied. "You'd be a beautiful daughter of a successful oil or cattle baron."

"Well, I'd rather be the marshal's woman," she said softly.

If he heard her reply, he was very casual in ignoring it. "Later, a disc jockey'll be in. Country music only. But the women love him because he does a lot of special requests just for them."

"Oh. And what do they request most?"

"Mostly slow music," he said. "Love songs. Stuff like that."

"Are we staying?"

"If you want to."

"I'd like that very much," she said, the drum beginning to beat in her chest. In the dim light she couldn't see that he was happy over her decision to stay. And undeniably she was unaware that the beating drum in her chest was no longer solo.

The long-awaited arrival of the disc jockey was greeted with rowdy applause and he, ever the gentleman, bowed to each wall and corner of the room. His flamboyant style only heightened the appreciative roar and the hand clapping and cheering continued until he reached the corner stage.

While he entertained the crowd with spicy words of praise and thanks for their greeting, J.D. and Tiffany walked to the bar and took two corner seats reserved for them near the wall.

The music began and immediately a young man approached and asked Tiffany to dance. She looked to J.D. who nodded and leaned forward to whisper in her ear. "It's okay. This song doesn't require you to get too close to the guy."

While she was on the dance floor he took the opportunity to look the crowd over for Mr. Mustang. He was certain the man wouldn't show up in western apparel, if he showed up at all, and would stick out like a wolf in a lamb's pen. Satisfied that the wolf wasn't preying on the lamb, he relaxed.

Tiffany danced almost nonstop for an hour before finally waving away her latest suitor and pushing herself back onto the barstool beside J.D. "My goodness," she said, breathlessly. "These guys are dancing machines."

"It's like this every Friday and Saturday night."

"Okay, ladies," The DJ said, his voice quieting the room. "This is what you've been waiting for. And tonight—tonight we have a very special request to play that slow lovin' music a little longer. So grab that man of yours and don't let him get away. Here, just for you, is ten hold and love your man songs in a row, beginning with a little something from Alabama."

A half dozen men stood by with broken hearts and shattered dreams as Tiffany took J.D. by the arm and guided him to the dance floor. The first steps were measured and the distance between them would've had the stamp of approval from Sister Mary Catherine at the monthly parochial school dances. They looked at each other and laughed and the gap began to close.

With each note and word of love the gap separating them diminished. By the end of the third song she was pressed against him, eyes closed and her head resting on his shoulder. Her breath, warm and soft, brushed the side of his neck and his arms held her a little tighter as the warning light flashed somewhere in his mind and told him to back away. But caught up in the moment he failed to heed the warning.

Soon, the only thing stopping their flesh from joining was the clothing they wore. This public display of lustful touching wouldn't be tolerated at the sectarian level and Sister Mary Catherine would've been storming through the crowd toward them, pushing up her sleeves and brandishing the yardstick. But, tonight, that wouldn't happen. Yardstick toting nuns seldom patronized One Step West.

When the music stopped they were both somewhat weak in the knees as they walked back to the bar. An ice cold mug of beer was placed in front of them and they sipped the frosty golden liquid in silence, thinking about the embrace shared on the dance floor.

By Friday night standards they were leaving early, but he was getting that little nervous twitch once again. They passed along thank yous and other compliments on their way to the door, while many single men watched the woman of their dreams stroll out of their lives on the arm of another man.

The light rain still fell as they started the drive back to the mansion, each lost in their own thoughts. She dreamed of the dance and feelings it stirred in her for the man beside her. And, like it or not, the "I can't let it happen" voice was beginning to fade rapidly. He, on the other hand, thought of the man in the Mustang and was ready to drop on bended knee and beg the powers above to grant him his wish of a much-wanted confrontation.

As he pulled the car into the driveway he stopped and looked around, hoping to catch a sign of the Mustang. Though he saw nothing, he was sure he could feel the eyes of the man peering through the darkness at them. Was he becoming more brazen? Or was he losing his edge and getting careless?

In the foyer the air was charged with the emotional energy that ignited when they first met and continued to simmer ever since. They looked for an opening, not for falling into each other's arms, but to say goodnight and graciously part.

"Thanks for a wonderful evening, Cowboy. I haven't had that much fun in a long time."

He took the opening and fell back to his Texas drawl. "The pleasure was all mine, ma'am."

"I have a confession to make," she said, slightly shuffling her feet on the marble. "I feel very comfortable around you. Almost like we've known each other for a very long time."

"Maybe we were friends in another life," he said, looking into her eyes. "Back in the old west."

"I guess I'd better get some sleep," she said, moving toward the stairs. "Goodnight."

She climbed a few steps and paused. "Cowboy," she called to him. "About that other life—the one in the old west. I think we were more than friends— much more." She turned and walked quickly up the stairs.

In the bedroom she leaned against the door, heart thumping, legs feeling as if they'd collapse and leave her on the floor like a wilted flower. She reached to unbutton her shirt, only to find her fingers wouldn't cooperate. *Damn,* she thought, *I'm beginning to feel like a virgin getting ready for her first date. What's wrong with me? Hell, I've been laid before. But it's been such a long time.*

At last she managed to peel off her clothes and walk on unsteady legs toward the shower. A hot burst of water, followed by a cold rinse and she was on the verge of regaining control of herself. She dried her body with the thick towel and reached for the silk robe that hung on the back of the door. She hesitated, pulled her hand back and walked boldly to the bed and slid naked beneath the sheets.

She'd forgotten how long it had been since she'd slept in the buff, but tonight she wanted to feel the cool sheets against her skin. She stared up at the ceiling and her mind started to drift, taking her back to another time and place.

The voices in the old saloon mixed with the notes pounded on the keys of the way out of tune piano. The beer and whiskey flowed freely as smoke from ten-cent cigars and hand-rolled cigarettes hung like a heavy cloud over the tables. Men with dust-covered boots and clothes challenged each other to raise the ante, while professional gamblers lurked nearby and waited for their chance to claim some easy money.

It was shortly before noon when the doors swung open and the handsome young stranger stepped into the saloon. Grime from a long ride on the trail clung to his black hat and shirt, yet no amount of grit could hide the badge he wore on his left pocket. Idle talk and rumors of a new marshal coming to town were laid to rest with the appearance of the man who looked them over with the eye of an eagle.

His stride as he walked to the bar was one of confidence and caused men to huddle over tables in smoky corners. Cautious glances were cast toward the gun on his hip as eager eyes searched for telltale notches on the polished walnut grip. To their dismay it held no cuts of bravado.

"Hello, Mr. U.S. Marshal."

"Good morning, ma'am," he said, tipping his hat to the lovely blonde-haired beauty behind the bar.

"Oh, and a gentleman too. I'm Tiffany, the owner of this fine establishment."

"Please to meet you, ma'am. I'm Marshal Jefferson Lewis."

"Well, Marshal Lewis, how can I help you?"

"I'm lookin' for this man," he said, casually removing a folded paper from his right shirt pocket. "And I'd sure appreciate it if you could help me out." He unwrapped the worn paper and put it on the bar. The startled look on her face told him that she was familiar with Johnny "Red" Warren.

"You're lookin' for Texas Red," she said, her voice carrying above the din and once more bringing a bizarre silence to the room.

"Yes, ma'am. Texas Red or whatever he's goin' by these days. I'm here to take him in."

"You're too young and too damned handsome to die tryin' to take the likes of him in. He's a cold-blooded killer and he's already killed over twenty men. He's the fastest gun around these parts."

"Yeah. So I hear, ma'am. But I'm here to take him back just the same—one way or the other for murder."

"Why don't you have a beer and think about knockin' off that trail dust," she said, reaching across the bar and touching his hand. "I'd be happy to help you. I'd like to wash your back for you and spend a little time in your arms. So, why don't you just forget Texas Red?"

"Ma'am, it sure would be a pleasure to spend time in your arms. But I can't do that until I've taken care of Johnny Warren."

She was sure he'd die and the cowhands, drifters and gamblers were quick to line up on Warren's side. Most believed it was a sure bet to place their money against the marshal in the upcoming gunfight. But there was a gambler wearing a derby hat and fancy bow tie who was willing, almost anxious, to cover all wagers placed against the marshal. He was a real smooth talker and quick to assure them he'd match their bets.

Word raced through town like a wind swept brush fire that a man with a badge was gunning for Texas Red. And the much praised gunfighter smirked when the talk finally reached him. He knew he was the best. He picked up his hat and went to meet the new man in town who'd soon be just another notch on his gun.

A storm was approaching fast as the two men stepped out into the street to face each other. Large droplets of water fell and began to pelt the ground around them, kicking up dust from the parched, dirt pavement. They moved closer, each searching the face of the other for a sign of fear, but neither flinched.

A mere twenty feet separated them when they stopped and glared at each other through the driving rain. Red drummed his fingers on the dark brown leather holster as the marshal stood stark still in the face of death. No one knew for certain who moved first, but the fight was over in less than a heartbeat and Texas Red lay dying in the rapidly muddying street.

The crowd who lined the wooden walkways stood frozen, shocked by the death of "the fastest gun in the land." His gun had just cleared his holster when the first bullet from the marshal's Colt Forty-four tore into the center of his chest, sending a shower of blood to blend with the rain. The second bullet ripped through the front of his skull just above the bridge of his nose as his knees buckled and sent him toppling face-first to the street.

While the crowd continued to gawk at the fallen gunslinger, the smooth-talking gambler collected his winnings and Tiffany led the young marshal to her private quarters above the saloon. "We've gotta get you out of those wet clothes before you catch your death of pneumonia," she whispered.

As she'd wanted to do the moment he stepped through the swinging doors into her saloon, she helped him peel off his clothes. "Now, if you'll just step into this nice tub of hot water , I'll wash away your troubles and then I'm gonna give you a real special reward for bein' so brave."

On a bed with squeaky springs the marshal was rewarded several times over during the course of the afternoon. And, while they held each other tight and the sun began to peek from behind the clouds, Marshal Lewis made her a very happy woman when he told her he'd found a reason to stay in town for a few more days.

The daydream ended and Tiffany stared back up at the ceiling. She swallowed hard when she realized just how easy it would be to walk to his room. No one would even know. At least no one would ever tell.

She clutched a pillow to her and squeezed her eyes shut, muttering, "God, why am I torturing myself like this?" She sat up, feeling the beat of her heart and the fire burning between her legs. A fire that screamed for satisfaction.

Twenty

Lewis had just slipped his boots off when he heard the unusual noise. He sat on the edge of the bed, head canted to the right, thinking that it might've been the wind brushing a tree limb against the house. But when he heard the barely audible sound once more he knew it wasn't the branch of a tree scraping the house.

He reached down and pulled the custom cut Model 870 shotgun from under the bed. He then picked his pistol up and tucked into the belt behind his back, took off his socks and sneaked out of the house.

A slight drizzle fell from the dark clouds and the grass felt cool on the bottoms of his bare feet. He moved carefully along the side of the house, staying in the shadows as he looked over the grounds searching for uninvited guests.

He dropped into a crouch and peered cautiously around the corner. There, not more than 30 feet away, was Mr. Mustang standing on a stepladder, trying to unlock a window. He was so caught up in his work he failed to see the detective dart from the corner of the house.

Lewis made no sound as he crossed the thick grass and came up behind the man he'd been so anxiously waiting to meet. He stuck the barrel of the shotgun between his legs and racked a round into the chamber. "Now, do exactly what I tell you or you're gonna get a sex change operation compliments of the Remington Arms Company."

"Jesus Christ!" the man squealed. "Don't shoot. Don't shoot."

"Put your fuckin' hands behind your head and ease your ass off that ladder."

"Okay. Okay. Just don't shoot."

Ezra, who was awakened by the commotion, called out as he rounded the corner. "It's me, Mr. Lewis. What can I do to help?"

"Call 911, Ezra. Tell them I have a prowler in custody."

"Yes, sir."

"Okay," Lewis said. "Let's walk around to the front of the house and be sure to keep your hands on top of your head."

When they reached the front of the house, Lewis ordered the man to put his hands against the wall and then removed his wallet from his pocket. "Let's see who you are." The barefooted detective moved backward several steps and flipped the black leather billfold open. "Winston Palmer, Private Investigator. Well, Winston, you'd better have a damn good reason for prowling around here."

Without the shotgun pressed firmly against his testicles, Winston Palmer felt a sudden surge of courage pulsating through his veins. "What I'm doing is confidential. I don't have to explain shit to you, cop."

"How'd you know I was a cop?"

When Palmer stood closed mouth refusing to answer, Lewis grabbed him by the nape of the neck and forced him into the front yard. He placed the shotgun between his legs again and shoved forward until the barrel protruded about two inches beyond Palmer's legs. He then calmly squeezed the trigger. There was a loud explosion, after which a ball of red and orange flame roared from the barrel of the gun. The recoil made the shotgun jump in Lewis' hand, slapping Palmer squarely in the groin.

"What the fuck're you doin'?" Palmer cried, his scream filling the night air. "You're crazy. You're fuckin' insane."

"Winston, I'm gonna ask some questions and you'd better have the right answers or the next shot might not be so far forward."

"Okay. Okay," he replied, feeling the discomfort in his testicles from the slap of the shotgun. "Okay. Tell me what you wanna know."

"Let's start with why you're here."

"I was hired by Zachary Barrows."

"Bullshit," Lewis said, jerking the shotgun up between his legs. "Don't lie to me, asshole."

"Man, I'm not lying," he said, making a gallant effort to escape the pressure of the gun barrel by standing on his toes. "Barrows hired me to make sure you were doin' a good job protecting his wife."

"You're serious," Lewis said, relaxing the tension on the gun.

"Yeah," Palmer said, still squirming. "Barrows agreed to pay me big bucks to test you."

"I guess he gave you the alarm and entry codes for the house and grounds."

Palmer nodded. "Yeah. He gave me everything—including the timetable for his wife's activities."

"Just what the fuck was Barrows trying to prove?"

"Look, the man told me he loved his wife and wanted to be damn sure nothing happened to her."

"I don't believe a word of this bullshit," Lewis said, grabbing his shoulder and spinning him around. He placed the barrel of the gun under Palmer's chin. "Not one damn word of it."

"I swear to God it's the truth," Palmer said. "I don't know anything else I can tell you. You've gotta believe me."

Lewis shook his head. "You know, I should have your ass hauled in and charged with every damn crime I can think of. But it's Barrows who should really get fucked for this."

"Look, I was only doin' what Mr. Barrows paid me to do. I didn't think it would go this far."

"Now I've gotta decide what to do with your ass before the cavalry arrives," Lewis said, shaking his head.

The Barrows residence was located on the border of the Southern District and Adams, Wallace and Hargrove were working the night shift. They raced like a pack of starving jackals with the scent of a fresh kill in response to the call. Their cars raced up the driveway with lights flashing, telling Lewis this just wasn't his day. "God, why me?" he muttered as the cruisers stopped in front of him.

"Who're they?" Ezra whispered.

"You met them at the station. Remember?"

"Oh yeah. I didn't recognize 'em in uniform."

"What's the problem here?" Adams said, tucking his thumbs in the waistband of his pants.

"It was just a misunderstanding, Lieutenant. I wasn't aware that Mr. Palmer here was an employee of Mr. Barrows. Isn't that right, Mr. Palmer?"

"Uh—yeah. Right," he stammered. "I—I forgot to tell him I was working for Mr. Barrows."

"You know what?" Adams said. "I think you two are lyin' to me."

"They're telling the truth," Tiffany said from behind them. "Mr. Palmer works for my husband. It's as much my fault as anyone's. I neglected to inform Detective Lewis when he was hired." She emerged from the shadows and walked toward them.

Heads spun like they were on swivels to look at the woman who stood in front of them barefooted and wearing a mid-thigh blue silk robe. In the ring of light cast around her by the overhead lamps she was a portrait of elegant, stunning beauty.

Seconds passed before Adams' vocal paralysis eroded. "Mrs. Barrows!

Sorry to intrude at this hour, but I'm sure you're relieved to know we're on the job."

"Oh, absolutely," she said. Then fearing they'd stay around longer, she heaped a generous amount of sugar-coated praise on him and stroked his ego, hoping he'd take his friends and simply vanish.

His self-esteem bolstered, he ordered Wallace and Hargrove to follow him. Soon the parade began again and curled down the driveway, lights rising and falling with the flow of the pavement, until they finally disappeared.

Lewis escorted Palmer to the gate and nudged him in the back with the shotgun. "Consider your job over. If I see you following us or catch you on the grounds again, I'm gonna make sure you spend some time in the hospital."

He didn't wait for Palmer to reply, but turned and walked back to the house. His anger over what Barrows had done was just reaching the boiling point when he opened the door and stepped into the foyer. His rage quickly subsided when he saw Tiffany standing by the stairs.

They stood in silence, staring at each other across the short span separating them. But in the stillness a thousand words were spoken with their eyes. Tiffany broke from her trance-like state and swiftly bridged the gap between them. Her hands quickly encircled his neck and her body pressed against him as her lips moved to his and parted. Her tongue, burning with passion, moved and danced over his while he struggled to pull her even closer. The heat from the fire burning in their souls seemed about to consume them when she suddenly pulled free.

"Oh, God! I'm sorry," she murmured, backing away. "I'm sorry." She turned and ran up the stairs, leaving him in a state of confusion on the cold marble floor.

"You know, I don't really believe she was sorry," Ezra said, stepping into the foyer and offering him a beer.

"You saw what happened?" he muttered, taking the bottle.

"Yes, sir. And, if you don't mind my sayin' so, I don't really think you were one little bit upset by it."

"Ezra, this sure could complicate things," he said, shaking his head.

"Complications," the old man said, smiling. "Yes, sir. Life's full of 'em." He took a long swallow form his bottle and chuckled. "But they sure can put some fine spice in your life. You should enjoy it. Be happy. Make her happy— but only if you think it's meant to be.

Twenty-one

Sleep was out of the question. At this moment emotional turmoil was taking Lewis on the roller coaster ride of his life. The adrenaline rush brought on by the confrontation with Winston Palmer and then the lighting of loves passions by the kiss he shared with Tiffany were more than enough to keep him awake.

He fought to force love and desire aside while he stroked the keys of the computer to record the evening's face to face encounter with Palmer the Private Eye. Although the meeting would be documented under a separate report number, he'd include a copy with the stalker murders. He was certain the P.I. had noting to do with the murders, but his presence was enough to add another wrinkle to the investigation and he knew he had to cover his steps completely.

With Palmer now out of the picture as far as the murders and Gary Wilson close to elimination as a suspect, he was near to rethinking his entire approach. And the very thought of the path he might have to follow sickened him. Could the killer be a man with a badge? If so, he'd have to heighten his level of caution because, in all likelihood, the murderer would be closely tracking his progress on the cases. Or course, if it wasn't a man wearing a badge and carrying a gun, he was still dealing with a very cunning individual.

He struggled to paint a mental image of all the policemen connected, in any way, to the Society Stalker killings. With uniformed officers, detectives, crime lab technicians and those reviewing the files, there were dozens; however, he did find a reason to smile when he thought of Adams and friends. If ignorance could truly be equated with bliss, they were the happiest people on the face of the earth.

He jotted down a list of things to do, beginning with getting a sample of Gary Wilson's blood. If his instincts about Gary were true he wanted him removed from the equation before someone else jumped the gun and made him the sacrificial goat. He then compiled a list of all personnel who responded to the crime scenes, collected and processed evidence or accessed the files.

When the list was complete he'd discreetly look over their records and backgrounds.

In bold letters he printed the name Zachary Barrows. He was furious, knowing Barrows had employed an underhanded tactic to check on him. Thinking of the countless other tragedies that could've been caused by the devious plot made him angrier. He'd deal with the Lord and Master when he came home on Tuesday.

Visions of Tiffany were beginning to cloud his thought process. He pushed the chair away from the desk and tried pacing to relieve his ever-building desire for her. But the room was too small. He walked briskly to the front door only to find the earlier mist had turned to a steady rain. He threw his hands into the air and went to his room, hoping a shower might chase away his forbidden thoughts.

He turned the water from hot to warm to cold and back again, yet neither steam nor ice proved to be the solution. *Man, wake up*, he thought. *This has gone far enough. She's married. You have a job to do and you can't let her interfere with it. Hell, I can't keep going like this. Maybe I should ask Captain Thomas to get me outta here.*

He turned off the water and began drying himself with the thick white towel. He brushed at his skin vigorously in hopes of ridding himself of the lustful demons that seemed to be trying to take over his mind and body. He wrapped the towel around his waist, opened the door and stepped into the bedroom. His heart jumped immediately into his throat.

Tiffany was standing beside the bed, her hands moving slowly to the sash that held her robe in place. "I overheard almost the entire conversation between you and Mr. Palmer." Her fingers wound around the sash and stopped. "I'm very angry over what Zachary did."

"So am I," he managed to say after swallowing hard.

"And another thing—I lied to you." She pulled the sash allowing the robe to fall open. "I'm not sorry about that kiss. Not at all." Her hands rose and slid the robe off her shoulders as she stepped toward him. It fell to the floor behind her as she reached out for the towel that covered his rising penis and tugged gently. Soon it too was on to the floor.

Their arms encircled each other as his mind screamed, *No!* But his body had already consented to join with hers and they fell across the bed, the point of no return being breached within seconds of falling to the mattress. Lightening flashed, thunder rumbled and fierce winds drove the rain against the windows of the bedroom. But the rage of the storm outside was meek compared to the torrid clashing of Jefferson Lewis and Tiffany Barrows. They pushed and pulled one against the other, panting and seeking to reach the same objective. He drove into her, hard and deep, until the volcano erupted. Their fireworks display seemed to overshadow most from Independence Day and would surely give new meaning to the phrase releasing of repressed lust.

She continued to cling to him tightly as the tension began to slowly subside. She knew she didn't want this to be the only passionate embrace shared with J.D. No. She wanted him to make love to her over and over, until they were physically drained and unable to move from the bed. "God, how I needed that," she finally whispered.

"God, how I wanted that," he said, taking a deep breath. "But where do we go from here?" He was more confused then ever, but it was too late to change what had happened. And in his tangled web of thoughts he somehow knew that he didn't want to alter the chain of events that led to their coupling.

"We don't have to go anywhere," she said, playfully nipping at his earlobe. "We can stay right here and just make love."

"I can't say that I don't like that idea, but we do have a few problems. You're married, you know. That—"

"Cowboy, for the last seven years I've been married in name only. What we just did was the first time I've had sex in seven years. And, to be quite honest, I guess I really stopped loving my husband some time ago. I made up excuses and pretended to care, even going so far as to try and seduce him recently. Only I failed miserably. I don't know why I didn't do this sooner. Maybe I just had to have the right man come along. Not long ago you walked into my life and I wanted you to take me the first time I laid eyes on you."

"Damn," he muttered. "When you confess, you tell it all." He recalled the sadness he thought he saw the first time they met and now he understood.

"Let's not talk anymore. Let's jump in the shower together. I'll wash your back and you wash mine and then we can make love until we collapse."

The shower was filled with much more than cleansing and washing. Hot, passionate kisses and sensuous touches seemed to raise the water temperature by several degrees. When the shower ended she toweled him dry, giving extra special and erotic care to certain portions of his anatomy. He just closed his eyes and enjoyed what she was doing.

When she stepped back he reached for a towel to dry her, but she objected. "No. No. I want you to kiss and lick me dry."

"What? I'm not sure I understand."

"Come on. I'll show you," she said, taking his hand and leading him back into the bedroom. She went to the plush chair in the corner and sat down. The look in her eyes told him this would be a pleasurable adventure for both of them. She would be the teacher and he the student. He knelt in front of her as she reached out to his muscular shoulders and gently urged him toward her.

She guided his kisses along her face, neck and shoulders, feeling the inferno starting to blaze once more. She led him on an arousing bodily exploration and soon her coaching chores lessened as he took the lead and added his tongue to the drying process. He worked very, very slowly over her breasts, lovingly kissing and licking them until her nipples were so hard she thought they'd burst. But she only wanted more. She didn't want him to stop what he was doing. It had been too long since she felt her fires burn this hot.

The journey from her breasts to her stomach was made on warm, firm flesh and his kisses were burning hotter as he moved lower. He teased her by flicking his tongue along the edges of the ginger brown triangle and over her thighs. He began to work down her legs, but she could no longer endure her body's cry for release. "No," she gasped, pulling him up. "There. Please. Kiss me there," she moaned, moving his head directly between her legs. "I can't wait. Kiss me there. Make me cry." He moved his tongue slowly over her clit and began an amorous assault of her sensitive flesh, feeling his own desire for her building to a peak. He worked his tongue very slowly over her at first and then faster until there was another brilliant display of fireworks and she groaned, "Yes. Yes. Oh, yes. That feels so good." And for a few moments tears of pleasure filled her eyes. She gently ran her fingers through his hair and couldn't remember the last time she felt so good. But it didn't matter. Everything was fine now.

They made love again before falling asleep in each other's arms and drifting away to their own world of special dreams.

On Saturday he managed to arrange for Gary Wilson's blood to be drawn on Monday and to collect the needed samples of printing from the computers. Much of his work was done between steamy love-making sessions with Tiffany, who seemed to be trying to recover seven lost years in a single weekend

Ezra walked into the kitchen where Lolita was preparing the evening meal. "It sure is a beautiful day."

"Ezra, you must be crazy," she replied. "It's pouring rain."

"There's plenty of sunshine if you only look in the right place."

"Well, I'm lookin' out the window right now and all I see is dark clouds and rain."

"Sunshine ain't always found on the outside," he chuckled. "You just need to look in the right places inside." Ezra, of course, was referring to the gleam he'd noticed in Tiffany's eyes earlier in the day.

At that moment Tiffany walked into the kitchen with a renewed spring in her step. "Good afternoon, Ezra. Lolita."

"Hello, Mrs. Barrows."

"Good afternoon, Miss Tiffany," Ezra said, nodding to her. "It's nice to see such a happy smile on your face."

"A beautiful day can bring a smile to anyone's face."

"I think everybody in this house has gone crazy," Lolita said, glancing over her shoulder in their direction.

"Why?"

"Mrs. Barrows, just look outside. It's rainin' cats and dogs and there's another big storm brewin'."

"Storm or not, I think it's a beautiful day."

"I guess I'd better go back to bed and start this day all over again, 'cause I sure don't see nothin' beautiful about today."

"You just have to know how to look at the day," Ezra teased. "Ain't that right, Miss Tiffany?"

"Yes, Ezra. It sure is."

"Dinner's just about ready, Mrs. Barrows," Lolita said, shaking her head and then mumbling something about the weather and insanity.

After a leisurely dinner, Tiffany led J.D. back to his room where, once again, he found her to be in a delightfully naughty mood. Locating his handcuffs, she threatened to place him in manacles and have her way with him, but soon found she didn't have to cuff him to take advantage of him.

Twenty-two

Sunday morning dawned with a brilliant sunshine, adding more sparkle to Tiffany's eyes, and soon after breakfast she was anxious to be off to the spa. She was still walking on air when she walked into the health club, where Rose Anna eagerly waited. "Where have you been?"

"Oh, busy," she said, looking down.

"It's not like you to miss a day," Rose Anna said, following her into the dressing room.

"Well, I had things to do."

"Well, whatever you did agreed with you. You're absolutely glowing. You look like...you—oh, my. Oh, my."

"What's wrong?"

"You did it," she said, smiling. "You did it."

"Did what?" she said as they sat on the bench.

"Took a tumble on the sheets with J.D. It's written all over you."

"It isn't." She tried to look away as her skin flushed to a deep crimson.

"It is," Rose Anna laughed. "Just look at you, you're a nice shade of red. Come on, Tiffany, you can trust me."

She looked at her friend for a moment before saying, "Oh, all right. We did it."

"God, don't leave me hanging. What was it like?"

"Well, the first time was sort of slam, bang, wow."

"The first time! How many times did you do it?"

"I don't know." She blushed again. "I lost track after the fifth time."

"Lost count after the fifth time! Wow, what a stud."

"Oh, Rose Anna. We just didn't screw nonstop. It's not like there was one love-making session after another. We did sleep and eat."

"That's right. You should make sure he gets plenty of nourishment. You don't want your love machine to run down."

"Oh, please. Remember, he's a policeman with work to do."

"Right now, honey, I'd say he's doing a fine job of working on you."

She opened her bag and said, "I can see I'm not going to win with you."

"Did you talk with him?" Rose Anna said, turning serious. "I mean, like have a serious talk?"

"Well, yes."

"Did you tell him about your other love affair?"

"My God, Rose Anna. That was before I married Zachary. I don't really think it's necessary to discuss that with him. At least not right now."

"Sooner or later you'll have to tell him."

"Maybe not. I mean this thing between us might not last long. It's just a physical thing we're having."

"Sure it is," she said, rolling her eyes back. "Who do you think you're kidding? I know you. If it was purely physical, animal craving, you would've jumped in the sack with some guy years ago. You can't do that. It's not your nature. Without some very strong emotional feelings you'd still be horny as hell."

She looked at her friend and touched her arm. "To be honest, I feel like a school girl with her first big crush."

"Uh huh. I thought so."

"My stomach is spinning. My heart's jumping. I feel like my feet can't touch the ground."

"My," Rose Anna laughed. "You do have it bad. But how does he feel?"

"I'm not a hundred percent sure, but I'm almost certain he feels the same way."

"This is beautiful. Really beautiful," she said with a broad grin. "You know, I'm really happy for you. But you do have some problems."

"Yeah, I know. And so does J.D. The biggest, of course, being Zachary."

"Honey, when I stop and think about it, I'm not too sure I'd get all that worked up over Zachary. You can bet he's stuck his dick in a few places where it didn't belong."

"I'm sure of that. But I'm not sure how I'll deal with the issue when it comes up. And, you know, sooner or later all of this is going to come out."

"That's true. You can't keep it a secret forever."

"Not around here. There're too many eyes and ears to hide it for very long. And to top it off, Zachary hired a private eye to check on J.D. to make sure he was doing his job."

"That's not good, Tiffany. That's not good at all."

"You're telling me. God only knows how many spies he has out there on his payroll. I wonder just how much information he gets from the trainers here or the employees at the club."

"The way Zachary throws money around, you can be sure it's plenty," Rose Anna said, shaking her head. "And some of these sneaky little shits around here would sell their mothers for a dollar."

"Sad, but true."

Rose Anna stood and pulled Tiffany to her feet. "Come on. Let's go work out. You have other, more important things to do later and I don't want to keep you from them." She smiled and for a moment was jealous.

"Yes. I do have something to do this afternoon," she said with a smile as a slight flush appeared in her cheeks again.

"It's probably good that Zachary's coming home on Tuesday. J.D. might need a few days off just to regain his strength."

The workout, although abbreviated, seemed to take forever. Tiffany's mind was elsewhere. Images of her and J.D. passing the afternoon away while sharing a passionate embrace kept spinning in her mind.

Later Tiffany sat on the library sofa and studied the young man who sat at the desk double checking his list of things to do. He was a portrait of firm resolve. A man who seemed determined to turn over every leaf and pick up each stone until he found the key to solving the murders. But she wondered if he'd find the key to the mystery.

Finally she crossed the room to the desk. "Are you any closer to finding the person responsible for the killings?"

"I don't know if I'm any closer to catching him, but I've eliminated one suspect and I'm on the verge of crossing another one off my list."

"Oh. Who did you eliminate?"

"Palmer."

"I didn't know he was a suspect."

"Right now, everybody's a suspect until I can prove otherwise," he said, pushing his notepad aside.

"When you finally arrest people for murder, do all of them stand trial?" she said, moving behind him where she began rubbing his neck and shoulders.

"No, not all of them. The courts rule some of them mentally incompetent and incapable of participating in their own defense. They usually wind up in an institution, and believe me, some of them played a game to get there. They were as sane as you and me, but they fooled everybody. Then others are set free because of insufficient evidence or a case that's poorly prosecuted. And some of the guilty ones don't like the idea of going to jail for the rest of their lives so they kill themselves."

"Do many kill themselves?"

"I'm not sure of the numbers. But we have some who commit suicide before we can arrest them."

"Why?"

"Lots of reasons, I guess. If they know we're closing in they might panic and kill themselves. Or they suddenly can't face their family and friends because of what they did. Some of them leave long rambling notes where they talk about their crimes and ask for forgiveness. Some just scribble a few words saying they're sorry for what they did and some just go without even leaving a note."

"The stalker, what do you think he'll do next?"

He closed his eyes and eased his head back against her. "I wish to God I knew. If things went according to his earlier pattern, you'd be his next victim. But he's changed his method of operation recently and now I'm not sure what his next move might be. Christ, he might be using you as a decoy and is actually planning to kill someone else."

"That scares me as much as my being his intended target," she said, feeling a chill race along her back. "All of those women were my friends. It's frightening to think that at this very minute he could be stalking one of my neighbors."

"And the son of a bitch always seems to know when they're alone. I keep asking myself if they advertised the fact that their husbands were going out for the evening or leaving town on business. Did they plaster a sign on their front door?"

"At the club anything's possible," she said, beginning to gently massage his face. "The gossip mill runs nonstop morning, noon and night. It's possible that all of them said something about their husband's comings and goings. You always have one trying to be one up on the other."

"Yeah. And anybody within earshot would know what was goin' on in every house in the area." He shook his head. "So attempts by Smith to out boast Jones just might've tipped off the killer."

"Well, why don't we save this unpleasant business for some other time? I'm sure a cold beer would help relax you. After the beer, I'm sure I know something that would really relieve your tension."

"Sounds good. I have a busy schedule tomorrow. Let's have a cold one," he said, pushing the chair away from the desk and closing the notebook. But in the back of his mind he knew he should really stay and work. A killer was out there waiting and right now he was only thinking of making love to

Tiffany.

"A cold beer and a hot woman," she laughed. "How do you like that?"

"I love it," he said, squeezing her hand. Then he wondered where this illicit romantic encounter would lead. The future was shrouded in a fog of uncertainty, but the present was clearly filled with passion and lustful pleasure.

Twenty-three

Lewis awoke early and sprang out of bed quickly as if he'd been launched from a catapult. He was anxious to start collecting the all-important evidence to his murder investigation. And today he'd swim through the murky waters and circle some of his colleagues while trying to find the scent of blood on their hands.

He first collected a sample of printed material from Ginny Mason's computer and then the computer at Weldon Landscaping. He carefully labeled each and attached them to laboratory requests asking for analysis and comparison with the letters taken from the crime scenes.

Next he accompanied Gary Wilson to the hospital where he stood witness to the drawing of his blood. In the presence of Wilson, his girlfriend and the doctor who drew the sample, the evidence was given directly to a crime lab technician. He was following departmental procedure to the letter, refusing all shortcuts, which if taken, would leave his methods exposed to attack.

Lewis was so deeply involved in his tasks that he almost forgot that he'd dragged Tiffany along with him. "I'm sorry," he finally said. "I got so wrapped up in my work I ignored you."

"No need to apologize," she said, rubbing at her eyes and yawning. "I'm still not awake. Remember, I don't usually get up at the crack of dawn, jump in a shower and then devour a big breakfast."

"Sorry. I wanted to get an early start."

"I still think you could've left me home. I would've been fine. Ezra was there."

"It's not that I don't trust Ezra, but if something happened and I wasn't there, I couldn't face myself, let alone the hammering I'd get from everybody else."

"Well, can we stop somewhere for coffee?"

"Need another caffeine fix?" he laughed. "Well, okay. We'll stop for coffee before we go to the police station."

In the coffee shop they sat side by side at the counter and slowly drained their mugs, unaware they were being watched closely from a corner booth. The crowd of people, many with eyes still at half mast and looking for that awakening jolt of caffeine, hid the three policemen.

"I'm tellin' you he's sticking the dick to her," Hargrove said. "Just look at 'em."

"They do look mighty friendly, don't they?" Wallace said, tearing open another packet of sugar.

"Well, we sure as hell just can't walk over there and ask 'em if they're doing the deed," Adams sputtered between bites of his chocolate donut. "But, damn, it would be nice to know they were."

Hargrove nodded. "Just look at the way she keeps whisperin' in his ear. And check the smile. Tell me that ain't a smile of pure fucked silly happiness."

"Look, we can't concern ourselves with his lickin' her muff or ballin' her silly," Adams said as he watched them leave. "I checked those reports you told me about and I think this prick is on to something."

Wallace slapped the tabletop. "I told you he was."

"Bill, after you two get outta court this morning, drop by the station and just sort of poke around his desk a little. See if he's turned in his latest reports. If he has, make me a copy and we'll look everything over tonight. We can still beat this miserable shit to the punch."

Lewis took a copy of his reports to Captain Thomas who looked unusually tired. He wondered if Thomas just had a bad weekend or if he was still suffering side effects from his divorce. He'd found out that the breakup of Thomas and his wife had been the talk of the town since the day he discovered her in bed with one of her co-workers from the computer sales industry.

Thomas had taken a half day's leave to finish a backyard barbecue project and found his wife pinned to the mattress groaning in ecstasy. Divine intervention must've played a major role in keeping him from pulling the trigger of the pistol he shoved in the mouth of the man he violently removed from atop his wife. The salesman survived; his marriage didn't.

The divorce proceedings, initiated by his wife, were ugly and at times the captain had been on the brink of physically battering her attorney. He was fined twice for contempt of court and threatened with jail if he failed to maintain proper demeanor throughout the rest of the hearing.

Suddenly Lewis found himself staring at Thomas and asking himself, *could this be the man I'm looking for? Did he snap from the pain of losing his wife? Is he venting his anger by killing innocent women?*

"Detective Lewis, have you got a minute?" Thomas said, looking up at him through bloodshot eyes.

"Yes, sir."

"I've been going over your reports and it looks like you've developed a pretty good suspect in the stalker killings. Will you be bringing Wilson in anytime soon?"

"Sir, I don't think Wilson's our man."

"What? Why not?"

"Well, he's cooperated fully with me. Including going to the hospital first thing this morning and giving a blood sample for DNA testing."

"You've done one hell of a fine job on this investigation," Thomas said, blinking and pointing to the report on his desk. "So far, everything you've laid out in this file points right at this Gary Wilson."

"Circumstantially, yes. But I don't think he's the guy responsible for killing those women. I know on paper he looks great and I know there's more than enough evidence to arrest him and question him here. On the other side of the coin I'm almost certain the killer's someone else. The DNA test should prove that."

"If you don't think he's our man, then who're you looking at?"

"Sir, I'm lookin' at every possible angle," he said, not wanting to reveal the path where his thoughts were leading him. "I'm not ruling anyone out of the picture."

"Well, I hope to hell you come up with something soon. There're people around here who're turning up the heat on my ass and demanding results."

"I'll do my best, sir."

Thomas leaned back in his chair and covered his face with his hands for a few seconds. "I know you will," he said, sitting up. "I'm not trying to jump down your throat. I just had a real bad weekend. The kids were over and both of them came down with the flu yesterday. Christ, what a time. Up all night long. Barfing. Crying. I don't think I slept an hour the whole night."

"Sorry to hear that, Captain," he said, figuring this was the most opportune time to leave. "I've gotta get some papers before I leave, so if you'll excuse me."

"Uh, sure. Keep me posted on your progress."

"Yes, sir."

Lewis left the office and made his way toward the records division. Halfway there he ran into Don Grayson who suddenly seemed very anxious to talk with him. He nervously extended his hand saying, "Look, I think I owe you an apology. I was way outta line for takin' sides against you. I'm sorry."

"Don't worry about it. It's okay."

"No. I mean it. I'm sorry."

"Thanks," Lewis said, shaking his hand. "Right now I'm kinda up to my ass in alligators. So, I can't stand around and talk. Maybe later."

"Yeah. And, listen, if I can help you with anything, uh—like the stalker cases, just call me."

"Sure. Thanks," he said, moving by and continuing on his way.

He looked through the Society Stalker files and learned that in all, 21 people had in some way taken part in or reviewed the investigation. On the surface, none of those listed stood out in an unusual fashion. So again he'd be sifting through personnel records and looking for other sources to find out if one of them would become a suspect.

He spent the majority of the day doing a preliminary background work up on the personnel whose names he got earlier. In the process he eliminated three of them as they'd signed reports or records with last names and first initials only and turned out to be female officers.

Later, over dinner, he noticed that Tiffany had lost her smile. "Hey, why the sad look?"

"This is the last night we'll have together for a few days," she said, dropping her napkin to the table. "I'm going to miss sleeping beside you and having you make love to me. And that makes me sad."

He looked across the table at her and thought he was surely violating every ethical code known to man. He'd become involved with a woman he was sworn to protect and at one time even thought might be responsible for mailing the letter to herself to regain her husband's attention. Now that thought was eliminated. "I'm sure gonna miss holding you and making love to you too."

"Well," she said, pushing her chair back and giving him a look that Rose Anna would've been proud of, "I'd like to make a suggestion. Why don't we go and indulge ourselves in something we can dream about for the next couple of days?"

"Let's go," he said, seeing ethics fall another rung on the ladder as his desire for her pushed conscience aside.

Their session on the sheets would've rivaled most tropical nights. Their flesh seemed aflame while they embraced and slowly rocked to love's rhythm, the rising heat causing perspiration to flow and coat them. They teased and fought to prolong the agonizing road to heaven until they could no longer hold the river back. The dam burst and with it came a rush of elation and they spun out of control, rising to dizzying heights and floating around in a world of dreamy passion.

Sometime later as she lay nestled in his arms she whispered, "Do you think I've lost my innocence again?"

"Maybe," he said with a smile.

"Ummmm. I probably have."

While she slept beside him he stared up into the darkness and thought about the loss of innocence. When was it really lost? Was it lost in one sweeping instant or did it erode over time? And he thought that it must ebb gradually, somewhat like the sands on a beach are swept away with the tides of time.

In his lifetime he imagined the age of innocence began to slip away with the death of his parents and the sadness that followed. The passing of virginity in the arms of Rachel on a warm, spring afternoon was a time of blissful growing. But he felt certain that innocence passed forever on a sweltering morning when he raised the rifle and peered through the scope, taking deadly aim at a man. A stranger without a name.

He and a small group of fellow Marines were sneaking and crawling around in a place where, in all probability, their mission didn't officially exist. They were looking for drug smugglers. Just following orders like good Marines, without questioning them. On a hill overlooking a small valley they found their target. A small group of men on their way to do business with someone who'd carry their product to the United States for sale in the streets. But he and the others would make sure that didn't happen.

The man in the scope was smiling and talking with his comrades as he moved among them. His smile stood out like a beacon against his olive skin and black beard. As the man turned to speak with a colleague the cross-hairs of the scope rested on their mark. He slowly squeezed the trigger and recalled how the smile seemed frozen to the man's face as the bullet ripped into his skull just above the left ear. There was a split second of silence before the morning air was again torn by rapid bursts of gunfire. A few minutes later the unofficial mission was accomplished. They'd obeyed their orders and it was time to go home. He slipped away quietly, leaving the remains of his once untainted soul baking in a sun-drenched pool of blood.

Twenty-four

Lewis went out of his way to make sure that he was the only member in the greeting party to hail the returning hero. There was no mincing of words when he told Barrows he wanted a private chat immediately. He slammed the door to Barrows' office and got right to the point. "What the fuck's the idea of hiring Palmer to check on me?"

"What? I don't know what you're talking about."

"Don't try and pull that bullshit with me. It won't work. I caught your hired goon outside and he confessed the whole scheme to me."

"I have a right to make sure my wife's being properly watched over," he snapped. "I have—"

"Listen, asshole," Lewis snarled, leaning across the desk. "What you did was toss Palmer into the ring as a possible suspect in the murders. So I started wondering if he was the killer. I had to keep lookin' over my shoulder because I thought there was a change in pattern and he might kill your wife outside the house."

"So what?" Barrows said, attempting to return to his usual pompous self. "I can do whatever I damn well please when it comes to seeing that my wife's protected."

"I have news for you," Lewis said, circling the desk and standing a mere arm's length from the man who was testing every fiber of his patience. "I could lock your ass up for hindering an official police investigation."

"Go right ahead," he replied, smiling and leaning back in his chair. "I'd be out before you could blow your nose. Threats from punks like you don't scare me. Hell, I buy and sell people like you everyday."

He could hear the voices of Mr. Higa and John Henry Johnson telling him to control his urge to the punch the bragging multi-millionaire squarely in the teeth. "I don't doubt that you'd buy your way out of it. But it would be an embarrassing headline for you. Every big shot at the country club would have something to talk about behind your back. And just think of all those questions you'd have to waste time answering, instead of spending it bragging about your latest squashing of some poor slob."

"Lewis, I don't like you," he growled. "When this is over it'll be my pleasure to teach you a lesson."

"Oh, believe me, I'm looking forward to it," he said, stepping back and glaring at him. "In the meantime, when you talk to Palmer, tell him to remember what I told him."

Barrows remained behind the locked doors of his office for over an hour before finally reaching for the telephone. "Palmer, this is Zachary Barrows. Now, what the fuck went wrong?"

"Uh—Mr. Barrows, that guy's nuts. I mean like stone cold fuckin' insane."

"Palmer," he bellowed, "answer my question."

"Well, I tested him like you ordered and somehow he caught me. I was tryin' to break in the house. I got by the security system with no problem 'cause you gave me the codes. But when I went to work on the window he must've heard me. That crazy son of bitch stuck a shotgun between my legs and when I didn't answer his questions he pulled the trigger. I damn near shit myself."

"So you just went ahead and spilled everything, is that it?"

"For Christ's sake," he whined, "you would've done the same damn thing if he jammed that fuckin' shotgun in your balls."

"Okay, Winston, calm down. What else do you have to report?"

"Not much. Except that the guy does his job. You wanted him to protect your wife and it looks to me like you got the right guy for the job. Nobody can get near her when they're off the grounds."

"Anything else?"

"No. But by your tone, I'm not sure what you mean."

"I think he might be doing a little more than just keeping a close eye on my wife," he said, lowering his voice.

"Damn! You don't think he's ballin' your wife, do you?"

"I don't know. I just can't be sure."

"The equipment's workin' okay, isn't it?'

"Yeah. Fine. Fine. I just happen to think they're too friendly. I want Mr. Lewis put in his place. Can you handle that?"

There was a pause. "Well, I don't think I should personally take care of it," he said. "I mean he can identify me. I could lose my license."

"Can you find someone to handle it?"

"Hell, the right money can buy anything or anybody, Mr. Barrows. I have two guys in mind who'd probably be willing to put that prick in his place."

"Why two?"

"Shit, that guy's spooky. I mean Lewis has that look in his eyes. You know what I mean?"

"Yeah. I know what you mean," he said, recalling his thoughts upon meeting the detective and the look he thought of as the eyes of a hunter. "Talk to your men. I'll be leaving again in about three days. Take care of it while I'm out of town."

"Sure thing, Mr. Barrows. I'll call you tomorrow afternoon and let you know if the arrangements have been completed."

"Fine. I'll be waiting for your call."

Over dinner Zachary noticed that Tiffany seemed aloof. Though cordial in every way, she was distinctly a different woman than the one he'd left behind only a few days ago. There was a noticeable radiance about her, a look he'd not seen in some time. But it was her chilly rebuff of his attempted embrace that sent his suspicions concerning her and the young detective soaring.

After dinner he set about on his own brand of fact-finding mission, questioning Lolita and Ezra. But the reception from them was even colder than Tiffany's rebuke of his intended hug. Their answers were blunt and filled with reluctance, which did nothing to ease his uncertainty.

Stunned three times by the cold shoulder given to him by those, who in times gone by would've nearly trembled before him, he went to his office. There in the room where he often schemed the overthrow of business kingdoms and gloated over past triumphs, he thought about his fall from grace.

Lewis waded into his work, reading files, placing telephone calls and making tactful visits to those he trusted. When his fast-paced activity finally slowed he'd narrowed his list of suspects in his field of coworkers down to two.

Mark Santos, a self-professed woman-hater, held his attention for some time. But as he worked through the files, notes taken during telephone conversations and information gathered during personal contacts, he found that Santos simply wore a mask of deceit. He put up a strong front to lure women who couldn't resist being taken advantage of by a man who claimed to hate them. And there were dozens standing in line begging for abuse.

Captain Karl Thomas, on the other hand, was a very bitter man. Betrayed by the woman he loved and adored, he seemed an almost perfect candidate for a man who wished to make a statement. Friends and relatives feared the worst and spoke often of how they were sure he'd snap and do the unthinkable.

According to his background check, the marriage of Irene and Karl Thomas spun out of control and crashed to the ground only two months before the first murder. His anger over being forsaken by his wife would seem to give him a motive for murder. And his position of trust as a police captain could surely get him into homes where a woman left all alone would have no reason to believe his intentions were anything but honorable.

The more he moved the pieces of the jigsaw puzzle around, the easier Thomas began to fit in the completed picture. As a cop he could gain valuable knowledge about the victims and their habits, providing him with the perfect opportunity to commit crimes of violence sparked by hate and an appetite for retribution.

Still, in his heart he prayed that his investigation wouldn't prove his present thought correct. To take one of his own into custody for the brutal crimes would only serve to add another blemish to the badge of honor for which so many gallantly sacrificed their lives.

Lewis had no aspirations to be the detective who held a fellow officer up to public ridicule, however, he realized that life's twisting path is sometimes filled with shattered illusions of those most admired and trusted. Therefore, if duty required that he bring a brother of the badge to justice, he'd fulfill his obligation and carry out his oath of office.

The report he'd turn in wouldn't be filled with details of his latest investigative leads. He wouldn't dare point an accusing finger at another officer without proof beyond a shadow of doubt. To do so would be professional suicide.

As he placed the file in the desk, his thoughts turned to Tiffany. He'd seen very little of her over the past three days and it looked as if Barrows was going out of his way to keep him from having contact with her. He'd suddenly taken on the role of the robin in spring, protecting the nest and keeping away marauding scavengers.

Lewis thought Barrows was displaying classic signs of jealously and wondered if he suspected what was going on between him and Tiffany. But Barrows' possessiveness began to surface almost immediately after his arrival and the assumption of his duties. A normal trait for the master of the house? Maybe.

Zachary would be leaving on another business venture early tomorrow and that meant Tiffany would be returning to share his bed. He felt the excitement race over him as his anticipation of holding her and making love to her pushed thoughts of an outraged husband aside. His anxieties over what would happen if their affair was discovered also vanished.

For now he was content to dream of tomorrow and the happiness he'd find in the arms of Tiffany. A time when her touch, her scent and her passion would engulf him and all else would be forgotten.

Twenty-five

As anxious as they were to fall together and smother each other with lustful flames of love, they waited. Zachary seemed too apprehensive before he left and they certainly didn't want him to come back unannounced and find them making love.

They toiled through their morning workout routine at the health spa while more and more suspicious glances were cast their way. Questions, in quiet tones of course, circled the spa and country club regarding their relationship. Although they exercised every precaution in avoiding public displays of affection, vocal finger pointing was rising to a feverish pitch.

Rose Anna was hounded almost daily with questions by telephone and in person from the poisonous rumor spreaders to the idle curious. But, true to her oath to Tiffany, she told them nothing or had a little fun in her own perverted way by quenching their inquisitive thirst with misinformation.

When they finished their workout they decided to go to One Step West for their famed luncheon specials. While taking a sip of water, J.D. noticed the two men at the bar and smiled. Like Palmer at the health spa, the men blended as well as an overweight rat in the middle of a starving rattlesnake's convention.

"I hate to say this," he said, lowering his glass and touching her arm, "but I believe we have two new friends sitting at the bar."

"They certainly are obvious, aren't they?" she said, raising her teacup and looking in their direction. "I'm not a detective, but it would be impossible not to spot those two."

"Yeah. You think it could be the way they're staring at us?"

"Staring! I'm surprised they haven't set up a camera and started filming."

"By their looks, I'd say they strong arm people for a living."

She frowned. "What's that?"

"You know, bill collectors. The kind who come knocking when you fail to pay a gambling debt or repay a loan."

"Oh, those kind," she said, shaking her head.

"I smell Palmer and your husband."

"I can't believe they'd send something the likes of those two to follow us."

"I don't believe they were hired for the purpose of following us," he said, signaling the waitress. "They're strictly assault and battery men."

"You don't mean…." She stopped in mid sentence and looked at the men seated at the bar.

"What can I do for you, Cowboy?" the waitress said.

"Is Jerico in?"

"Mr. Jerico's in his office."

Lewis left the table, walked to the corner of the bar where the two men sat and summoned the bartender. "Give Dickhead and Dickhead here a refill and put it on my tab." Satisfied that he'd thoroughly pissed them off, he patted both of them on the shoulder and walked into the office of Ernest Jerico.

The meeting with Jerico was brief, but certainly long enough for them to enter into a conspiracy. A handshake sealed their agreement and Lewis left the office. He stopped a short distance from the men at the bar. "If you assholes are ready, we might as well go out back and get it on."

Lewis turned quickly and walked toward the back of the restaurant, looking back to be sure the men weren't overtaking him too quickly. He cut sharply to his right and ducked into the hallway marked Emergency Exit Only.

"Where'd that cocksucker go?" one of the men growled as they stepped into the dimly lit passageway.

The door at the end of the corridor clicked shut and they raced blindly toward it while visions of tearing Lewis into small unrecognizable pieces danced in their one-track minds. When they reached the exit both men grabbed the metal bar and stopped when they heard the barking. Seconds later they chuckled, knowing the incessant yapping belonged to a small dog. A very small dog. With an exaggerated heave they shoved the door open and came face to face with the dog that brazenly stood there and blocked their path. Chico the Chihuahua.

The men stepped out onto the concrete and reached to shield their eyes from the sun's brilliant rays. They squinted and looked around for Lewis while Chico continued to yap, but yield ground to the advancing men.

They stopped when the hinges on the door behind them creaked and alerted them that it was closing. Their eyes first focused on the grinning man in the black sweat pants and tee shirt who was pulling the heavy metal door shut.

But it was the bold letters on the sign just above the left shoulder of Lewis and the smirk on his face that slapped them like a brick between the eyes. It plainly said, Warning. Do Not Enter. Attack Trained Dogs.

They lunged for the door, but it was too late. The resounding dull thud told them they were left to face the yapping little menace that greeted them. But it was strangely silent. Almost as if he'd gone away. Of course, the sign did say something about attack dogs.

They turned quickly and to their dismay Chico had vanished. He'd been replaced by more than a half dozen German Shepherds. Even more disheartening to the men was the fact that the dogs were not barking and growling. They simply stood side by side, displaying rows of sparkling white teeth and staring at them. Large dogs that glare and show lots of pearly white teeth usually mean business and will surely bite.

The pounding on the door mixed with frantic cries for help clearly indicated that someone was in distress. But Lewis didn't rush to open the door and allow them to escape the beasts that seemed to cause them such anxiety. A little dispiriting now and then was good for the soul and it sure as hell delivered a message to those who wanted to spy on him, or in this case, give him a sound beating.

When he finally opened the door, only a single blur could be distinguished running down the hallway, followed by a very small, brown, yapping blip. Chico was in hot pursuit and announced to the world that he had the intruders on the run. They raced out into the restaurant and dashed between the packed tables with the killer dog rapidly gaining ground. The ferocious Chihuahua caught up with them at the front door and gave each of them a bite on the ankle before they fell outside onto the parking lot.

Chico made three rapid circles while snapping quickly at his tail as if telling everyone in the restaurant they were now permitted to cheer his heroic deed. To the sound of applause he strutted between the tables, head high, chest out, and tail arced to tell everybody he'd reestablished himself ruler of the roost.

"I don't know about you, but I enjoyed that," Lewis said, returning to the table and passing a thumbs up to Ernest Jerico.

"I loved it, but how'd you arrange it?"

"I asked for a favor. Ernest Jerico's wife, brother and sister-in-law train dogs on the property and in the building next door. Big dogs. German Shepherds. The property and the restaurant have a pretty large area between them, connected by a fence and a walkway. Sometimes the dogs are allowed to roam around in that area, and today they were there to form a greeting party for our two friends."

"And what about the Chihuahua?"

"Chico," he laughed. "I guess you could say he hosted the party. And for whatever reason, the big dogs love the little shit."

"How did you avoid their greeting?"

"Hey, I'm no fool. I hid in the janitor's closet after I pushed the door open far enough to bait them. They were in such a hurry to kick my ass they didn't see the sign."

"Wait a minute. If those dogs were there, why didn't they get chewed to shreds?"

"Simple," he said. "The dogs were put on alert, but told not to attack."

"Do you think we'll see them again?"

"I doubt it. My guess is they'd be too embarrassed to show their faces again. If your husband and Palmer had anything to do with hiring them, it's another slap in their faces. I don't think they enjoy looking like fools. So, I don't think we'll see them again."

It was early afternoon when she suggested a trip to the sauna and today they'd find it much hotter than usual. Slippery bodies joining and touching added a more erotic sensation to their lovemaking. When it was over perspiration flowed from every pore of their bodies and she panted, "We should do this again."

"Yes," he panted.

She led him to the shower where she made a playful game of washing him and shocking him with bursts of icy cold water. But eventually it was the slow soapy massage she applied to his lower abdomen that brought a more serious note back to the shower. She rubbed the bar of soap over him until he was thoroughly lathered and then slid her hand softly around him and brought his penis to full staff. He closed his eyes and enjoyed the sensation while she continued to stroke him. She pulled and pushed her hand back and forth until she obtained the desired results. He exploded and groaned, "Maybe we should do that again too."

"Why not," she said, kissing him lightly on the lips.

Twenty-six

After enjoying an early dinner, J.D. insisted he had work to do. She feigned injury to her womanly pride, working hard to display her best pout. When she realized she couldn't persuade him to forget his duties, she followed him quietly to the library.

For what seemed like a very long time he was lost in silent examination of the stalker case files. His eyes scanned the pages over and over, top to bottom and from time to time he jotted a note or two in his book or highlighted a segment on one of the pages. Finally he said, "You know, as many times as I've gone over these, I can't help but think something's still missing."

"What could be missing?"

"I'm not sure," he said, standing and stretching. "But there's another link in all of this that we've missed. I've missed it and so did the others."

"Like I said earlier, I'm not a detective, but maybe I could help if you feel like confiding in me."

"I haven't really picked your brain over this, have I?"

"No, you haven't"

"Okay, let's take it from the beginning," he said, nodding. "We have four attractive women in their forties. They're killed in their homes in a room specified by the killer in a letter sent to each of them. In each instance they're found with a piece of black rope knotted around their throats and they've been sexually assaulted. Now, either the killer is one slick dude or has one hell of a knack for con games."

"Why do you say that?"

"Listen and tell me what you think." He paced for a few seconds and went on. "In each case, the butler and maid are given the night off and we end up with a corpse on our hands. That's too much of a coincidence to suit me."

"Amanda French was the only one who had live in help," Tiffany said, moving from the sofa to a chair beside the desk. "Of course, Ezra and Lolita have their own quarters here."

"Yeah. I know that. But for some strange reason she gives them the night off and insists they go into town to a movie or do whatever they want to do. So they leave. In the other three households they were supposed to work late—10 o'clock or so. But each victim practically orders them to leave early and then they're murdered. I can't believe all of these women had some hot lover on the side and wanted to get the hired help out of the house so they could get laid."

"As far as I know they were faithful to their husbands. Besides, if they wanted to get laid, they didn't need to run the help off. They would've trusted them with the secret. No. It had to be something else."

"That brings us to the next problem. The alarm system. Let's forget a lover on the side. How'd the killer get in without tripping the alarm?"

"They let him in," she said, shrugging her shoulders.

"Why? What'd he do? Ring the buzzer at the gate and say, 'Hi, I'm your friendly neighborhood stalker and I'm here to kill you. Let me in.' And presto, they opened the door for him."

"Okay," she said, shifting in the chair. "It was somebody they knew."

"Let's suppose that's true. Is that reason enough to give the butler and maid the night off?"

"Damn," she muttered. "No, it's not."

"Right. So why, out of the clear blue sky, do they want the house to themselves?"

"I don't know."

"Now, you're alone in your home and you've received a letter from the killer telling you you're next," he said, turning several pages in his notebook. "The doorbell rings and it's your friendly handyman from the landscaping company, do you let him in?"

"Ummm, no. He's not a close friend and I'm alone. No. He'd have to come back when someone else is home."

"Good. Now, let's say a smooth-talking cop punches the bell, tells you he's in the neighborhood and just wanted to check on your safety. Do you let this guy in?"

"I'm not sure. How do I know he's a cop?"

"He's in uniform or he presents his shiny badge and ID card, complete with his picture in the corner."

She turned away, rolled her eyes and thought about the situation before replying.

"Right now, sitting here and having time to think about it, I guess I'd let him in. I mean he's there for my protection. I should trust him."

"So, you'd let him in."

"Yes," she said, nodding. "Oh, wait. Wait a minute. You don't think the killer's a policeman, do you?"

He paced back and forth, looking down at the carpet as he walked. He stopped in front of her and said, "Right now I have one who fits nicely into the puzzle. But I just can't seem to find that one small thing that says I'm a hundred percent on the money. And that bothers me."

"Why don't we go through the rest of the maze?" she said, looking at him. "Maybe then you can sort it all out."

"Why not?" he said, sitting down again. "From the top. All the victims were wealthy and lived in mansions. They attended formal parties. Traveled about most of the time in chauffeur driven limos. Worked out or exchanged bits of juicy gossip at the spa. They were married to very successful businessmen. They...."

"Don't forget," she said. "They were successful in their own right."

"I don't follow you. What're you saying?"

"You mean you don't know? They were businesswomen. They ran their own businesses. Owned their own small companies."

"Damn it," he muttered. "None of the reports show that. And dumb ass me just assumed they were living off their husband's wealth."

"Well, most of the wives around here do live off their husband's income. Only a handful run or ran their own companies."

"I guess you'd better fill me in," he said, picking up his pen and giving her his complete attention.

"Let's see. Amanda French owned a greeting card company. Cynthia Wellington ran a tennis wear and equipment store. Alexandra Upchurch owned and managed a swim wear company. And Kimberly McDougal owned The Huntley Manor Golf Shop."

"Why'd they run their own businesses?"

"I think it started out more as a hobby than anything else," she said, nodding. "Then it became a challenge to see if they could compete in the money market. I think in the beginning when their husbands bought the stores for them or set them up in business, they were just looking for tax write-offs or some loophole in the tax laws."

"Okay. So it was their husbands who bought companies for them or set them up."

"Yes."

"How many other women run their own businesses?" he said, working his pen with an almost savage fury across the note pad.

"Just two. Monica Swanson owns a jewelry store and Madeline Jennings has an antique company."

"And their husbands set them up in business?"

"Yes. Why?"

"I think I might've found the link I'm looking for," he said as he continued to write. "But at the same time it's probably gonna toss out the other suspects. Anyway, I can't worry about suspects right now. I have to call these two women—immediately."

"Only Madeline Jennings is home. Monica Swanson's with her husband touring Europe."

"Do you have Mrs. Jennings' phone number handy?"

"Sure."

"Call her and ask—no. Tell her we have to see her right away."

"Okay."

"Oh, by the way," he said, as she got up to leave. "Do you own or have you ever owned a business?"

"Yes. I owned a candy company. I sold exotic chocolates. But I sold the company several years ago."

"Did your husband set you up in business?"

"No, that wasn't necessary. I had enough money to start and run the business myself."

He gave a nod. "Okay. Now, make that call for me please."

The image of a killer was again changing, altering in the back of his mind to another hazy face without a name. He saw Captain Thomas slip a rung on his ladder of suspects, but certainly he didn't fall completely from the scenario.

Lewis thought the killer's choosing successful businesswomen as targets could be purely coincidental. But he realized the odds of that happening by mere chance were one in a million. No, he thought, these women pissed somebody off big time because they ran a profitable business.

Tiffany's voice shook him from his trance like state. "Madeline isn't answering her phone."

"Tell me her husband isn't out of town—please."

"Sorry," she said, her concern showing in her expression. "He left early yesterday morning for a business conference."

"Let's go," he said, grabbing his Stetson from the desk and taking her by the arm.

"We've gotta get to her house now."

"Oh, God," she whispered. "Oh, God."

"How many people know her husband's out of town?" he said as they reached the police car.

"Probably everybody at the club and spa."

"I guess that would include staff and anybody else who happened to be working around the buildings or grounds?"

"That's certainly possible. Every time somebody leaves or plans to leave, it's the topic of the day. I'm sure staff and workers listen in on the conversations and, in some cases, they might even be a part of them."

"They'd talk about somebody's trip, even if they leave town every week."

"Oh, yes. Gossip's gossip. And, it's important to be one up on everyone in the group, even if it is weekly news."

"Damn," he mumbled. "A ready made pipeline of information for anybody and everybody, including a killer."

Tiffany was silent for most of the drive, but as they neared the entrance to the Jennings property, she said, "You think she's dead, don't you?"

He didn't really want to answer her, but knew there was no way to avoid it. "Yes," he finally said.

"Why?"

"A feeling. A cold knot in my stomach. And it fits the pattern. Or at least a part of it."

He braked to a stop in front of the gate and looked for signs of life, but only grim darkness filled the night sky. He stepped from the car and pushed the intercom buzzer, knowing he wouldn't receive an answer. The only sounds filling the air were that of the car's engine and the crackling voices over the police radio.

He returned to the car and reached for the radio. After taking a deep breath he pressed the small red button on the mike and said, "Dispatch, send a uniformed officer to the Jennings residence at 36 Huntley Manor Road. I need assistance gaining entrance to the house."

He dropped the mike to the seat beside him, closed his eyes and rested his head on the top of the seat. There was nothing to do now but wait for the uniforms and think about what they'd find when they went into the house. And surely they'd find that death had once again left its gruesome calling card.

Twenty-seven

Tiffany stayed in the foyer, a uniformed officer beside her, while J.D. and other officers searched the house of Madeline Jennings. Tiffany was also beginning to feel the icy knot tightening in her stomach.

On the second floor in the master bedroom, grisly reality reared its ugly face and death's eyes showed the corpse of Madeline Jennings to searching officers. She was lying face up on the king-sized bed, a portion of black rope knotted around her throat and eyes fixed in a glazed afterlife stare.

For the next several hours, police officers, crime lab technicians and the medical examiner came and went, while a crowd of sightseers and news reporters swarmed around the entrance to the property. The spectators gathered with hopes of catching a glimpse of the macabre as reporters looked for a headline story.

Lewis wasn't shocked to see Adams and his two friends arrive at the house and try to enter the crime scene. When he refused to give them permission to enter the bedroom, a heated argument ensued. Adams said, "I'm a lieutenant and I'm ordering you to let me in this room. If not, you'll face charges of insubordination."

"All due respect to your rank, sir, but I'm the investigating officer and I'm in charge of the crime scene. I'm not giving you permission to enter."

"On what grounds?"

"You have no need to enter. You're not investigating the crime and at the present time you have no connection to the investigation in any way."

"We'll see about that," Adams said, trying to step into the room.

Lewis blocked his path. "Lieutenant, you can't come in."

"Get out of the way, you...."

"That'll be enough, Lieutenant," Captain Thomas said. "I'm sure you wouldn't want to go in there and possibly contaminate valuable evidence, would you?"

"Uh, no, sir."

"I thought you and the others would agree that following proper crime scene procedure would be the thing to do."

Captain Thomas entered the crime scene only after requesting and being granted permission by the case investigator, Detective J.D. Lewis. He stood beside the bed, looking at the corpse and listening to a synopsis of the initial findings. Satisfied with the preliminary report he nodded and left.

Lewis backed up to the wall beside the door and once again looked over the crime scene; however, the conversation in the hallway distracted him. It wasn't loud voices that disrupted his train of thought. It was the topic that caught his attention. Adams and Wallace were talking about Captain Thomas.

"Man, that was a shock seeing Thomas show up here," Adams said, as he strained to get a look at the woman lying on the bed.

"Probably couldn't sleep," Wallace replied. "He's probably still steamed over his ex's latest conquest."

"Oh. What's that?"

"I take it you haven't heard. Christ, it's in all the papers. She just nailed some big promotion and a fat salary to go with it."

"Why should that bother him?" he said, looking back at Wallace. "I mean they're through. Divorced."

"Yeah, I know. But I stopped by the office late this afternoon and I was there when she called him just to stick it up his ass. Man, was he pissed. Actually, I think that's an understatement. I don't even know if furious is the right word to describe his reaction to the call."

"Damn. I'm sorry I missed it. What happened?"

"Christ, Lenny, you should've heard it. He was screamin' that her and bitches like her should be killed. He said if somebody killed her, he'd pay for the guy's defense attorney. Then after she was buried, he'd shit on her grave. I'm sure everybody in the office heard him."

Lewis scratched his head and tried to make sense of Captain Thomas' actions. The divorce had been very messy, with fights over child custody and thoughts of another man in his bed sharing his wife's affections. The dazed first seconds of finding her wrapped in another man's arms soon turned to anger and later to pain. He wondered if what Thomas said was said in a moment of extreme anger fueled by her taunting.

He shook the thoughts from his mind and returned to the business at hand. There would be time to sift through facts and analyze Thomas' state of mind after he finished his work here.

Dawn's first light was showing above the trees when Madeline Jennings' body was taken from the house. As the black hearse rolled quietly down the driveway, songs of waking birds announced the arrival of a new day. Robins and crows alike took flight in search of earth's delicacies to feed their ever-hungry offspring, too busy to notice death's dark wagon pass by.

Lewis and Tiffany remained at the scene of the ghoulish crime. He wanted to look it over once more before leaving. He walked into the room and meticulously scanned every inch of the sleeping quarters, searching to make sure he hadn't missed anything.

Tiffany stood just inside the doorway, trying not to dwell on the loss of another friend. But her thoughts kept returning to the companion she'd known for many years, as her eyes wandered about the spacious room. She took a long look at the vanity table, fascinated by something she saw. "That's odd," she said, pointing to the object as she walked toward the table.

"What's odd?"

"This," she said, pointing to the bottle of Night Heat perfume. "Madeline Jennings was allergic to perfume. She'd break out in a terrible rash if she used perfume of any kind."

"Are you sure?"

"Positive."

"Damn. Why would…." He stopped and looked at the bottle. "Hey, you know, there was a bottle of Night Heat on Amanda French's vanity table," he said. He paused for a moment and muttered, "And a bottle in Gary Wilson's apartment."

"Well, it's a very popular perfume. A top-selling brand, in fact. But I can tell you Amanda didn't use it."

"What about the other victims? Did they use it?"

"Cynthia and Kimberly did, but I'm not really certain about Alexandra."

"Damn. I've gotta do some fast backtracking."

"Why?"

"Well, if Amanda French didn't use it and Madeline Jennings was allergic to it, it sounds to me like the killer left it."

"Why would he do that?"

"It's his calling card. A perverted signature. His way of telling the world this is his crime."

"That's sick."

"Yeah, it is," he said, nodding. "But I also think our killer's been taking pictures of his victims."

"God! Why would he do that?"

"Another signature. Some guys like to keep mementos of their work.

Sometimes it's an article of clothing or something personal belonging to the victim. And some like to take pictures of the victim after they've killed them."

"How can you be sure this one's taking pictures of his victims?"

"Tonight, while going over the crime scene, one of the lab techs found what he's sure is a piece of a Polaroid film box. It looks like the killer dropped it and kicked it under the bed when he opened the box and this time he didn't do a real good job of cleanin' up."

"You think he's getting careless?"

"I don't know," he said, reaching for the perfume bottle and easing it into a plastic baggie. "Maybe he was in a hurry for some reason."

"Could it be a different killer?"

"I don't think so," he said, holding the bag up to the light and looking for a telltale sign. "But the pattern changed again. Madeline Jennings didn't get a letter—at least not that we know of. The rope, the sexual assault and the neatness all point to the same guy."

"Do you think one of your suspects is responsible for these killings?"

"On the basis of circumstantial evidence, one looks great. On motive alone, the second seems more suited to fill the killer's shoes." He put his arm around her waist and began walking toward the door. "And right about now, that makes me think that it's neither of them."

"But are you sure?"

"Not a hundred percent. Not yet. But there's something else about the killer. Something drives this guy to commit these crimes. What he's doing shows a deep hatred for women, but there's more to it. Something happened in this guy's life to drive him to do this and right now I don't know what that is."

"That doesn't necessarily eliminate your suspects, does it?"

"No, it doesn't. But—how did Ezra put it? I'm not sure of his exact words, but something like, 'sometimes what you see right in front of you just ain't so.' And that sounds like what I have here."

"Well, Ezra's a very wise man."

"That he is."

"You told me one of your suspects is a policeman. You're not looking for a way to prove this man innocent just because he's a cop, are you?"

"No, I'm not. It's my job to work just as hard to prove a man innocent, as it is to prove him guilty. But in these cases it seems the more I struggle to point the finger at a suspect, the more something keeps telling me I'm going down the wrong road."

"There's one thing you might want to keep in mind while you're sorting all of this out."

"What's that?"

"Night Heat perfume is very expensive. If your killer's leaving that as a calling card, it's a very high-priced one. Of course, I guess he could always steal it."

"Yeah, he could steal it," he muttered. And suddenly Captain Thomas slipped another rung down the ladder. He could picture Thomas as many things, but he certainly didn't wear the cloak of a common thief. And, for some reason, Gary Wilson also seemed a step above the shoplifter's league.

"I don't know about you, but I'm ready for some sleep," she said, clinging a little tighter to his arm.

"For me, that's out of the question. I have too much to do. Besides, I'm too fired up to sleep."

"You're not going to leave me alone, are you?"

The concern in her voice was quite clear and he stopped and looked at her. "No. I'd never do that. I'll make sure a police officer's assigned to stay at the house while I do my backtracking and go to the autopsy."

"I guess I should've known you wouldn't abandon me. But I'm so frightened. Very, very frightened. I'm wondering what the killer's next move is. I received the letter and Madeline's killed. This whole thing is so crazy. I just wish it would end." Tears were forming in the corners of her eyes.

"I can only imagine how you must feel," he said, taking her in his arms and gently hugging her. "But sooner or later I'll find this guy. In the meantime, I won't let anything happen to you. I promise."

"You know, there's another thing that bothers me, Cowboy. What happens when this is over? To us, I mean?"

He shook his head and squeezed her tighter. "I don't know. We'll have to cross that bridge when the time comes."

"I don't want what we have to end," she said, fighting to swallow the lump in her throat. "I feel alive for the first time in years and I sure don't want to let go of that feeling."

"I don't want this to end either."

Twenty-eight

Lewis was standing on familiar ground again, the cutting room of the Chief Medical Examiner's Office. Doctor Wexler's voice was a dull, droning hum as with scalpel and saw he set about dissecting the body of Madeline Jennings. Mundane medical terms and words buzzed in Lewis' ears.

He drifted back once more on a hazy cloud recalling that lovely woman who cared for him when he was so very young. She was a portrait of beauty and caring, a bright spirit on dreary days who gave him warmth and love. And suddenly he wondered why Tiffany didn't have any children. She seemed like a women who'd enjoy them. Maybe he'd bring the topic up when the time was right.

Doctor Wexler coaxed him back from his faraway land and told him that the Society Stalker was responsible for Madeline Jennings' murder. They knew that, of course, when they met earlier in her bedroom, but, as always, it wasn't official until the autopsy was complete.

After witnessing Madeline Jennings' autopsy, Lewis retraced the killer's steps beginning with the French residence. Although he'd gone over 24 hours without sleep, he was running with throttle open. Adrenaline was his fuel again.

Jonathan French still showed signs of his devastating loss. His face was pale and drawn, while dark circles under his eyes told of his many sleepless nights tortured by his wife's death. But he willingly, almost eagerly, agreed to talk with Lewis about his wife's murder.

"I know this is difficult for you, Mr. French, but there're some new developments and it's necessary to go over certain facts again."

"That's quite all right. I'll do anything I can to help catch the man who killed my wife."

"Okay. Can you tell me if your wife used Night Heat perfume?"

"No," he said. "No, she didn't. In fact, I bought Amanda's perfumes for her and that wasn't one of my choices."

"Any chance that she might've bought a bottle for herself?"

"I doubt that," he said, shaking his head. "As I recall, she didn't particularly care for Night Heat."

"Mr. French, in the photographs taken on the night of your wife's murder, a bottle of Night Heat is on the vanity in one of them."

"That's certainly strange." He scratched his head and looked away for a moment.

"I'm sure Amanda never bought any for herself. I can't understand why there'd be a bottle in one of your pictures."

"Well, it's right there on the vanity table."

"Then it would still be there. I haven't touched or moved a thing in our bedroom since Amanda was killed."

"I'd like to see the room, if you don't mind."

Jonathan French escorted him to the room on the second floor and with a slightly trembling hand reached for the door. Lewis could see the tears welling up within the sunken eyes of the man as he turned the heavy brass knob and opened the door.

Lewis judged from the amount of dust forming on the furniture that the room hadn't been entered, even for the purpose of cleaning, since the death of Mrs. French. He walked to the vanity table and there, just as in the photograph, was the bottle of Night Heat. He took a plastic bag out of his pocket and carefully picked up the bottle and lowered it into the bag. He looked it over and hoped the crime lab techs could raise a fingerprint.

His re-tracking of the killer continued and by the time he reached the third stop on his journey he was convinced the perfume was left by the stalker. Cynthia Wellington and Kimberly McDougal were within the circle of fans of Night Heat perfume, but there was an extra bottle on their vanity tables. And at house number four, on Alexandra Upchurch's vanity there was a bottle of Night Heat, though her husband swore it was not her perfume of choice.

Lewis went to the station and walked into the crime lab carrying six plastic bags labeled as evidence and started filling out request forms to have the contents processed for fingerprints. "I took two bottles from Wellington's and McDougal's," he said, as he signed his name on the papers. "All of them looked like they had about the same amount of perfume and I couldn't tell one from another."

"Hey, what the hell's one more piece of glass to us?" Bob Benson, the lab supervisor said with a laugh as he nudged his glasses up with the knuckle of his index finger. "We'll process all of it."

"I knew I could count on you, Bob."

"Naturally. By the way, J.D., I have the results of the tests we ran on those printing samples you brought in."

"And?"

"Hewlett Packard printer."

"Hewlett Packard," he said, rubbing the back of his neck. *That sure helps Wilson out*, he thought. *Neither Ginny's nor Weldon's printer was a Hewlett Packard. The police department has dozens of HP printers, so that tosses a bag of shit right back at Thomas.* He started for the door and stopped. "I guess nothing's back on the DNA yet."

"Still a little too early. But I did call and ask if they'd push us toward the top of the pile. They'll try and speed things up a little for us because of the nature of the crimes, but they can't promise anything."

"I'm pretty sure they won't get a positive result there. I just need to be sure it's not Wilson. You know, before someone gets all nervous and jumps the gun."

Benson laughed. "I think I know exactly what you're sayin'."

"Well, I'm gonna try and get a few hours sleep."

He went back to the mansion by mid-afternoon and managed to steal three hours of what surprisingly turned out to be very restful sleep. He awoke with a roaring hard-on and wished Tiffany was there to relieve his problem. But right now he'd have to settle for a cold shower and have his problem taken care of later.

He downed three cups of coffee with dinner and felt the caffeine kicking him to a nervous edge. He was anxious to get on with his work and Tiffany vowed she wouldn't interfere with his duties; however, she did promise to stop by later and check on his progress.

She stood aside as he got up to go to the library. When he left the room she asked herself if she truly wanted him to identify and arrest the killer as soon as possible. The sooner the murderer was in the custody, the quicker other decisions would have to be made. She cursed herself for being so selfish.

Lewis sipped a fourth cup of coffee while looking over the country club membership list, giving it a very thorough going-over. He was crossing the line by stepping over the wall that shielded society's upper crust from prying eyes such as his. Here was a man with the nerve to look them over and say to himself, it might be one of you.

Until now, no one presumed to step on the toes of those who cast a sometimes arrogant eye over the rim of crystal glasses and glared at their neighbors. And suddenly, a brash young detective was considering raking their very ancestry through the fires to see what came up.

He started at the top of the list and entered their names, including those of Zachary and Tiffany Barrows, into the computer. It was a long process, but he was determined not to miss even one of the elite, and surely at least one of them had a skeleton somewhere in his or her past. Yes, the women too would fall under his microscope, because it just might be a ghost from their closet that sent a husband over the edge.

While the computer processed and printed the information, Lewis pulled a heavy scrapbook from one of the shelves and began leafing through its many pages. He wasn't surprised to find the scrapbook filled with magazine and newspaper clippings detailing the many conquests of Zachary Barrows.

As he slowly thumbed through the pages, it looked like a relatively young Zachary Barrows had stormed into the business world and was immediately hailed as a wizard of industry. He put failing companies back into the mainstream and climbed to the top, pulling in millions in profit, while showing no signs of faltering in his relentless pace.

Lewis admitted to himself that he was impressed with the accolades and awards heaped upon a man he personally didn't admire or like. Barrows had managed to accomplish the nearly impossible and, at the same time, he gave to others far less fortunate. He set up trust funds for the homeless and the sick, donating hundreds of thousands of dollars yearly for their benefit.

Like him or not, Lewis admired the man for giving to those who had nothing. "Well, Mr. Big Shot," he muttered. "I'll certainly bow to you for caring for others. That shows a lotta character—even for a prick like you."

At the back of the heavy scrapbook he found a news clipping not attached like the others. He glanced over the bold headline relating to a corporation changing hands and thought it was out of place in this book. After all, why should Ester Wentworth-Fox's selling of her company, specializing in women's toiletries, to Elizabeth Ames mean anything to Zachary Barrows? Then again, it was probably a way of staying abreast of the competition. It seemed to make good business sense.

He put the book back on the shelf and began reading over the information that the printer spit out. He searched the pages for a smudge on the squeaky clean image that was always held up for the world to see. But another letdown was in store for him. No criminal flaws floated to the top.

He reversed course and looked over Gary Wilson and Captain Thomas one more time. Still, he was growing more and more certain that neither was the killer he was looking for. The man he wanted entertained a deep hate for women. He couldn't see it in Wilson and the anger displayed by Thomas was, in all likelihood, due to the fact that he was still in love with his wife.

It was time he gave very serious attention to the belief he'd held all along. The man responsible for these brutal slayings was one of their own. A man who walked, lived and moved freely among the elite and was held in their highest esteem. Maybe it was the husband of one of the women who'd already been killed.

"I think you've been working too hard, Cowboy," Tiffany said from the doorway. "You need a break."

She was standing in the doorway wearing a sheer black teddy, black high-heeled shoes and a seductive smile. She stepped inside and closed the door behind her, the clicking of the lock sending a very clear "do not disturb" message.

"Was there any particular recreation you had in mind for my work break?" he said, while recalling his earlier erection. It looked like the relief he'd dreamed of a few hours ago was now very close at hand.

"Let me help you out of those clothes and I'll show you exactly what I have in mind."

While the printer completed its programmed assignment, she very deliberately traced a burning trail with her lips and the tip of her tongue over his body. She began by kissing him on the lips. Then sliding lower, she worked over his shoulders and chest while he stood in front of her. The passage she took, though irregular, left no doubt as to her intended destination.

She guided him to the chair and dropped to her knees, smiling as she once again lowered her head. She took him in her mouth and began rolling her tongue over his hard organ. He sighed deeply and closed his eyes as she worked up and down, taking her time and doing everything she could to prolong the journey to ecstasy. The whir of the printer stopped sometime into the passionate journey, but neither of them was certain when it ended. It didn't matter. She was bringing him to the top of the mountain. A slow roll of her tongue and a long swallow sent him over the side of the mountain as he clutched the back of her head and gasped, "Oh, God, yes."

Twenty-nine

Ezra waited until the breakfast dishes had been cleared from the table before he went to J.D. "Mr. Lewis, I know this might not be anything of interest at all to you, but I wrote it down anyway." He handed Lewis a small piece of paper.

"What's this Ezra?" he said, looking at the paper.

"It's the license plate number of a car I saw the night Miss Madeline was killed."

"Where'd you see the car?"

"Well, sir, after dinner I got a little restless. So, I decided to take a walk and I ended up down by the gate. While I was there I noticed a car drivin' real slow and the driver kinda lookin' everything over. I didn't pay much attention to him at first, but then he came by a second time. He was just actin' real funny and I figured I'd better write down the plate number of his car."

"Did you get a look at the driver of the car?" he said, his heart beginning to beat a little faster.

"Not a real good one. It was gettin' dark and it was a little hard to see inside, but I know he was white. That's all I can tell you 'bout him."

Lewis nodded. "That's good enough. Did you notice anything else about the car? What kind it was?"

"I'm not much on tellin' one car from another, but it looked something like your police car."

Lewis nodded and glanced at the paper again. He knew almost immediately from the combination of letters and numbers that in all probability it was an unmarked police car. "I'll check on this right away," he said, pushing his chair away from the table and leaving the room.

In the library he made a call to the department's motor pool to check on the tag number. Within seconds the pool supervisor gave him a reply. "Detective Lewis, that vehicle's assigned to Captain Thomas."

"Damn it!" he spat, balling up the paper and hurling it across the desk. "Damn it! Why the fuck is it that every time I'm just about convinced you

146

had nothing to do with the murders, you try and prove me wrong? What were you doing out here?"

His dismal beginning to the day fell even darker when the Lord and Master made a sudden unannounced return to the home front. But his arrival this morning lacked its usual flair for the dramatic.

He appeared with almost stealth like silence and did away with his normal show and showering Tiffany with an overabundance of affection. Instead, he brushed her lightly on the cheek with a kiss and headed straight to his office study where he slammed and locked the door.

Soon he was on the telephone to Winston Palmer. "Okay. What went wrong this time?" he snapped.

"Christ, Mr. Barrows, that maniac set a pack of dogs loose on my men. They were lucky they weren't torn to pieces."

"Bullshit, Palmer. That's not what I'm hearing from my independent sources around town," Barrows growled. "Your men were made to look like complete fools by Lewis and a fuckin' Mexican Chihuahua."

"Uh—well, that's not what they reported to me, Mr. Barrows. They said there were six or seven German Shepherds that came after 'em."

"Okay. Okay. Let's forget that. There're other more pressing issues at this time. Your surveillance equipment confirmed my suspicions regarding my wife's infidelity. I was right. She's having an affair with Lewis."

"Oh, I'm sorry to hear that, Mr. Barrows. But you can get rid of him now."

"I can't do that. Not yet. I need him around for the time being, no matter what he's doing with my wife."

"Damn. Aren't you even a little upset about what he's doin' to your wife?"

"Of course, I'm upset, you idiot," he said, slapping the desk. "But other matters take precedence over my feelings. Until the killings are resolved, I'm inclined to allow things to remain as they are."

"Hey, every man to his own taste. But if some guy was doin' a number with my old lady, I'd want his ass gone in a hurry."

"Palmer, she's not your wife," he yelled into the phone. "And, if it'll ease your mind, let's say I can't afford to let him go right now. Besides, I believe your old lady was fuckin' one of your hired hands and skipped town with him."

He banged the telephone down and beat a hasty path from his study to the kitchen, bellowing for Lolita to prepare a pot of fresh coffee and some pastries for him. He paced in circles over the sparkling white tiles, while she looked over her shoulder now and then at the fuming man.

As the scent of perking coffee filled the room, he seemed to relax as though the aroma of the Colombian blend had some sort of hypnotic effect on him. He broke with tradition and sat at the table in the kitchen, eating several of Lolita's French pastries and drinking three cups of coffee. When he was finished, he stunned her by passing on a few complimentary words.

His quiet manner vanished in a hurry when he went back to his office and found Ezra seated behind his desk. "What the hell are you doing?" he yelled. "Get away from my desk."

"Mr. Barrows, sir," Ezra said, pushing himself away from the desk and getting to his feet. "I was just tryin' to tidy up and dust a bit. I didn't have time to do it before you got home."

"Get away from the desk. I have important documents there and I don't want you nosing through them, do you understand?"

"Sir, I haven't touched a thing. I haven't seen nothin'," he stammered, backing away from the desk.

Barrows pointed to the door. "Get out and don't ever come in here again unless I tell you. Do you understand me?"

"Yes, sir. Yes, sir," he stuttered, as he lowered his head and walked quickly toward the door.

Barrows locked the door, walked to the entertainment center and again pressed the play button on the VCR. The images flashed before him on the large screen; the backdrop for Tiffany and Lewis' tryst was the library he'd set up for him as an office.

His anger reached the boiling point one more time as he watched Tiffany perform an erotic ritual on the young man. The act she was performing with the naked policeman was something with which she'd thrilled him in years gone by. He wanted to turn the VCR off, but the sight of her when Lewis returned the favor held him captive.

Memories raced by like so many fast cars in flashy splotches of color. But these were recollections of lusty times and the brilliant array that danced in his eyes was of her negligees and fancy garter belts, over a firm, tanned body. A body he'd touched and savored for a long time. The body of a woman he'd once made squirm and groan as she was doing now on the screen with another man.

When the tape ran its course and the screen went blank, he realized that he was to blame for her fleeing to the arms of another man. Reality shocked him much like a glass of ice water spilled over exposed flesh on a hot summer's day. It was he who'd failed to give Tiffany the love and affection she craved. He, the icon of business, had now suffered a setback in the world of love.

For a brief instant he entertained the idea of buying a gun and shooting Lewis. But that would only bring further humiliation when he was arrested for murder. No, he wouldn't kill the young detective. But he could have Jason, his chauffeur confidante and friend, do it. He'd delivered messages for him in the past, messages of a physical kind. He'd hold that thought for later.

He turned his attention away from love's collapse and back to his desk and the documents stacked neatly in order of importance. He wondered if Ezra had rummaged through the papers and other items in the desk and he began a slide back to a slow burn.

Thirty

Ezra's flight to escape the wrath of Zachary Barrows led him to seek out his friend. But he discovered that J.D. had left the house in a big hurry only seconds after receiving a call from Gary Wilson's girlfriend.

Lewis was burning up when he arrived at the police station. He brushed formality and the chain of command aside and stormed angrily into Captain Thomas' office. "Sir, did you know that Wallace and Hargrove arrested Gary Wilson for the stalker murders?"

"What? When?"

"This morning," he growled. "Goddamn it! They dumped those cases on me and now they're tryin' to cut my fuckin' throat. Wilson's not the killer."

"Okay. Try and calm down. I'll see if I can get to the bottom of this."

Lewis was right on his heels as he headed for the cellblock. "Sir, if you don't mind I'd like to come along. I gave Wilson my word nothing would happen to him and now I'm the one who'll have to explain things."

"Not my first choice," he said, hoping Lewis wouldn't rip Hargrove and Wallace to pieces. "But come along anyway."

By the time they reached the detention area, Lieutenant Adams had arrived. He expected Thomas to spout words of praise for a job well done, but soon found he was in a very bad mood.

Thomas looked from Adams to Wallace and then to Hargrove while Lewis stood behind him with his fists clenched, trying to decide which of the trio to punch out first. Finally Thomas raised a hand and pointed to Adams. "Step out here in the hall and explain this to me."

"Lewis was movin' a little too slow on this guy," Adams said, looking like a peacock about to spread its tail as he strutted into the corridor. "Christ, it's obvious he's the man we want for the killings, so I told Wallace and Hargrove to go ahead and bring him in and grill him."

"Lieutenant Adams, you and Wallace took it upon yourselves to assign those cases to Detective Lewis," he said, calmly. "Why, all of a sudden, did you feel it was necessary to jump back in with both feet?"

150

"Like I said, Captain, he was moving too slow. He—"

"Bullshit. Have you closely looked over all of his reports or spoken with him about his investigation?"

"Well, not recently, but—"

"Well, Lieutenant, I've looked over his reports and taken the time to talk with him about his progress on the investigation. I'm satisfied with the way he's handled the cases so far and I also agree with him about this particular suspect. In other words, you dumb shits jumped the gun."

"Captain, I—"

"Have you officially charged him with the crimes?"

"No, not yet. I thought we'd question him first and then call a press conference to announce his arrest."

"Release him."

"What?" Adams said, blinking.

"You heard me. Release him."

"Captain, this is entirely irregular," Adams said, feeling the dampness in his armpits. "Everything points to Wilson."

"Only circumstantially," he said, his level of tolerance beginning to slip. "Are you aware that Wilson voluntarily went to the hospital with Lewis and gave a blood sample for DNA testing?"

"Uh—no, I wasn't."

"Now, if he's the killer, why'd he beat a path to the hospital to give blood? Just so we could prove he's guilty?"

"Maybe he's trying to throw us off track."

"I'm not gonna argue with you," he said, jabbing a finger at him. "Release him. That's an order."

"Yes, sir."

Adams, Wallace and Hargrove glared at Lewis as they left the cellblock. "I hope you're satisfied," Adams whispered as he passed. "When this guy kills somebody else, it'll be your ass."

Lewis ignored the comment and turned to Wilson. "Jesus, Gary, I'm really sorry this happened."

"Christ, do you know what those bastards did? They jerked me outta Ginny's car right in front of all the guys I work with. They pointed guns at me and threw me on the ground. Then they turned around and told everybody I was the stalker."

"Damn it," he snarled. "Fuckin' assholes."

"And even worse, Mr. Weldon was just gettin' out of his car. He saw and heard everything. I'll probably lose my job over this."

"Look, I'll call and explain things to him. Try and smooth them over."

"I'd really appreciate that. I can't afford to lose my job. Not with me and Ginny gettin' married."

After making a call to Weldon Landscaping and releasing Wilson, Lewis went back to Captain Thomas' office. "Sorry I blew up, sir. It's tough enough working these cases without having Adams and his friends tryin' to fuck everything up."

"That's okay. I know what they were trying to do. They were looking to grab the glory before they bothered to look into all the facts. Adams is bucking for captain and he's desperate to score points in the press."

"Yeah. He'd make a great captain—in the fuckin' motor pool."

"He'd probably fuck that up too," Thomas said, leaning back in his chair. "Anyway, do you have any new leads or suspects in the murders?"

Shit, I can't very well tell him he's near the top of my list, Lewis thought. *What do I say? Hey, Captain, can you tell me why you were prowlin' around the neighborhood the night Madeline Jennings was killed?* He took his Stetson off and sat down. "I have one possible new lead."

"Oh. What's that?"

"Ezra Dawkins, he's the butler—anyway, he saw a car the night Mrs. Jennings was murdered."

"Did he get a description of the car or a tag number?"

"Unfortunately he didn't," he said. "He just saw it go by twice, but couldn't see the tag."

"That's too bad. Did he say he could identify the driver?"

"No, sir. Couldn't see him either."

"Hummm. I was over in that area that night. Maybe it was my car he saw. Do you know what time he saw it?"

"Uh, well...." Lewis was surprised by Thomas' answer. "I believe it was right around dusk. In fact, I think he said it was almost dark."

"I don't know. Maybe it was me." Thomas looked right at Lewis. "I didn't feel like sittin' at home. The place sort of gets to me. Anyway, I decided to take a ride and I just drove over to Huntley Manor Road. Figured I'd look around a little."

Nice of you to provide yourself with an alibi for being in the area of a murder, he thought, then nodded. "I guess you didn't see anything out of the ordinary?"

"I wish I could help you. I didn't see a thing. As a matter of fact, the only other cars I saw on the road were the fancy chauffeur driven type."

While Lewis and Captain Thomas continued to talk, Zachary Barrows was busy plotting the downfall of Jefferson Daniel Lewis. Although the brazen young detective had succeeded in wooing his wife to his bed, he would not reign triumphant over the king of industry. He'd see to it that the policeman would be scorned by his colleagues and ridiculed by the public. He had the power to bring him down and he'd use it to the fullest to make him fall.

Barrows put his plan into motion early in the evening by dining with Tiffany at the country club. He was careful to avoid overindulging in alcoholic beverages, but was quick to ensure that his wife received an abundance of attention. He poured on the affection for all of their friends, sugar-coating every word to her. Regardless of what she and Mr. Lewis were doing, which was fucking each other while he was away, he'd be the loving, caring husband in the public eye.

It was well after dark when Lewis finally got back to 21 Huntley Manor Road and parked his police cruiser. He was crossing the driveway, lost deep in thought, when something interrupted his thoughts. He stopped, looking to his left and listening for the sound that had caught his attention.

He remained very still in the shadows for several minutes before walking on to the house. When he reached the door he stopped again and waited, looking around and listening for the noise again. But he didn't hear a sound. He opened the door and stepped into the foyer as a feeling of uneasiness swept over him.

The house itself was unusually quiet and he thought it was odd that Ezra didn't meet him when he walked in. The old man was like a magician, arriving almost immediately every time he came in, no matter what hour of the day or night.

He walked to the kitchen thinking Ezra might be there with Lolita, sharing a little late night conversation or pleasing himself with just one last slice of apple pie. The room was empty and everything was in its place as usual. As he turned to leave, Lolita walked into the room and he could see that she was upset. "What's wrong?" he said.

"Have you seen Ezra, Mr. Lewis?"

"No, I haven't. I was looking for him because he didn't meet me at the door like he always does."

"I can't find him either," she said, sniffling. "And Ezra wasn't himself all day long. He's been terribly upset."

"Why?"

"Mr. Barrows screamed at him for cleanin' his office. He yelled at poor Ezra, sayin' he was snoopin' around his desk. Told him never to come back in there again unless he was told."

"Maybe Ezra's in his room."

"No, sir. I knocked on his door and when he didn't answer, I went in. It looks like he hasn't been there since this morning."

"Do you think he might've gone to town?" he said, again feeling uneasy.

"Oh, no. Ezra would never do that unless he told me."

"Damn," he muttered, pushing his Stetson back. "What about family? Does he have any family in the area?"

"No, sir. His family's in Baltimore and Atlanta."

"Look, why don't you try and get some sleep. I'll make some phone calls and see if I can find him."

He left Lolita in the kitchen and went straight to the library. He started calling the local hospitals and clinics, asking about the distinguishable white-haired man, only to be told that Ezra Dawkins hadn't been admitted or treated at any of the facilities.

Over two hours passed before the high pitched *beep, beep, beep* of his pager shook him from his trance like state. He rubbed his eyes and tried to bring the numbers into focus. As the cobwebs cleared, he reached for the telephone and called the number.

After identifying himself, the voice on the other end of the line struck like a bombshell. "Mr. Lewis, we have Ezra Dawkins here in the emergency room. He's been badly injured and the doctor would like you to come in right away."

"I'll be right there."

He sped to the hospital, his mind spinning with questions about what happened to his friend. He pulled the car into the first available space and sprinted for the emergency room entrance. As he neared the door he saw Officer John Stark pacing on the sidewalk. "Jack, what the hell happened to Ezra Dawkins?"

"Looks like the old guy was the victim of a robbery."

"Robbery?"

"Yeah. Took a pretty nasty shot to the head," Stark said, turning a page in his notebook. "Wallet and watch're gone. The only thing on him was a paper with your name and pager number."

"Where'd it happen?"

"He was found on the back lot of the Huntley Manor Health and Fitness Spa. But I don't think it happened there. I think the old guy was assaulted somewhere else and dumped there."

"What about witnesses?"

"Sorry, J.D. You know the story. Nobody saw or heard shit."

"Bullshit."

"Hey, man, that's all I have."

"Sorry, Jack. I'm not saying you didn't do your job," he said, shaking his head. "I know the routine."

He stepped by Stark and into the emergency room, going straight for the cluster of men and women dressed in white, faded rose and mint green smocks. "What can you tell me about Mr. Dawkins' condition?" he said, looking from one to another.

"I'm Doctor Harper," a man wearing a mint green smock said, turning to him. "And you are?"

"Detective Lewis."

"Ah, yes. Mr. Dawkins had a paper in his pocket with your name and number on it. Are you a friend?"

"Yes, I am. Now, can you tell me about his condition?"

"He's still unconscious. He received a very hard blow to the left side of his head and he has a broken left forearm. His injury would probably be far more serious, but it looks like he was able to deflect the blow, which is probably how his arm was broken."

"Will he be alright?"

"Mr. Lewis, anytime a person's struck on the head, it's serious. A blow to the head can be fatal. That's why we insist on keeping people for at least a day when they've received a blow to the head. We want them to remain in the hospital for close observation. As for Mr. Dawkins, only time will tell. He appears to be in good health and he's quite strong for a man his age. He'll be moved from here to our Critical Care Unit where he'll be closely monitored."

"Can I see him?"

"You can look in on him, but only for a minute. He's in cubicle eight."

Lewis drew the curtain around the cubicle and looked at the man lying on the gurney. He was hooked to monitors, which flashed wavy green lines on a screen above the bed and emitted a low harmonic peep. IV lines were stuck in his right arm, the white tape standing out against the dark color of his skin.

He stood beside the gurney, leaned down and whispered in his ear. "Ezra, don't give up on me. Fight. I wanna know who did this to you. Get your strength back. I'll take care of everything."

Lewis left the cubicle and pulled the attending physician aside. "Doctor, I want you to do me a favor."

"Name it."

"Can you see to it that he's not allowed to have visitors?"

"I could, but I'd need a valid reason."

"Let's just say I believe this man's life's in grave danger. Is that a valid reason?"

"Yes," the doctor said. "More than valid, I'd say."

"Okay. I don't want him to have visitors unless you or somebody from the staff clears it with me. That includes anybody from the police department. I'd like to be able to interview Ezra before anybody else talks with him. Believe me, it's important."

"I'll do what I can to help."

"Maybe you could make sure he just kind of gets lost here. Know what I mean?"

"Yeah." The doctor smiled. "I think I can handle that."

"Thanks. I really appreciate it."

Lewis drove slowly around the parking lot before leaving the hospital grounds, carefully looking over each parked car. When he was satisfied that everything was okay he drove off and tried to figure out what happened. But that strange sixth sense was calling to him again, telling him the motive behind Ezra's beating wasn't robbery. There was another reason and the growing knot in his stomach said it was somehow connected to the stalker murders.

Thirty-one

Lewis' thoughts were a jumbled mass and ran together in slow motion as he fought to keep his eyes open. His thinking process had bogged down with the onset of fatigue and his body cried for rest. He'd slept little in the past few days and realized it was useless to try and mix old evidence with newly discovered clues until he was alert.

He stretched out on the sofa and closed his eyes while the haunting sight of Ezra lying unconscious in the hospital flashed through his mind again before he collapsed into a deep sleep.

He still woke up long before the others in the household and, in a groggy stupor, stumbled to his room. He peeled off his clothes and staggered into the shower, welcoming the burst of cold water. The icy fingers shooting from above stabbed his flesh, sending frigid shock waves through his body and he trembled from the chill. He numbly reached out and gradually turned the water from cold to warm and finally to hot. As steam began to fill the room, his mind started to work and went back to sorting out his tangled thoughts.

Ezra had survived a brutal assault and lay unconscious in the Critical Care Unit. He was certain the blow was meant to permanently silence the old man for something. But what was it? Did Ezra accidentally stumble across a piece of evidence or did the Society Stalker think that he could identify him?

However, dumping the old man behind the Huntley Manor Health and Fitness Spa was another matter. It was incredible to think that a person or persons would assault and rob him somewhere else and then take him to the back lot of the spa and dump him there. There were dozens of places where Ezra could've been dropped where he would've gone undiscovered for days or maybe weeks. Of course, that would've meant death for him. If his assault was a spur of the moment thought, he could've been tossed out there in a fleeting moment of panic. But he wasn't satisfied with that idea. There was another explanation.

The stalker murders and the brutal assault of Ezra weren't the only issues bothering him. He hadn't seen or spoken to Tiffany since the unannounced return of Zachary. It was almost as though her husband was holding her hostage in the mansion and forbidding her to have contact with him. He missed the sound of her voice and her warm, loving touch.

He dressed and walked down the stairs, asking himself how their forbidden relationship would survive. Could it survive? What would happen when their romance became public knowledge? Would fingers be pointed at them like so many loaded guns? Would voices cry out for them to be stoned in the city square for adultery? He pushed the thoughts aside when he walked into the dining room where Lolita was serving breakfast.

"Mr. and Mrs. Barrows," he said, trying not to look at Tiffany too long. "I'm afraid I have some very unpleasant news."

"What is it?" Zachary said, lowering his cup and staring at the detective.

"Ezra's been the victim of a serious assault. He's at the hospital in the Critical Care Unit."

"Oh, God," Lolita sobbed.

Tiffany gasped. "Is…will…will he be all right?"

"Right now, it's hard to say. He's still unconscious. He took a very nasty blow to the head."

"When did this happen?" Zachary said, putting his napkin on the table and pushing his chair back..

"Some time last night."

"Where did it happen?"

"I really don't know, Mr. Barrows. It looks like he was beaten and then dumped behind the Huntley Manor Spa."

"Do you have any idea who's responsible?"

"The investigating officer told me there were apparently no witnesses and so far everybody he's talked to at the spa didn't see or hear a thing." He shrugged his shoulders. "Of course, that's not unusual. Even if people do see something, they'll deny it because they don't wanna get involved."

"By God, I'll post a ten thousand dollar reward. That should help jar somebody's memory, or make them get involved. What do you think?"

"Well, sometimes money does have a way of bringing out the reluctant witness."

"I want the person responsible for this brought to justice," Barrows said, reaching for his coffee cup. "If ten thousand dollars isn't enough to bring a witness out, then I'll double it."

"That's very generous of you," Lewis said, wondering if his motive was actually something more than just grandstanding.

Then Barrows proved that he might be an Oscar nominee for his acting ability as he walked over and put his arm around Lewis. "Look, I know you're busy with the murders, but if you can keep an eye on the progress of this investigation as well, I'd deeply appreciate it. Ezra's a loyal employee and trusted friend."

Lewis nodded. "I'll do my best, sir."

"Can he have visitors?" Tiffany said.

"Not right now," he said, wanting to tell her she could see him, but deciding against it. "The doctor wants to keep him isolated until his condition improves—if it improves."

"Keep me up to date on this," Barrows said, patting him on the shoulder.

"Yes, sir."

Lewis took the cup of coffee Lolita offered him and headed for the east wing and the library. Something was gnawing at him and he wanted to review the stalker files again. As he drained the last drops of coffee from the cup, he suddenly realized that an all-important document was missing. He cursed himself for not having noticed earlier that the paper was not in the file.

He reached for the telephone and called the department's records division. "Good morning, this is Detective Lewis. Would you check your files on the stalker murders and pull the psychological profile on the killer?"

A few minutes passed before the clerk came back on the line. "I'm sorry, Detective Lewis, but that information's not in any of our case folders."

"Damn. Thanks anyway."

He hung up the phone and angrily slapped the desk. *You bastards got me. You took the psychological profile out of the reports. That's what's been bugging me all this time. The profile wasn't there when you unloaded the cases on me. Ah, hell, it's my fault for not noticing it wasn't there.*

He picked up the telephone again, this time placing a long distance call. "May I speak with Lieutenant Bowers please? This is Detective Lewis calling."

"Lieutenant Bowers. May I help you?"

"Yes, sir. This is Detective Lewis calling from Huntley Manor. I'm working the stalker murders now and—"

"I thought Hargrove and Grayson were working those cases."

"Not any more, Lieutenant. I am."

"Okay. So, what can I do for you?"

"Well, sir, it seems the psychological work up you did for us on the killer somehow managed to disappear from the reports and I can't seem to locate it anywhere."

"I see."

"I'd like to get a copy so I can try and sort things out," he said. "I know you're a very busy man and I'm really sorry to bother you like this, but could you send me another copy of the work up you did for us?"

"It's not a bother," Bowers said. "I'll get it out to you this morning."

"Thanks, Lieutenant."

"I hope it helps. You've got a real tough case on your hands."

"I'm sure it'll help, sir. And, thanks again."

As their conversation ended, Tiffany slipped into the room and closed the door behind her. "Are you busy?"

"Well, yeah. But I can sure as hell steal a few minutes for you. I mean, if it's safe for you to be here."

"Zachary's in the shower."

He crossed the room and embraced her. "I've missed you."

"God, I've missed you so much," she whispered, squeezing him tightly. "I've been going crazy not seeing you."

"Is everything okay?"

"I think he suspects something," she said, looking into his eyes. "He's really acting different. He's smothering me."

"How? What do you mean?"

"It's like he doesn't want me out of his sight." She ran her fingers through her hair and sighed. "We went to the club for dinner last night and he wouldn't even let me walk to the ladies' room unescorted. God, he's never been that way."

"Did he say anything at all that sounds like he's on to us?"

"No. It's just the way he's acting."

"Maybe one of his business deals fell through."

"Maybe," she said, nodding. "But there's something else that's odd."

"What's that?"

"He and Jason seem to be having a lot of quiet talks since they came home. I mean more so than usual."

"I guess he discusses his business deals with Jason, right?"

"I know they have in the past. Jason's been Zachary's personal chauffeur for almost fifteen years and he also acts as his bodyguard. He trusts Jason. I guess that's why he takes him along on so many of his business trips. I think he feels more comfortable discussing business with Jason than with me."

"Well, maybe it's nothing. Try not to get upset over it."

"I feel terrible about Ezra," she said, reaching to touch his face.

"So do I. I really like him. We've become pretty good friends."

"Have you called to check on him lately?"

"That's on my list of things to do."

"Call now, please."

He called the hospital while she stood beside him, softly scratching his back. "This is Detective Lewis. Is Doctor Harper still there?"

"One moment please."

"You must be psychic," Harper laughed as he answered the phone. "I was just about to call you."

"How's Ezra?"

"There's really no change. He's still holding his own. But that's not why I was going to call you."

"Oh?"

"Are you familiar with a Captain Thomas?"

"Yeah. Why?"

"He was in here about a half hour ago asking about Mr. Dawkins. He also asked to see him, but I told him that wasn't possible right now. He said he understood and left."

"Did he say he'd be back later?"

"No."

"Okay. If anybody else shows up, I'd like to be called or paged right away."

"Sure. I'll post it at the nurses station and make a note of it on his charts."

"Thanks, Doc."

"Ezra's holding his own," he said, hanging up the phone.

"Thank God. I just hope and pray he'll recover."

"Jesus. So do I," he said, squeezing her to him. "And there's another thing."

"What?"

"Doctor Harper said Captain Thomas was in this morning asking about Ezra and that's not like him. Not at all. He usually just asks the case investigator about a victim's condition."

"Well, could he possibly be more concerned over Ezra than he has been in the past over others? Or do you suspect something else?"

"Christ, I don't know what to think about him or anybody else right now. I mean it's getting so, I might even start looking at myself as a suspect."

"Something else's bothering you. What is it?"

"Hell, I just realized this morning that the psychological profile of the killer was removed from the case files before they were turned over to me. I was so wrapped up in looking over the other evidence I didn't notice the profile was missing."

She shook her head. "I hope it's not because of what's been going on between us."

"No. No. It's not that," he said, but wondered if she was right. "I just overlooked it, that's all."

"Surely there're other copies."

"That's what I thought too. It seems all of the copies somehow vanished. I called Lieutenant Bowers earlier. He's the expert who profiled the killer. I asked him to send me another copy."

"He'll do it, won't he?"

"I should have it later today."

"That's a relief."

He kissed her softly on the lips and muttered, "God, I wish we could strip and do each other right now."

"Oh, God, don't say that. You don't know how much I want you. I have an itch that needs scratching so bad. But I'd better go before Zachary gets out of the shower. If he found me here, he'd sure as hell put two and two together."

"Yeah. And we don't need that right now. I'm just glad we were able to steal a few minutes together."

"So am I."

He walked her to the door where they shared a loving, passionate kiss. Tiffany pressed tightly against him as their tongues entwined and danced. The fires were lighting and they fought to regain control of their burning desires. At last she broke away and left the room, feeling her legs tremble as she walked down the hallway.

Thirty-two

Zachary vigorously lathered his body while thinking of a way to completely destroy Jefferson Lewis' character. He'd destroy young Mr. Lewis, although he recognized that by doing that he'd also tarnish the image of his wife. But, in a strict business sense, it was sometimes necessary to trample upon someone near and dear.

Zachary Barrows was viewed by many as brutally ruthless when it came to closing a sweet business deal. He was not beyond digging deep into an adversary's life and dredging up dark secrets with which to blackmail them. But what he presently faced was on a very personal level and on that plain his business figure would pale.

He'd carefully watch out for his prey and, at precisely the right moment, raise his sword of vengeance and slice through the heart of Mr. Lewis. The attack would be swift and, of course, venomous. A complete execution of his opponent's honor.

As for Tiffany, he'd allow sufficient time to pass before permitting her to grovel at his feet and beg for forgiveness. Naturally, in due time, he'd grant her absolution and show everyone around him that he was capable of accepting the role of scorned husband and maybe he'd rise to sainthood in the eyes of his friends for his kindness.

His victory would be total and he'd bask for a very long time in the glow of success. In the end he'd rein as champion and grind Lewis into dust under his feet and walk away clutching the sought after trophy, Tiffany. But toward that end he needed a beginning. A way to start tipping the scales back in his favor.

His mind wandered back to the videotape of his wife and the detective naked in the library, engaging in lustful sexual acts while he was away from his domain. He felt a surge of excitement race through his penis and smiled. Yes, that was it. He'd take his wife and have his way with her. He turned off the shower and began to towel dry, listening for her to come into the bedroom.

He heard the door open and he cautiously peeked out and watched her undress as she prepared to shower. She was reaching for her robe when he stepped into the room and said, "Don't bother."

"What?" she said, turning quickly and seeing him walking toward her, his penis at full staff. She held the robe in the front of her and stared at him.

"I said don't bother." He pulled the robe from her hands and dropped it to the floor. "Get on the bed."

"What?"

"Damn it. You heard me. Get on the bed."

"Zachary, are you okay?"

"Oh, I'm fine. I just want to make love to my wife," he replied, pushing her back against the bed.

"Why? Why now after all these years of leaving me alone?" she stammered and hoped he'd go away.

"You're my wife. I want to make love to you—now, Tiffany. So get on the bed."

When she hesitated, he pushed her down. She was surprised by his almost cat-like movements as he positioned her beneath him and, while holding her down with one hand, inserted a finger from his other into her vagina. It slid into her easily as she'd gotten worked up while sharing a passionate embrace with J.D. He pushed his finger in and out, continuing to hold her down. He flashed a crooked, cruel smile.

He roughly pulled her legs apart, placing them on his shoulders as he positioned himself above her. He pressed his penis against her and lunged forward, plowing into her flesh and burying himself as far as possible inside her. He wasted no time. He pounded against her with a fury, his flesh pummeling her with each thrust.

Well, Lewis, he thought while ramming himself into her. *How do you like this? I'm fuckin' my wife while you're here in the house and there's not a damn thing you can do about it. He slammed into her even harder. You could only fuck her while I was off on business. Who's on top now, cop? Me. I'm fuckin' her right now while you're downstairs. This is how men of real power do things, Lewis. They take what they want, when they want it. And right now, I've got her. I'm up to my balls in her. That's right. I'm gonna be the one shootin' a wad in her*. He slowed down, groaned and lunged against her one last time before collapsing on top of her.

A few moments later he rolled away from her and strutted across the floor to the bathroom, savoring his victory. He didn't look back at her. He just left her lying there while he walked off in triumph. He smiled, thinking how he'd showed her who was the ruler of the house. *I'm back on top of the heap*, he thought, turning the water on once again, *and I'm there to stay.*

Tiffany lay stunned from what he'd done, staring up at the ceiling. She couldn't think at the moment, at least not clearly. She knew Zachary had taken her by force, but why? It had been so long since he showed an interest in her physically. Then to appear from the bathroom and, in reality, rape her in her own house. What was going on? What was he trying to prove?

Suddenly she felt very dirty. Violated. The body she now shared so willingly with a younger man had been breached. She felt sick and for a brief instant thought she might vomit on the bed. She buried her face in the pillow and cried instead, wondering how she'd face J.D. again. How could she tell him what Zachary did? How would he react?

Lewis was once again digging into the backgrounds of the high and the mighty. He'd be unrelenting in his pursuit of some secret step from the straight and narrow, be it business or personal.

He wasn't really shocked to learn that Rose Anna Guilford had seduced a young man on his 18th birthday. Then again, she didn't exactly go out of her way to hide her adventure and had openly bragged of finding several new positions in which to make love on a weight bench.

However, he was a little stunned when he learned of her husband's dalliance with the young daughter of a foreign business magnate. She was but a few weeks beyond her 16th birthday when her loud groaning attracted her parents' attention. They walked into her room and found Thurston Guilford planting a rather amorous kiss on a very sensitive part of her anatomy. The mother fainted while the father forcefully pried Thurston from between his daughter's legs.

Public humiliation was avoided when Thurston Guilford agreed to sign a multi-year, multi-million-dollar business deal with the young lady's less than happy father. Though the scandalous frolic was never headline news, it circulated for several months among cooks, butlers and chambermaids.

As his prying continued, he learned of many shady dealings and back door hanky-panky among society's elite. The art of back-stabbing was alive and well in the ranks of the rich and many unsuspecting people had their throats slashed, not with a knife, but the stroke of a pen.

Glitzy parties were often spiced with what he called closet fucking. And there were many instances of alcohol-induced wife-swapping. Wives were exchanged openly while drink glasses were filled again and again. And, on occasion, a chauffeur took an extended stroll in the moonlight while the back seat of a Rolls Royce, Mercedes Benz or Lincoln Town Car proved to be more than an adequate bedroom substitute for adulterous liaisons. Then there were some who didn't even try to find a secluded spot for their tryst.

His research carried on well past the dinner hour and he slipped quietly from the mansion and went into town. He ate dinner at One Step West and then made a visit to the hospital to look in on his friend.

Doctor Harper reported that Ezra still remained comatose and showed no signs of improvement. But he was hopeful that the old man would recover from his attack and be able to give Lewis a description of his assailant.

With the hospital rounds behind him, Lewis drove to the Huntley Manor Country Club. He wanted to look over the displays of its members' conquests, professional and private, if possible. The club proudly boasted of its upper crust membership and their many achievements.

As he walked to the door he thought about the affairs and less than forthright corporate deals and mergers that had gone on behind closed doors. The actions of some of these men and women, whether on a whim or inhibitions that had been thrown aside because of too much to drink, might provide a motive for murder.

He presented an air of nonchalance as he strolled around the lobby looking over the photographs and thumbing through the endless mounds of leather bound scrapbooks. But he was aware of the nasty glances cast his way by those who saw his presence as an unwelcome invasion of their privacy.

It took him several hours to skim through the scrapbooks and look over the photographs flaunting company successes and mega-corp takeovers. When he closed the last of the books, his head was spinning from all that he'd tried to absorb about the county club's elite membership.

His eyes felt as though someone had placed hot coals over them as he walked into the mansion. He was in desperate need of sleep and walked trance-like toward the bedroom, knowing his body was on the verge of revolting from exhaustion. He'd pushed himself to the limits of his endurance and it was time to rest.

He slept soundly, although his dreams were filled with the faces of business hot shots and headlines detailing their rise to ever greater fame and fortune. There were men and women with smiling faces and frowning faces, shaking hands and slapping backs.

It was the ringing of the telephone that caused the happy and not so happy faces to vanish in a haze. He pulled the receiver from its cradle as the first hint of morning was just beginning to peek through the curtains. The familiar voice of Captain Thomas was a hollow echo as he told the sleepy detective he was needed immediately at the apartment of Gary Wilson.

He dragged himself from the bed and managed to make it to the shower. He went straight for the steamy hot spray, hoping it would help his blood pump through his body and ignite his thinking process, because he was still having trouble understanding what Captain Thomas told him.

Thirty-three

The scene in front of 3006 Spring Valley Drive was a maze of red and blue flashing lights, marked and unmarked police cars, ambulances and rescue trucks. The whirling red and blue beacons announced a tragic beginning to the day and, like a magnet, attracted a crowd of the curious. Lewis parked his car a block away and walked to the entrance of the building.

Captain Thomas stood on the sidewalk waiting for him to get there. "I think we'd better talk before you go inside."

"What the hell's goin' on?"

"It's Wilson. He committed suicide."

"What?" Lewis stopped in mid-stride and looked at him in disbelief. "That's crazy. Why would he kill himself?"

"It turns out he was the killer after all."

"No," Lewis said, shaking his head. "No fuckin' way."

"Christ, will you listen to me?" Thomas said. "He left a note for his girlfriend and in it he says he killed those women. There's evidence of the crimes in there too."

"Evidence? Ah, bullshit. What evidence?"

"Pictures. The same kind of rope used to strangle the victims. Hell, he even hung himself with a piece of black rope."

"Hold on. Let's go back to the pictures, Captain. What's in the pictures?"

"Well, he has one photo of each victim. It looks like he took a Polaroid shot just after he killed them."

"And there's just one picture of each victim?"

"That's what he left out on the table with the note."

Lewis took a deep breath and slowly exhaled. "And you say he hung himself," he said, again shaking his head.

"Yeah. In the bedroom closet. Tied the rope around the clothing support pipe, put a loop around his neck and just bent his knees. Hell of a way to strangle yourself."

"So he writes a note and—"

"No. It was printed. Looks exactly like the print on the letters sent to our murder victims."

"I'm not buyin' it," Lewis stated bluntly. "Doesn't this sound a little bit like a too-neatly-wrapped package?"

"What're you sayin'?"

"Captain, without even taking a look inside, I think this is a frame-up by the real killer. Somehow he knew Wilson was a suspect and…." He caught himself, realizing that he looked at Thomas as a possible suspect.

"Go on."

"Forget it. It's probably too far-fetched anyway."

Thomas reached out and put his hand on Lewis' shoulder. "Look, you did a great job on your investigation. You were just sidetracked by a theory or a gut feeling. Don't worry about it. It happens to all of us. Hell, you've only been assigned to the Bureau for a few months. You still have a lot to learn."

"But Captain, I thought you agreed with me on my theory."

"I went along with you, sure. But maybe I got caught up with your enthusiasm. I mean, you've gotta admit there was enough circumstantial evidence to arrest him."

"Then why'd you order Adams to release him?"

"Ah, hell, that was probably just a personal thing. I didn't want him to get credit for clearing the cases. If I'd listened to him maybe we could've prevented this."

"Who's assigned to Wilson's suicide?"

"Adams, Wallace and Hargrove were first on the scene. I guess it's their case."

Lewis threw his head back and raised his arms in a gesture of hopeless surrender.

"Great. Just fuckin' great. Do you think I could get a look at the scene before they fuck it up?"

Thomas nodded. "Hell, I owe you that much. Come on. I'll keep them off your ass while you look around."

Inside, Ginny Mason sat on the sofa rocking back and forth and sobbing, her arms crossed in her lap. Her face registered the horror of what she'd found when she opened the door to the bedroom closet. She looked at Lewis as he walked into he room and shook her head quickly from side to side as if to say she didn't believe Gary committed suicide.

In the bedroom he found an almost circus like atmosphere as Adams and Wallace laughed while slapping each other on the back and sharing an occasional high five with Hargrove.

Hargrove jumped back and snapped to attention, raising his hand to salute Lewis.

"Make way for the hotshot ace of the Criminal Investigations Bureau."

"That's enough," Thomas said, glaring at him. "Just let Lewis take a look at the scene without all your personal comments."

"Don't touch anything," Adams said, pointing a finger at him.

He disregarded the three men and walked to the closet door where he paused and studied the lifeless form of Gary Wilson. The body still hung from the pipe, the black rope knotted on the right side of the throat.

He carefully inspected the entire setting, beginning with the area where the rope was tied to the pipe. He followed its trail down to the right side of Wilson's neck and worked his way downward until he reached the floor. There he noticed the feet were to the rear of the body, almost touching. But the oddity of the sight was the fact that the feet rested squarely on the insteps. He scratched his head and thought, *had Wilson simply bent his knees and strangled himself, the legs should've swung to one side or the other with the feet coming to rest in an angular position.*

He turned and left the room without saying a word to Adams or the others. He went out to the dining room and looked over the precisely arranged photographs lying beside a printed note and again he shook his head. "This is all too neat," he muttered. "The damn pictures are even lined up in the exact order of the murders."

"Detective Lewis," Ginny sobbed. "Can I talk to you—in private?" she said, eyeing Thomas suspiciously.

"Let's go outside," he said softly, placing his arm around her waist and guiding her toward the door.

When they were clear of the building she blurted, "I don't understand any of this. It just doesn't make sense. Why would Gary kill himself? I know he didn't commit those murders."

"Ginny, I wish to God I had some answers for you, but I don't. And I sure as hell don't believe he committed the murders."

"What makes this even crazier is that Gary suggested we move our wedding date up," she said, brushing her arm across her eyes as she fought to control her sobbing. "He wanted to go to the courthouse, buy the license and just get married by the Justice of the Peace."

"When did he suggest this?"

"The day before yesterday. We were gonna get married next Friday. God,

170

I was so happy."

"Ginny, do you feel like you can answer a few more questions for me?" he said, as he touched her shoulder.

"I'll try," she whimpered.

"What was Gary's state of mind? How was he feeling?"

"After he gave the blood samples he felt like everything was behind him. He was positive those tests would prove him innocent and it was like somebody pulled a five-ton weight off his back."

"Was he happy?"

"Oh, yes. He was really excited. He was looking forward to us getting married."

"Was everything okay at work? I mean after his run in with the other detectives?"

"Sure. Mr. Weldon was very understanding. Especially after you talked with him and all. Just yesterday morning he found out Gary and I were getting married and he gave Gary a pay raise."

Suddenly the death of Gary Wilson became more intriguing. It was positively beyond comprehension that a man would move his wedding date up, get a pay raise, have a very positive outlook on his status as a suspect in the stalker slayings and then take his own life. Although he'd doubted Wilson's death was a suicide from the start, these few additional facts only heightened his suspicions.

First, Ezra's found beaten and unconscious and now Wilson's found hanging by a piece of black rope in his bedroom closet. There was a definite connection between Gary's death and the stalker killings and Lewis was sure Ezra's beating was in some way linked to those incidents. But convincing others that his suspicions were right would be very tough to do.

He escorted Ginny back to the apartment and pulled Captain Thomas aside. Suspect or not, Thomas was one of his few allies and he'd have to play a cautious game with a man who, if in fact he was the killer, could very well make him his next target. "I didn't want to hit her too hard. So, could you fill me in on what led to the discovery of the body?"

"The first officer on the scene told me Wilson's girlfriend showed up to give him a ride to work. Apparently his car's in the shop for a tune up or something. Anyway, she waited on the lot for him and when he didn't come right out, she knocked on the door. A minute or two went by and he didn't answer, so she let herself in and started looking for him. Eventually she went to the bedroom, opened the closet and there he was."

"Do you mind if I read the note?'

"Not at all."

Lewis leaned over and read the note where it had been placed on the table. He didn't want to handle the paper, hoping that Hargrove would have it processed for prints. But he had a hunch that Gary Wilson's prints wouldn't appear anywhere on the paper.

My Dearest Ginny, the note began:

> *I can't go on like this anymore. I've done some terrible things and I know it's only a matter of time until the police have the proof of my involvement in the murders of those high-society women. I'm a sick man and I know I can't be helped. The only solution is to end it now before I'm caught. I know I couldn't stand being sent to prison. But most of all, I don't want to see the embarrassment you'll have to face when everything comes out. I know how hurt you'll be and I hate myself for doing all those things that will cause you so much pain. I pray you'll find it in your heart to forgive me. I love you. I'll love you until my dying breath.*

Lewis straightened up and looked at Thomas. "You know, this is a very strange suicide note."

"Why's that?"

"Well, for one thing it doesn't seem to say much. It looks like it was just thrown together to offer us a reason for his death. And don't you think it's a little odd that he didn't bother to sign the note, or at least print his name on it?"

"You're right," he said, nodding. "That is odd."

"And another thing, where's the damn computer he used to write it? I don't see a computer here in the apartment."

"He probably wrote it somewhere else."

"Ah, come on, Captain. How many people go some place else to write a suicide note? Hell, that's gotta be the last thing they do before killing themselves. It doesn't make sense to go to the library, or use the computer at work to write the last letter of your life. I think that would be a very private, very personal thing. I know damn well if it was me, I wouldn't want somebody hanging over my shoulder or bumping into me while I was writing down my last thoughts."

"You know, Lewis, if you keep this shit up, you'll make a believer outta me," he said, rubbing the back of his head and staring at the note again. "This doesn't make one damn bit of sense, does it?"

"No, sir. Not at all," Lewis said, stepping away from the table. "That's why I think this whole thing's a set-up."

"Yeah. Anyway, I'd better get outta here and get ready for the media onslaught. You know we're gonna take a beating over this from the press."

Lewis nodded. " I'm sure you're right about that."

As Captain Thomas left, Doctor Sidney Wexler walked into the room, looking as if he'd been called from a very sound sleep. After a healthy yawn he said, "I understand we have a suicide here."

"I'm not too sure about that," Lewis said, glancing over his shoulder toward the bedroom. "Personally, I think the guy was murdered. Could you give this an extra look to be sure?"

"Always do. But, I'll give it an even closer look for you. You're the investigator, right?"

"Uh, sorry. Afraid not, Doc. Adams, Wallace and Hargrove were here first. They're in there now," he said, nodding in the direction of the bedroom.

"Oh, shit. You mean I have to deal with them first thing this morning?"

"Sorry."

Doctor Wexler looked closely at the setting in the closet, noting the position of the body before ordering Wilson cut down. As the body lay on the floor he examined the area of the neck where the rope still remained tightly wrapped. At a quick glance it appeared to be a suicide by hanging, but scratch marks on the throat immediately cast a suspicious shadow over the death.

Wexler said nothing to the detectives in the bedroom. Instead he left the room and spoke to Lewis. "You might be right. Of course, I won't know for sure until I complete the autopsy, but something's not right here."

"I know this is a strange request, but could you leave it listed as a suicide for the time being?"

"I could, but why? Especially if he was the victim of foul play?"

"To throw the killer off track. I need time to nail the bastard and if he thinks it was ruled a suicide, it might give me the time I need."

"You know, the talk in the other room is that this guy's the society stalker. How do you feel about that?"

"I don't believe it. I know there's a note confessing to the crimes and photos of the victims neatly laid out on the table, but I'm sure it's just something to throw us off the trail of the real killer."

"Well, I'm inclined to go along with your wishes for the time being,"

Wexler said. "I'll try and sit on this for a few days to give you time to search for your killer."

"Thanks, Doc. I owe you one."

As Wilson's body was being carried from the apartment in the dark bag, Hargrove muttered to Lewis, "Hey, hotshot, you gonna give the grieving girlfriend a quick hump before you leave?"

"Yeah," Wallace chuckled. "You can give this broad a quick bang and then sneak back over and do your rich bitch. By the way, what's it like ballin' rich pussy?"

Lewis ran headlong into Doctor Wexler as he tried to reach Wallace. The doctor thought he was trying to stop a runaway locomotive as he pushed against the angry cop.

"No. No, it's not worth it," he said, struggling to hold him. "You'll lose your job if you hit him."

Hargrove, looking to score favor with Wallace, tossed his notebook aside. "You wanna go a few rounds, hotshot?"

"I'd love to, you worthless cocksucker," Lewis snarled as Wexler pushed him to the other room.

"Maybe that can be arranged," Hargrove yelled. "Just name the place and time."

"Whew! For a minute there I thought I was going to have another autopsy to perform this morning," Wexler panted, continuing to restrain Lewis. "Then maybe there wouldn't have been enough left of him to examine."

"Thanks again, Doc," he said, his rage beginning to subside. "Now I owe you two. You just saved my career."

Thirty-four

Lewis took a badly shaken Ginny Mason out and drove her to her mother's home. There he assured her he'd do his best to find out what happened in the apartment, but his words did little to console her.

On his way out to the car Lewis wondered why he, Adams, Wallace and Hargrove couldn't work together. *It would sure make everything much easier if we worked as a team instead of fighting each other*, he thought. *Maybe I should consider taking Grayson up on his offer and ask him to help me. But, hell, I'm not sure I can trust him. I don't know if he was suckin' up to get information out of me, or what. Damn, what a screwed-up mess.*

He found his troubles were growing when he returned to the mansion where he was greeted by Jason. "Mr. Barrows wants to see you in his office right away."

Barrows went straight for the nerve center. "Your services will no longer be needed. I want you to pack your belongings and get out of here immediately."

The blow was quick, but effective. "What? What are you saying, Mr. Barrows? Is there a problem?" he said.

"No," he said smugly. "None at all. Now that the killer's out of the way. Haven't you heard about that?"

"If you're referring to Gary Wilson, I don't believe he's the man responsible for the murders."

"Look, Detective, it's all over the news. This guy Wilson committed suicide after leaving a note confessing to the crimes. According to all the news reports there was evidence in his apartment linking him to the killings."

"Sir, I don't care what the reports—"

"Listen, I'm not going to argue with you over it," Barrows yelled, jumping to his feet. "You're through here. Now pack and get out. Or should I call Chief Greenberg and inform him that you're refusing to leave my residence."

"That won't be necessary," he mumbled, turning for the door.

Lewis was devastated as he packed his suitcase, his mind spinning in search of an answer. Things were happening too fast to understand, almost as though some vile plan had been set in motion. And where was Tiffany? He didn't see her or any signs of her in the house. Naturally, it wouldn't be very smart to ask Zachary Barrows where he was keeping his wife.

By early afternoon he'd returned to his apartment, confused and feeling a burning ache in his heart. But the cracks in the walls of his world were widening and he wondered if it was just a matter of time until the bricks tumbled down around him.

The first brick spun from the top of the wall and crashed in front of him when it was announced that the print on the note left by Wilson matched that of the letters sent to the murder victims. But this only served to reinforce his belief that Gary's death was a clever mask used by the killer to shield him from unwanted attention.

He was sure he'd wear the carpet through from pacing anxious circles while he was trying to sort out the rubble and find the truth. He learned the answer to one of his questions by making a telephone call to the former Mrs. Karl Thomas. Posing as a survey analyst he learned that her former spouse didn't have a computer in his home.

His bleak mood turned a shade darker when the evening news began by pointing an accusing finger at him, alleging incompetence. The newscast mounted a blistering attack on his handling of the Society Stalker murders and went so far as to imply that he was directly responsible for the death of Madeline Jennings.

The reporter glaring at him from the television paused only to catch his breath. He turned his attention to Gary Wilson, whom he identified as the killer of innocent women at the top of the broadcast. His assassination of Wilson's character included every personal segment Lewis had gathered during the course of his investigation. The reporter was careful to air every piece of dirty linen, including the fondling of Betty Haskins during biology class. Lewis was outraged, knowing that information was only contained in his police report.

He turned the television off, feeling that he'd not only been publicly humiliated, but also betrayed by someone close to the investigation. Was it Adams or one of his henchmen who released the information to the media? Or was it Captain Thomas? If Thomas was the killer it would seem reasonable for him to want to destroy both the investigator and the man being identified as the killer. A public crucifixion of both of them would take any attention away from Thomas.

The telephone rang and, for the moment, his mind turned away from the gloom that surrounded him. Doctor Wexler's voice carried its normal business like tone as he told him it was his opinion that Gary Wilson was murdered. The scratch marks on Wilson's neck were made when he tugged at the rope in an effort to free himself. This was verified by scrapings from under his fingernails that revealed traces of skin.

"I believe Wilson was strangled with the rope and then placed in the closet by the killer in an attempt to conceal the murder by making it look like suicide," Wexler said.

"Christ, it's a relief knowing I was right about his death. But our killer has to be a pretty strong guy to hang him on the support pipe after he's dead. Hell, Gary Wilson wasn't exactly a little boy."

"Yeah. That, or he had help," Wexler said casually.

"Jesus, Doc, thanks a lot. Like I don't have enough problems already. Now you wanna add the possibility of another person. But, what the hell, I agree with you. I've gotta look at every angle."

"Good luck. Oh, by the way—I'm sorry about those ugly stories on the news about you."

"Thanks. Shit, I guess they need to make somebody the scapegoat and, for right now, that's me."

Later he tried to reach Tiffany by calling Lolita. But his hopes were crushed when she said, "I'm sorry Mr. Lewis, Miss Tiffany isn't here."

"Do you know where she went?"

"No, sir, I don't," she said. "But Mr. Barrows and Jason took her outta here and I don't expect that they'll be back anytime soon."

"Why?"

"They put a lotta suitcases in the car before they took Miss Tiffany out."

"Damn it," he spat.

"And another thing, Mr. Lewis, I don't think Miss Tiffany was happy at all about goin' with them."

"Why?"

"Well, Mr. Lewis, she sure seemed awful upset to me. It almost looked like they were forcin' her to go with them."

"Thanks, Lolita."

It was a restless night, filled with tortured thoughts and damning voices calling for him to be fired. But it was a picture that would not come into sharp focus that tormented him most. A woman with something dark tied on the right side of her neck laughed and said to him, "Look at me and find a clue."

Thirty-five

There seemed to be no end in sight for Lewis' somber mood. His day began with a visit to the hospital and there he found no reported change in Ezra Dawkins' condition. Yet Doctor Harper remained optimistic, saying, "No change also means there's no decline in his health."

He called Lolita again, praying that she'd heard from Tiffany, or at least found out where she was. But there was no word from her and Zachary and Jason hadn't come back to the house. As for Lolita, she was becoming increasingly nervous staying alone at the mansion and was thinking about leaving to stay with friends.

Lewis sat at his desk in the Criminal Investigations Office, putting forth a gallant effort to concentrate on the pages of the psychological profile sent by Lieutenant Bowers.

He found himself having to read certain segments of the report over and over because his mind was so crowded with other thoughts. This was a somewhat new experience for him. In the past he'd had no trouble applying himself to the tasks at hand. But then he hadn't faced such pressures professionally and personally.

Hargrove walked into the office and, seeing Lewis at his desk, decided he'd have a little early morning fun. He strolled over and stopped in front of the desk, muttering, "Hey, I guess you can fuck that Barrows broad without havin' to worry now. I mean, since we solved the murders for you, you can get on bangin' her hot ass and you won't have to stop to do any police work."

"Get away from me," Lewis growled, fighting to hold his rage back. "This isn't the time to be fuckin' with me."

"I bet she gives a great blow job. She has the perfect mouth for it, doesn't she?" He placed his hands on the desk and leaned toward Lewis, saying, "Tell me, does she swallow?"

Hargrove's first mistake was failing to make sure that he wasn't alone in the office with Lewis when he began his attack. His second mistake was leaning over the desk and sneering at him.

The dam holding back the fury burst and Lewis sprang to his feet. His hands flashed like lightening bolts, grabbing Frank Hargrove behind the head as a terrifying scream roared from deep within. His grip held Hargrove like the jaws of a steel trap while his arms pulled down with the force of a large piston.

Hargrove's eyes widened as it looked as though the top of the desk was rising to meet his face. There was a sickening splat as his nose met the desktop and flattened, spewing blood over the papers, his face and shirt. The rockets exploded in his head while white stars of varying sizes danced in front of his eyes before finally vanishing.

Lewis let go of his grip and Hargrove slid back and dropped, like a wet rag, to the floor. Lewis walked around to the front of the desk and noticed a nasty gash had been opened above Hargrove's right eye.

He was still standing over Hargrove when Captain Thomas walked into the office through the back door. "Jesus. What the hell happened to him?"

"Uh, well, sir, he—"

"Looks like he took a mean fall. Did he trip over something?"

"I guess you could say that, but—"

Hargrove groaned as his friends arrived and rushed to his side. "The fucker assaulted me," he mumbled through cupped hands.

"Damn. Look at all the blood," Wallace stammered as he looked around at the desk and floor.

"You did it this time," Adams said, grinning like an alley cat in a canary cage. "I mean, you really fucked up. Okay, Frank, tell me exactly what happened."

Hargrove tried to sputter an answer, but Captain Thomas cut him off. "Hell, it looks like he tripped over the phone cord and hit his head."

"But he said Lewis assaulted him," Adams protested.

"Yeah. I know. But he's probably hallucinating from the blow to his head. It must have jarred his brain pretty good. Why don't you take him to the emergency room and get him patched up? Maybe he'll see things differently after he's cleaned up a bit."

"Okay. Whatever you say, Captain."

Thomas tapped Lewis on the shoulder and pointed to his office. "Let's talk."

"Yes, sir."

Lewis stood in front of Thomas and told him about his run-in with Frank Hargrove. He tried to recite the lewd description Hargrove gave of Tiffany's oral sexual skills and about his relationship with her without losing his temper again.

"I didn't hear his comments," Thomas said when he finished the story. "But I did see what you did to him."

"Huh? Then why'd you stick up for me?" he said.

"Lewis, I haven't known you a very long time, but I've known you long enough to know you're not foolish enough to strike a fellow officer for some chicken shit reason. I figured he did something that really pissed you off, so I took your side."

"What happens now?"

"Maybe I can convince him to change his story. I don't condone what you did, but if he'd kept his big mouth shut, he wouldn't have gotten his ass kicked—not that he didn't deserve it. I'm surprised that mouth of his hasn't gotten his ass in trouble before this."

"Sir, I don't understand why you're doing this," he said, shaking his head. "Hell, you're sticking your neck—your career—out on a limb for me."

Thomas pointed to the newspapers he'd dropped on his desk. "Have you read any of those?"

"No, sir."

"Right now we might be each other's best friend. Maybe only friend," he said, trying to laugh. "Christ, they tore us a new ass. You for allegedly screwing up the investigation and me for backing you. And wouldn't you know it, they don't have a damn thing in there about Adams and his friends, except what a fine job they did in closing out the stalker killings."

"The evening news didn't exactly do me any favors either," Lewis said, lowering his head and staring at the floor.

Thomas nodded. "I think for the next couple of days they'll pound us pretty damn hard. Right now they need somebody to sacrifice and I guess we're the ones who'll get tossed in the fire. You—we'll just have to tough it out."

"Hell, I can take it," he replied with a shrug of his shoulders. "What I don't like is the fact that my friends have to eat this garbage too. And I can only imagine what Ginny Mason must be going through. The press corps butchered what was left of Gary Wilson's character."

"I'm sure it'll pass after his funeral. Things'll get back to normal and they'll run around looking for somebody else to hack up. The circle always goes on."

"Yeah. I guess you're right."

"Look, you've been through a lot lately," Thomas said, looking at Lewis. "Why don't you take a few days off? Get your head back in the game."

"I appreciate the offer, Captain, but I can't take off," he said, starting for the door. "I have too much work to do. The stalker's still out there. He'll kill somebody else if I don't find him."

"You're convinced Wilson's not the man, aren't you?"

"Absolutely. Gary Wilson was murdered. That was just an attempt by the stalker to cover his ass. Nothing more." He hoped to see some reaction from Thomas, but he simply nodded, agreeing with him.

"What's your plan of action?"

"I want to finish reading the psychological profile—which, by the way, managed to vanish from the case files before they were given to me. Then I'll start digging all over again. Maybe this time I'll come up with the right guy."

"Well, the offer still stands if you want a few days off."

Lewis cleaned off his desk and picked up Lieutenant Bower's report, highlighting a number of points in it such as, white male. Intelligent. Mid-thirties to forties. Dominated during childhood by an older woman. Possibly mother, grandmother, or older sister. He suddenly realized his ability to concentrate had come back. For now he was right on course, although many things bothered him.

Gary Wilson's death, with its almost ceremonious placing of a note and pictures of the victims, seemed to be no more than a gift-wrapped package. It was an offering from the killer saying, "Here's a way to solve your murders. Leave me alone." Naturally, Adams and his friends were willing to accept the gift and conclude the investigation.

As he continued to sift facts and coincidences he had the feeling that the killer was almost reading his mind and using his very own thoughts to stay a step ahead of him. His most personal thoughts regarding the cases weren't included in his reports and yet it looked as though the killer knew about them.

The days leading up to Gary Wilson's funeral were filled with scathing editorials, in print and on screen. Lewis found his picture on the front page of every newspaper in town and filling the TV screen morning, noon and night. He and Captain Karl Thomas became the topic of local radio talk shows and there was no lack of listeners willing to call in with an opinion.

What troubled him most about the scorching publicity was that by now it had reached John Henry Johnson and Mr. Higa. The men who taught him to observe a strict code of honor and to be forthright in his dealings with everybody would also endure his pain. He felt they were also being disgraced by the unwarranted attacks on his integrity.

While he was being smeared by the media, Adams, Wallace and Hargrove were taking daily bows in front of the cameras, patting themselves on the back as the steadfast investigators who solved the stalker killings. They jumped at every opportunity to find fault with the way Lewis and Captain Thomas handled the cases.

Wilson's funeral almost became a circus as local and out of town newscasters tried to get the best location to film the burial of the Society Stalker. Even in death Gary Wilson was given no peace and the woman who loved him had to be helped from the bizarre scene by friends and relatives. Screaming "Why?" over and over, Ginny Mason was led away while cameras rolled to record her grief which stations would later broadcast for everybody to see.

Thirty-six

With the funeral of Gary Wilson over, Lewis hoped it would signal the end of the hounding by the press. He wanted to walk in anonymity again and not see heads turn and fingers pointed as he walked by. He was tired of being in the limelight and the subject of four star editions.

He continued to hope that soon he'd be left alone as he parked his car on the lot at the police station. But when he walked through the front door he was summoned to the Internal Affairs Division. There he was met by Lieutenant Wayne Joseph and Captain Thomas.

"Do you have any idea why you were called in here?" Joseph said, directing him to a chair.

"Well, Lieutenant, I'd damn well bet it ain't a social call," Lewis said, shaking his head.

"Detective Lewis, before we get to the formalities, I want you to be aware of some very serious allegations being leveled against you by Mr. Zachary Barrows."

Lewis' heart jumped. "What's he accusing me of?" he said.

"Look, rather than wait and possibly jeopardize your rights, I'll go over them with you at this time," Joseph said, as Thomas looked on in silence. He picked up the papers and read, item by item, the rights afforded Lewis and had him initial the appropriate boxes to indicate he understood them. When he completed the advice of rights, Joseph said, "I know I got ahead of the normal procedures by not informing you of the charges first. But I wanted to be sure you were aware of your rights before we did anything else."

"Yes, sir."

"Detective Lewis, Mr. Barrows is accusing you of seducing his wife while you were assigned to protect her and with carrying on an illicit affair with her over the past several weeks." Joseph had hurled a bombshell across the desk and into his lap. Indeed, Tiffany's suspicions had been correct and now he waited for the bomb to go off.

He shook his head slowly, muttering, "Yes, sir."

"In addition to his accusations, Detective Lewis, Mr. Barrows provided me with a videotape of you and his wife engaging in various sexual acts in the library of his home."

The bomb had exploded. "This is a very serious breach of conduct."

The once-sturdy walls of his world were toppling and tumbling down around him. Brick by brick his shelter had been torn like a paper doll and tossed aside to reveal his human vulnerability. The voice of good reason that once warned him to avoid becoming involved with Tiffany now cried, "I told you so."

"Of course, you have the right to see the film, if you so desire."

He was about to turn down the offer to preview his pornographic film debut when he had second thoughts. "Yes, sir. I'd like to see it. I guess I might as well see the evidence against me."

Joseph retrieved the remote and turned on the television and VCR that occupied a corner of his office. There in living color, J.D. and Tiffany performed on the screen, the sights and sounds of their lovemaking filling the room. For a fleeting moment he was almost overcome by the memory of the passion they shared. But soon he was looking beyond the writhing bodies. He was searching for the location of the hidden camera that was planted to spy on them.

"I've seen enough," he said, looking away from the screen.

"Do you wish to say anything at this time?" Joseph said, stopping the tape and looking at Lewis.

"No, sir."

"Okay. Now, Detective Lewis, by order of Chief Greenberg, I'm officially informing you that you're being placed on administrative leave until further notice."

"Yeah," he replied with a slight sarcastic chuckle. "I believe that's the polite way of telling me I've been suspended."

Joseph nodded and went on. "When my investigation's complete you'll be notified, at which time a decision'll have to be reached regarding a trial board."

"Yes, sir."

"By the way, I think you should know—Barrows is going public with this."

"Jesus Christ," Lewis muttered as he closed his eyes and lowered his head. "Here we go again."

"I'm sorry. I tried to talk him out of it, but he wasn't about to listen to anything I had to say."

"Yeah. He's about as warm and cuddly as a King Cobra."

"I gathered that the minute he stormed into my office," Joseph said with just a hint of a smile.

Captain Thomas walked outside with Lewis and said, "I'm really sorry about all this shit."

"Thanks, Captain."

"What're you gonna do now?" Thomas said, looking around.

"I don't know. Shit, it's tough putting up a defense when you're one of the stars of a video that's to be used as evidence against you."

"Think everything through very carefully. Don't make a hasty decision. Think it over for a little while."

"Maybe I'll do that. Thanks for the advice, Captain."

"I take it you're still gonna pursue your theory about the stalker?"

"More than ever. I'm good and pissed off now and I won't rest until I've got the bastard by the balls and I'm draggin' his ass off to jail."

"Be damn careful," Thomas cautioned, looking around again. "You know you're not supposed to be working cases when you're on admin leave."

"Yes, sir. I know. I'll try to be as careful as possible."

"You'd better split," Thomas said, pointing behind Lewis. "Here comes Channel Eight's Instant Eye News Team and I have a feeling they're looking for you. I'll try and occupy them while you get the hell out of here."

Lewis walked quickly to his car and left the lot through the back gate. The last thing he needed was to be interrogated by the vultures of the press about his affair with Tiffany. Other questions were beginning to bother him and he believed he was getting close to the answers, but to find them he couldn't stop to entertain the inquiring minds of the public.

By evening he'd read through the killer's profile again and was regrouping to go on the offensive. He'd gained a valuable insight into the workings of the killer's mind and was forming a clearer image of the man he'd hunt down and arrest for the murders.

He broke away from his strategy session to watch the evening news; however, he was very reluctant to do it. He was sure the lead story would be filled with the wretched details of the Lewis and Barrows love affair.

It turned out to be much more than he'd anticipated. Zachary Barrows, dressed in a tuxedo and carrying his personal cue cards was stepping up to a cluster of microphones. It was obvious that this would be another award-winning performance.

He cleared his throat and raised his right hand to tug at the collar of his shirt. He stared straight into the cameras and began. "Ladies and gentlemen, it is with a sad heart that I stand here before you today," he said, bowing his head. "I'm deeply hurt by what I must confess to you my friends, my neighbors and business associates. My lovely wife, Tiffany, in a moment of weakness fell prey to the advances of a young man and permitted herself to be lured to his bed. Now I know you might be asking why I should be standing here telling you that my wife has committed adultery."

He paused for a moment, looking over his audience and continued. "I believe it's my duty to inform you that the young man I speak of is none other than Detective Jefferson D. Lewis. A man sworn to uphold the law, but more importantly he was assigned to investigate the Society Stalker murders. And what did he do? He took one look at my wife and lust possessed him day and night. He pursued her in a neverending fashion. He wooed her until she finally gave in to his perverted charm and satisfied his immoral cravings. He seduced my wife while flagrantly disregarding the safety and well-being of the citizens he'd sworn to protect. He shunned his duties while dragging my poor unsuspecting wife down into a vile, lustful pit.

"I believe we should stand up and demand that he be made to answer for his gross misconduct. He should be punished for failing the citizens of this community. He should be held accountable for the death of Madeline Jennings. If he had investigated the crimes with the same zeal with which he pursued my wife, Madeline Jennings would surely be alive today. In every sense of the word, Detective Jefferson Lewis is guilty of murder. He killed Madeline Jennings."

"You low-life fuckin' prick," Lewis yelled at the TV screen. "I can't believe you're low enough to drag Tiffany through the mud like this."

He turned the television off and angrily hurled a pillow from the sofa to the floor, wishing he could do the same to Zachary Barrows. Was the Lord and Master looking for sympathy from his friends and neighbors, or was he trying to firm up a faltering business deal by acting the part of a martyr? Regardless of his reason, it only made Lewis hate him that much more.

He suddenly felt drained and stretched out on the sofa. He closed his eyes and tried to rest. Somewhere in between the worlds of slumber and wakefulness he saw Tiffany's smiling face. He reached for her hand only to see her face suddenly change to that of another woman.

He closed his eyes tighter, trying to force the other woman to go away when he saw the object tied around her neck. It was a black scarf tied on the right side of her neck and knotted in the same fashion as the ropes on the murder victims. The woman laughed and said, "Look at me and find a clue." He sprang up on the sofa and opened his eyes.

"I know who you are," he blurted, staring at the wall. "I remember where I saw you. Somehow you're a part of this and I'm gonna find out just what your role is."

Thirty-seven

Lewis tried to sleep after completing a list of things to do the following day. The list flashed by as he closed his eyes, tossing and turning while he tried to sleep. Faces and names turned up again and again in his semi-restful state, each vying for the top spot on his list.

By 3:30 he was awake and within a half an hour he'd showered, dressed and left the apartment. His first visit of the day would be an early wake up call for Winston Palmer. He was sure the underhanded PI had installed the camera for Barrows and he wanted answers to a lot of questions.

"Good morning, Winston," Lewis called softly while pressing the barrel of the 870 Remington shotgun against the sleeping man's head.

"Wha—who's there? Palmer stuttered, opening his eyes and raising his hand to shield them from the light Lewis was shining in his sleepy baby blues. "What the fuck's goin' on?"

"No, Winston, I ask the questions. You give me the answers."

"Lewis?" he said, still groggy.

"Yeah."

"How the fuck did you get in here?" Palmer sputtered, propping himself up on one elbow.

"Maybe Scotty beamed me in, asshole."

"By God, you burglarized my home!"

Lewis laughed. "Yeah. But, you ain't gonna report it, right?"

"Okay. Okay. I won't report it. Just what the hell is it you want?"

"Answers, dickhead."

"About what?"

"Well, let's start with the hidden video camera in Barrows' library. Did you install it for him?"

"Yeah."

"When?"

"When the house was built."

"Why'd Barrows want the camera in there?"

Palmer cleared his throat. "Well, there was a time when he used to hold a lot of business meetings there. He wanted the camera there so he could go off later and study a client's reaction to his offers."

"Are there any other cameras in the house?"

"Yeah. In his office."

"I take it that camera was there for the same reason?"

"Yeah. He held some of the meetings there instead of the library," he said, trying to sit up.

"Careful, Winston," he said, tapping his head with the shotgun. "Don't get any dumb ass ideas."

"Hey, I ain't that fuckin' stupid."

"So these cameras have been there since the house was first built."

"Yeah," Palmer said. "And actually I just upgraded all the equipment."

"When?"

"The day before you moved in."

"Okay," Lewis said, relaxing the pressure on the gun. "Now, are there any other cameras in the house? And don't lie to me, Palmer. I'm not in the mood."

"Uh—yeah. There're two others."

"Where?"

"There's one in the bedroom they shared and another one in the bedroom where his wife's been sleeping off and on for the past few years."

"Why'd he have them installed?" he said, though he suspected he already knew the answer.

"He wanted to see if his old lady was doin' the number with anybody else."

Lewis shook his head. "Where the hell does he hide all this spy apparatus?"

"There's a small room behind the bookshelf in his office. One of the sections swings open into a sound proof room."

"How does he open it?"

"I don't know."

"Palmer, don't bullshit me," he snapped, shoving the gun tighter against his head.

"Man, the fuckin' door's open when I get there. I never saw him open it."

"So you have no idea where the button or control for the door is?"

"No."

"How big's this room?"

"I don't know. Maybe 10 by 10. I'm not really sure."

"What else does he have in there?"

"Uh—well, he had me bug all the bedrooms in the west wing of the house. The listening and recording equipment's in there with the video cameras."

"What?" he said, shaking his head. "Why the hell he'd have you bug all the bedrooms in the west wing?"

"He'd bring prospective clients in from outta town and put them up there. After a meeting they'd go to their rooms. That's when he'd listen in on their phone calls or the talks between them and the advisors or attorneys they brought along."

"You mean you tapped their telephones?"

"Yeah."

"Shame on you, Winston," he said, poking his shoulder with the shotgun. "That's against the law."

"Yeah. Yeah, I know."

"Okay. Now, where's he keeping Tiffany?"

"I don't know."

"Wrong answer, Winston," he snapped, moving the gun back to his head.

"All right. All right, goddamn it. He has a place somewhere in the country."

"Palmer, I'm not in the mood to play 20 fuckin' questions with you every time I change the topic. Now where the fuck is it?"

"It's about a hundred and seventy-five miles northwest of here."

"That's a start," Lewis said, moving the gun. "Now, what else can you tell me?"

"It's some ritzy community. Homes on ten, fifteen and twenty acre lots. A big country club. Golf courses. Stables. Swimming pools. Hiking trails. Fishing streams and lakes."

"But you don't know the name of it?"

"No. I can't help you there."

"Let's go back to the hidden room for a minute. Exactly where's it located?"

"When you face the bookshelves behind his desk, the center section's the door."

"Does it swing in or out?"

"In. Why?"

"I wanted to know where the hinges were. If it swings in, the hinges are inside the room."

Palmer nodded. "You're pretty damn slick for bein' so young."

"I've still got a lot to learn," he muttered. "Okay. Is there anything else in that room besides the cameras and recording equipment?"

"No."

"What about file cabinets?"

"No."

"A desk?"

"No."

"Palmer, are you sure?"

"Yeah. I'm sure."

"Just how friendly are Zachary Barrows and Jason Dantley?" he said, pulling the gun away from Palmer's head and resting it on his shoulder.

"I know Zachary trusts Jason completely. I mean, they've been together for a long time."

"It looks to me like Jason sticks pretty close to him. Plays bodyguard for him as well as chauffeur."

"Yeah."

"You know, I didn't see him lurking in the background yesterday when Zachary gave his little speech to God and the rest of the world."

"I don't know anything about that," he muttered.

"You don't think Jason's up at that lodge or whatever it is, makin' sure Tiffany doesn't leave, do you?"

"Ah, shit, man," Palmer said, pushing himself up higher on the bed. "Don't get me involved in their domestic shit. I don't need grief like that comin' down on me."

"Winston, I'm gonna pass a little advice along to you before I leave and I want you to pay real close attention."

"Yeah. Okay."

"I don't want you trying to get in touch with Saint Zachary and telling him I paid you a visit. If you do, I'm comin' back and me and Remington here are gonna give you that sex change operation I promised you the first time we met. Do you understand?" he said as he lowered the shotgun to Palmer's groin for emphasis.

"Jesus, yeah. Every word. Every damn word."

Lewis left Palmer's house hating Zachary Barrows more than ever. He felt it was disgusting for Barrows to stoop so low that he'd have cameras installed in Tiffany's bedroom to spy on her. After all, it was he who made the decision to have nothing to do with her. Was it the old double standard or insecurity on his part?

His spirits lifted somewhat, knowing the general location where Tiffany was staying. Or was being held a better term? In an odd sort of way he was happy she wasn't around. Not that he didn't want to see her, but for the time being she didn't have to face her friends and neighbors after Zachary's public address. Of course, many of those friends and close neighbors lived in their own glass houses and weren't in a position to cast the first stone.

He stopped for breakfast at the Green Ridge Diner and took a seat at the far end of the counter, hoping to avoid curious and accusing glances. A few whispers buzzed around the restaurant when he took his Stetson off, but for the most part the customers ignored him.

Lewis went back to his apartment to begin the job of finding out what role Ester Wentworth-Fox, the woman in the scarf, played in the stalker murders. He thumbed through the telephone book but couldn't find a local listing for her, and directory assistance was also unable to give him any information. A quick check with the police records section also didn't help. But it was the long distance telephone call he made that hit him like an uppercut. As the conversation went on he blurted, "She's Zachary Barrows' grandmother!" And suddenly piece after piece of the scrambled puzzle fell into place. By the time the call ended he was certain he knew the answer he'd been trying to find for so long.

"Sweet Jesus!" he muttered getting to his feet and reading his notes again. "She was your grandmother, Barrows. One more thing and I've got your ass. It was you. You killed those women. You son of a bitch, I know you did."

He was so overwhelmed by his good fortune he almost didn't hear the telephone ringing. He crossed the room, grabbed the receiver from its cradle and rasped, "Yeah. Lewis."

"Christ, did you just run a marathon?" Captain Thomas said.

"Uh—no. No, sir. I just came in."

"Okay," he said.. "Anyway, I just called to see if you've come up with anything on your theory."

"No, sir. Not yet."

"Shit," he muttered, unable to hide his disappointment. "Look, if you come up with anything—anything at all—let me know right away."

"Yes, sir."

As he hung up the phone he thought, *sorry, Captain. When I get the last piece of information I'm gonna drop a grenade in your shorts. Under the circumstances I'm not sure you'll want to come along for the ride.*

He walked into the kitchen, poured a glass of water and sat down. He jumped to his feet almost immediately and began pacing circles around the table, stopping from time to time to glance at what he'd written in his notebook. It was as though he was trying to be sure that he'd written everything down correctly.

As he paced slowly around the table, sipping his water, he realized that he had to be one hundred percent right when he made his move. If he moved to make the arrest without all of the facts in place, the media and citizens, as well as a few of his fellow officers would probably call for a public lynching.

Furthermore, he knew he was crossing the line by pursuing the investigation while on administrative leave. That in itself would probably lead to disciplinary action, even though he was certain he'd identified the man responsible for the slayings.

The sound of his pager interrupted his thoughts and he glanced down at the now-familiar number of Doctor Harper. He picked up the telephone and called the hospital, all the while holding his breath and praying.

"Doctor Harper speaking."

"Doctor, this is Detective Lewis."

"I didn't expect you to call so quickly, but I'm glad you did. Ezra Dawkins has regained consciousness."

"Can I see him?"

Harper laughed and said, "I was going to suggest that you come down right away. Mr. Dawkins asked to see you and threatened to get out of bed and leave the hospital if we didn't call you."

"Yeah, that sounds like Ezra."

Lewis went straight to the old man's side when he arrived at the hospital. Ezra's face looked drawn, but, as always, he somehow managed to light up the room with his smile. The two men clasped and squeezed each other's hands.

"How do you feel, Ezra?"

"I'm not ready to go ten rounds with anybody just yet," he said, smiling again. "But give me a day or two."

"It looks like you lost a few pounds."

"When I get outta here maybe we could go and sample some more of that cornbread, fried chicken and apple pie."

"You're on."

Ezra's smile faded. "But first you gotta do something for me. You gotta even the score for me."

Lewis shook his head. "In this case I don't think I'd like to even the score. I plan on us being way ahead when the game's over. After I leave here I'll start putting the papers together to nail that son of a bitch."

"Then you already know who you're looking for."

"Yes. But I'm hoping you can give me enough information so I can drive the last nail in his coffin. Can you tell me who assaulted you?"

"Yes, sir, I sure can. It was Jason. Jason did it," he said, reaching for his glass of orange juice. He took a sip and began telling a tale of a bizarre discovery and of trying to reach Lewis to inform him. His efforts to pass on what he'd found were stopped when he was beaten and dumped behind the health spa.

When Ezra finished his story, Lewis fitted the last corner into the jigsaw puzzle. Now it was time to write a search and seizure warrant, and this time he'd willingly step into the limelight and rock the boat.

He waited until he was certain the CIB office was clear and sneaked in through the back door. He moved quickly to finish his task before someone happened to come in and find out what he was doing. His greatest fear was having word leak out before he moved to arrest Barrows. An arrest situation is always touchy, but a suspect who's warned ahead of time increases the danger for the police and innocent passers-by ten-fold.

It took him just under two hours to finish writing and printing the search warrant. Satisfied that it was in order, he left the station and went back to his apartment. Normally he'd have a senior officer or supervisor review the warrant before going to a judge and asking him to sign it. But the circumstances surrounding this case were anything but normal.

But he wanted to get an opinion from an expert on the warrant and he knew of only one man who fit the description almost perfectly. Even though it was 2:30 in the morning, he dialed the number of John Henry Johnson.

"At this hour it damn well better be good," the deep, sleepy voice grumbled.

"Ah, come on, Pops. I thought you'd be happy to hear from me."

"J.D.?"

"Yes, sir."

"Is everything okay?" he said, the anxiety clear in his voice.

"Sure. I just needed to tap into your expertise on the matter of a search warrant."

"Why me? Can't you contact your people?"

"Well, in this case, I'd prefer not to involve any of them. I'm afraid word of what I'm doing might get out."

"This sounds serious. Let me get to the other phone." A few moments passed before John Henry picked up the other line and said, "Just how serious is this?"

"Let me put it this way. I'm about to nail the man who's actually responsible for the stalker killings."

"Huh," John Henry grunted. "According to all the damn bullshit publicity the press is dumpin' on your ass, the stalker killed himself."

"That's a crock. It's a cover."

"Okay then, what about this other bullshit? The story about you and the Barrows woman?"

"Uh—I'd like to get into that, but I don't have time, Pops. I'm afraid other lives, including hers, are in danger and I've got to move fast."

"Okay. What do you want from me?"

"I'd like to read my warrant to you and get your opinion on its content and see if you think it'll fly."

J.D. began with page one of the application for the warrant and read the entire document, word for word, to John Henry. When he was through there was a low whistle from the other end. "Man, that's some piece of work. You didn't miss a thing."

"Thanks. I feel a lot better hearing that from you."

"But, Jesus, the killer's Zachary Barrows. Man, that's sure gonna rock the town."

"Yeah, I know."

"Now, who's helping you with the arrest?"

"Nobody. I'll take care of it myself."

"J.D., you shouldn't go it alone," John Henry scolded.

"I know. But I'm not sure who the hell I can trust."

"Think it over, son. I know you're in a hurry, but think it over. There's gotta be somebody you can trust."

"Well, maybe. Anyway, I'll think about it."

"Good luck."

"Thanks," he said and hung up the phone.

He walked slowly to his bedroom, pulled off his boots and dropped to the bed, but he knew he probably wouldn't sleep. He was anxious to get on with it. The day of reckoning was at hand and the man in the black Stetson was about to come calling.

Thirty-eight

Sleep was a stranger to him that night. Concerns for Tiffany's safety overshadowed his need for rest, and the anxious knot rolling around in his stomach kept him on edge. He wondered what would happen if Barrows found out that he knew he was the killer. Would he hurt Tiffany? Maybe even kill her? But without her, Zachary Barrows would have no aces to play. It would be better for him to keep her healthy. But in this case sound thinking almost seemed out of place.

He was up at the first light of dawn, thinking about his next move. John Henry's advice to ask someone in his department for help made sense. Lewis reached for the telephone and called Captain Thomas. "Sir, I hate to wake you, but we need to meet right away."

"Yeah. Okay," he mumbled. "Where? What's up?"

"I've identified the stalker."

"Holy shit," he blurted. Suddenly Thomas sounded wide awake. "My office in 20 minutes."

"How about the Bagel Bin? They open in 15 minutes. Your office might have ears and what I have to tell you—well, it shouldn't get out."

"Yeah. Sure. I'll see you there."

The two men huddled in a booth in a back corner of the shop. Lewis forced an onion bagel down and hoped he wouldn't puke. His stomach continued to churn from anxiety over Tiffany and what he was about to face. He thought that today would probably be the longest day of his life.

"Who did you finger as the stalker?" Thomas said after a sip of his coffee.

"Zachary Barrows."

"What!" he sputtered, nearly choking on his coffee. "Jumpin' Jesus, man, do you know what you're saying?"

"Yes, sir. And I have proof positive he's the man."

"Christ, fill me in."

Lewis gave him a brief rundown of the facts, including what Ezra saw in Barrows' office. He then gave him a copy of his search and seizure warrant to look over and sat back anxiously awaiting Thomas' comments.

Thomas read the warrant over, giving a low whistle from time to time, or muttering, "I'll be damned." He shook his head when he finished reading the paper and leaned toward Lewis, saying, "You sure know how to stir up a hornet's nest. If I didn't see this with my own eyes and hear the facts from you, I wouldn't believe a word of it."

"Yeah. I can understand why."

"Where do you go from here?"

"First stop's the courthouse to get this signed. Then to the mansion to seize the evidence. After that I've gotta find the exact location where he's keeping Tiffany and get up there as fast as I can. I really think she's in serious trouble. When she's safe I'll take him into custody."

"Right now, it's your ball game. What can I do to help?"

"I think we need to get somebody out to Barrows' house and make sure nobody destroys the evidence before I get there with the warrant. I'm not sure that anybody's there, but I don't think I should take the chance. Could you take care of that?"

"I'll see to it personally."

"Oh, you might wanna ask Grayson to go along," Lewis said, putting his Stetson on and getting to his feet. "He volunteered to help me not too long ago. I guess I might as well take him up on the offer."

Thomas was surprised by his suggestion, but agreed. "Yeah. If that's what you want, I'll call him in."

Lewis was among the first to walk into the town's old stone courthouse. With warrant in hand he searched for a judge who was available to review and sign the papers. The predator had the scent of blood and was eager to get on with the hunt.

Much to his dismay, the only judge available was Weldon O'Boyle, a man with a colorful, if not tainted, reputation. O'Boyle was notorious for his courtroom antics and had often made headlines by hurling his gavel at prosecutors, defense attorneys and even some defendants. On one occasion he'd left the bench, marched to the defense counsel's table and poured a glass of water over a defendant's head who had nodded off while he lectured the prosecutor on interrogation procedures.

It wasn't his courtroom behavior that bothered Lewis. It was the talk in cobweb-filled corners and after-hours chatter in pubs that made him feel uneasy. His Honor was rumored to be in the hip pocket of a number of crime figures as well as one or two politicians with shaded reputations. There'd also been idle gossip linking him to several high-ranking police officials.

Although he was unhappy about presenting the warrant to O'Boyle, Lewis had no other choice and entered his chambers. "Good morning, Your Honor."

The judge looked up from his morning newspaper and a scowl appeared on his puffy red face. He pushed at his gold rimmed glasses and rocked back in his chair, studying the young man who stood in front of him. "What can I do for you?"

"Your Honor, I need a search and seizure warrant signed and I—"

"Just like that," O'Boyle said, snapping his fingers. "You want a warrant signed. I think I'd better review it first, don't you? I'm the one who'll make the decision as to whether or not probable cause exists for the issuance of a search warrant."

"Yes, sir. I—"

"Hand it here."

He reached out to pass the search warrant to O'Boyle only to have the papers ripped from his hand by a man who seemed to be growing more irate with each tick of the clock. The judge read quickly through the first few paragraphs before stopping abruptly and staring icily at the young detective. His reading suddenly became unhurried and his billowy red cheeks turned a darker shade of crimson. "Detective, is this your idea of some perverted joke?"

"No, sir. It's not a joke."

"You're a liar," O'Boyle roared, leaping to his feet.

"No, sir."

The judge hurled the papers at Lewis. "You take this shit and get outta my office.I refuse to sign my name to such an atrocious pack of lies. By God, what you've written is pure slander and I won't be a part of it."

"Your Honor, I've named the source for some of the information and he's willing to testify in court."

"He's a bigger fool than you. No jury with an ounce of sense would believe such outrageous accusations. Not against a man like Zachary Barrows."

All the wrong buttons were being pushed and J.D. Lewis had finally had enough of the system, the media and playing the part of everybody's whipping boy. "You're fulla shit. You're in his back pocket. Everything I've heard about you's true. You're a judge with a price tag and you can be bought for the right dollar amount."

"When I'm through with you, you won't be able to get a job cleaning toilets in this town," O'Boyle said, shaking his finger at him. "You just wait till the press gets a hold of this."

"By then, Your Honor, I'll have Barrows in custody," he snapped. "Maybe you'll be the one cleanin' shithouses for a career when it's all over." He spun on his heels and charged out of the office.

"We'll see about that," O'Boyle called after him.

Lewis had taken but a few long strides in the dim hallway when he stopped and walked silently back to the door. He stood with his back pressed against the wall and listened to the judge talking on the telephone.

"Lewis was just in my office trying to get me to sign a search warrant for your residence," the judge said. "He made some pretty strong and incriminating statements in the affidavit for his warrant. I think you'd better make damn sure the items he's referring to disappear for good."

Lewis heard what he expected and now he felt that he had to move quickly to prevent the destruction of the evidence. Without the items listed in his warrant, he'd fail to prove his case. He could ill afford to go down to defeat. It would certainly place others in grave danger and Tiffany would have to be near the top of the list. Maybe he'd already picked her as his next victim.

Lewis raced out of the courthouse and stopped in his tracks. There, standing on the sidewalk, the morning sun behind him highlighting the outline of his massive frame, was John Henry Johnson. "Jesus. What the hell're you doing here?"

John Henry grinned. "You didn't really think I'd let you go off on your own to take care of this, did you?"

"Well, I guess not. But I did take your advice," he said, embracing the man who still remained as rock solid as the first day he'd met him in the karate dojo. Now, the only noticeable difference was a slight trace of silver showing in his dark, curly sideburns. "I called my captain and told him what was going on."

"Good," he said, nodding. "Good thinking."

"By the way, how'd you get here so fast?"

"Took the first flight out," he said, putting his hand on the young man's shoulder. "Did you get the warrant signed?"

"No. I had a problem with the judge."

"What kinda problem?"

"It seems Judge O'Boyle is more than a little chummy with Zachary Barrows. He refused to sign it and then the cocksucker called Barrows and tipped him off."

"What about another judge?"

"None available. Everybody but O'Boyle's stuck in some bullshit workshop for the whole day."

"You call the shots, J.D. Whatever you wanna do, I'm with you."

"Let's get out to the Barrows Mansion. Captain Thomas and Detective Grayson should already be there. At least, I hope they are."

Many miles away, Tiffany nervously walked around the floors of what amounted to her prison cell. Zachary refused to allow her to contact anyone. He removed the telephones and hid them, and personal contact was out of the question. When Zachary was gone, Jason became the menacing compound guard.

She wanted to get out of this prison and put everything, including her marriage to Zachary, behind her. She'd grown to hate her role as a possession and a mere object flaunted at his will. She'd grown tired of his declarations of love and token trinkets in place of real love. The sands of life were beginning to fall too fast to the bottom of the hourglass, and it was time to stop the game. Of course, his brutal assault of her only pushed her farther away from him and made her decision easier.

She opened the door and walked out onto the porch, her bare feet giving only the slightest hint of sound. The voices from around the corner told her that Zachary and Jason were having another of their many secret talks. She moved toward the sound of the low-pitched chatter, stopping just short of the edge of the cabin to listen to their conversation.

At first, the words Zachary spoke seemed more suited to a conspiracy in a third-rate movie. But as he continued to talk, the cold reality of what he was saying slashed through her like a razor's edge. She started to tremble, her knees growing weak as she struggled to understand the orders he was giving to Jason.

"This has to be dealt with immediately," he said, jabbing his fist in front of him to drive home the point. "I've rented a helicopter to fly you back to the house. It should be here shortly."

"I'll take care of everything. Don't worry."

"While you're gone I'll...." A noise from behind them on the wooden deck caught their attention. "What the hell was that?" Barrows said.

Before either man could move, Tiffany staggered into view, clutching the front of her pale blue blouse with both hands. "My God, it's you! It's you. You killed them. Oh my God. Zachary, how could you? They were our friends." She turned and tried to run away on badly shaking legs.

"Get her," Barrows commanded. "Get her back in the house."

Her flight was short. Within a matter of seconds Jason ran her down and yanked her off her feet. Although she was in excellent physical condition, her attempts to resist being dragged back to the cabin were useless and she soon found herself face to face with a very angry Zachary.

"What should I do with her, Mr. Barrows?"

"Leave her. I'll deal with her. Right now the most important thing is to get rid of everything in the desk at the house."

"Okay," he said, hearing the helicopter in the distance.

As the door closed behind Jason, Tiffany looked through still disbelieving eyes at her husband. "My God, Zachary, why? I…I'm shocked. You of all people. You have almost everything a man could want. You'd be the last person on this earth that anyone would suspect."

"Not everyone, my loving wife," he spat. "Your boyfriend figured it out. He just tried to get Judge O'Boyle to sign a search warrant for the house."

"What're you going to do?" she said, trying to think of some way to keep Zachary talking. If J.D. knew Zachary was the killer, he'd somehow track him to the resort and rescue her.

"Right now, I don't know," he said, rubbing the back of his neck. "I thought I had everything under control, but it seems I underestimated the abilities of Detective Lewis. Hell, I should've known better. I knew he was different the first day he walked into the house. He just doesn't give up. He's like a goddamn mongrel hanging on to somebody's leg. The son-of-a-bitch won't let go. You know," he laughed, "in a way, I admire the young punk. He'd be one helluva businessman."

"What about me?" Tiffany said, searching his eyes for a sign that he still cared for her in some way. "What're you going to do with me?"

"Ah, Tiffany," he said, stepping behind her and grasping her by her shoulders. "If Jason—I'm sorry. When Jason destroys the evidence, it won't leave young Detective Lewis with much of a case. It'll be the word of a jealous lover against mine. And right now his word's not worth much. So, my dear, I'm afraid you'll suffer a very tragic accident. And you were such a terrific security screen."

"I see," she said, trying to push the sinking feeling that suddenly surrounded her out of her mind. "With me out of the way, there'll be no one to verify his story. And you, the poor grieving husband'll say that my accidental death was because I was so upset over losing my young suitor. Or will I commit suicide over it?"

"Bravo, darling," he said and started clapping. "What keen insight."

She shook her head. "Still, I don't understand why you killed those women. I'm really shocked. Did you hate them for something they did?"

He walked around the room in silence, his rage growing with each step. He suddenly spun around and stared wide-eyed at her. "Yes," he shouted. "Yes, I hated them. Those fuckin' bitches trying to take over the business world. And their damned husbands not only condoned it, they gave them a helping hand. They had no right stepping into my territory."

"Zachary," she said softly, "you don't have exclusive rights to run the whole world's business."

He laughed. "That's just what my loving grandmother said right before she sold her women's toiletries company. By God, I ran that company from the time I was 16 up until the day she sold it out from under me. The great, the lovely, the grand madam of business, Ester Wentworth-Fox, castrated me in front of the entire industry. That damn worthless bitch sold out to Elizabeth Ames when I should've been given the reins to the company."

Things were beginning to take shape as she sank to the sofa and looked, almost sadly, at the man pacing in front of her. He'd mentioned little of his family during their courtship, but she recalled the photographs of Mrs. Wentworth-Fox and her trademark black silk scarf knotted neatly on the right side of her neck.

"And to top it off," Zachary continued, "that whore, Elizabeth Ames, didn't have the money to buy the fuckin' company. So her pussy-whipped husband bought it for her. A week later I'm out on my ass with nothing. That was the thanks I got for making the company a success."

Tiffany couldn't ever recall hearing Zachary talk the way he was now. Nor could she remember seeing him so enraged. He was normally very reserved, being more sarcastic than angry when upset.

He went on with his dialogue. "About seven years ago I decided to get the company back. I made a most generous offer to Mrs. Ames, hoping she'd part with the business. Do you know what she did?" he yelled. "The brazen slut just laughed at me. Laughed at me, Zachary Barrows. I tried to reason with her, but she only laughed louder. Of course, my loving grandmother even got a real big chuckle out of me trying to buy the business back. I should've squashed that fuckin' bitch when I had the chance, but she died before I could give her what she really deserved. I was no more than a damn slave to her. I did everything but kiss her ass in Times Square on New Year's Eve to please her. I don't know why, after the way she treated me."

"I'm sorry, Zachary," she said, looking for a way to defuse the situation and calm him down. "I didn't know about any of this. You didn't confide in me about your family when we dated or after we married."

"I had nothing good to say about any of them. My parents never had time for me. They were always traveling around the world spending the money they inherited, leaving me at the mercy of granny dearest. Hell, I became my grandmother's slave when I was a child. Can you believe she used to take me to work with her when I was only six years old? The old lady had me running errands for her when I was six! If I delivered a message to the wrong office, she'd punish me when we got home. She'd lock me in a dark room and leave me there for hours. When my confinement was up, she'd tell me what room I'd be locked in the next time I fucked up. Then she resorted to writing me notes, telling me where I'd do my next penance. When the note-sending became boring, she stopped writing them and started randomly choosing a room for me. Usually one where I'd already served time."

The man walking back and forth in front of her was suddenly a pitiful sight. But she realized that his mournful display concealed a violently hateful man, and at any moment he could unleash a fatal attack on her. She bowed her head and prayed that somehow she'd be delivered from the fate that had befallen her friends.

Thirty-nine

When they reached the house on Huntley Manor Road, Lewis wasted no time punching in the entry codes at the gate. He started up the driveway just as the sickening knot started to tighten in his stomach again. He faced a lot of problems, but he was worried most over Tiffany's safety. He whispered a silent prayer that she was still okay.

"Damn, what a layout," John Henry said as they neared the top.

"Hell, you ain't seen nothin' yet."

When he reached the top of the hill he decided to hide the police car in the garage. After parking his car inside, he took Captain Thomas' car and somehow managed to squeeze it inside as well. He hoped Zachary would be in too much of a hurry to check the garage for strange cars.

Inside the house he made a quick round of introductions and then the four men went to Zachary Barrows's office. Lewis went straight to the desk and saw that it was still locked. "Well, the bottom left drawer is where Ezra saw the pictures."

"You have a choice," Thomas said. "You can break it now, or wait for him to show up and open it."

"I thought I'd wait and catch him in the act of trying to destroy the evidence. If we break it now and take the pictures and any other evidence that might be in there, we could lose it in court. I'm sure there're arguments for seizing it now. Then again, I guess there're arguments for seizing it later. But it doesn't matter. We can't present the case to anyone until after the fact. I think we'd be better off nailing him in the process of removing the evidence."

"That's smart thinking," John Henry said.

"Yeah, it is," Thomas agreed.

"Christ, the way things are going, we might all get our asses jammed for breaking and entering," Lewis said.

"Let's worry about that later," Thomas said. "Why don't we start looking for a way to get in that room behind the bookshelf."

They stopped talking and, while John Henry kept watch for approaching vehicles, J.D., Captain Thomas and Grayson started searching for the controls that opened the door to the room behind the bookshelves.

J.D. worked around the center panel, running his hands and fingers along the smooth wood surface feeling for a button. He didn't find any switches or buttons on the wood's surface. He began checking the bottom shelf, pulling the books out to look behind them for a switch. He worked his way up to the fourth shelf and about one third of the way in from the right edge of the shelf he pulled a book that released the latch. The door opened slowly and he said, "I'm in."

The room was just as Palmer had described it. There was only recording equipment and videotapes inside. J.D. walked around the room and looked over the elaborate setup. He thought it was a shame that a man would become so obsessed with corporate takeovers and spying on his wife. Before leaving the room he checked and found that all of the equipment was loaded and in working order.

"Son of a bitch," John Henry said. "There's a fuckin' helicopter landing in the front yard."

"Shit," Lewis spat.

John Henry quickly moved away from the window and said, "Captain, why don't you, me and Grayson duck in the spy room there and let J.D. confront him?"

"That sounds like a good idea."

Lewis hid in the shadows of the hallway until he heard the sound of the desk drawers opening in the office. He moved very quietly into the room and called to the man behind the desk, "Looking for something?"

"What? How the fuck did you get in here?"

Lewis was shocked when he saw that it was Jason Dantley sitting behind the desk. "Goddamn! I wasn't expecting you. I thought Barrows would come back."

"Well, he's busy."

"So you came instead. You know, this makes you an accessory to murder."

"Really? Well, you haven't arrested me and right now you don't have one damn shred of proof."

"The proof's in the bottom left drawer," he said, nodding his head. "You see, Ezra pulled through and told me what he saw in there."

"Damn it. I should've killed that fuckin' nigger when I had the change. I wanted to go to the hospital and finish the job, but Barrows said no."

"Are you saying you're the one who beat Ezra?"

"Yeah."

"Nice of you to confess."

"It won't do you any good, punk. You ain't gonna leave this house alive. Hey, I came back here to check on things and surprised a burglar and shot him in self-defense when he attacked me."

"Slick plan—if it works," he said, seeing Jason's hand slide behind his back. He knew he was reaching for a gun, but decided not to go for his own, hoping and praying that his gamble would pay off.

The gun came into view and Jason leveled it on his mid-section. "Oh, it'll work. Remember, Lewis, your name's mud in this town."

"Yeah, I guess you're right," he said, shaking his head. "Christ, when Barrows and the press get through with me this time, I probably won't even be able to get a funeral around here."

"Probably not," Jason said with a grin.

"I guess you've known about Zachary's hobby all along. Very unusual hobby—murder. Anyway, did you just cover for him or did you help him plan and commit the murders? Wait—before you answer that, I should advise you of your rights."

"What the hell for?" he laughed.

"Police procedure. Besides, I don't wanna fuck the case up with something like failing to inform you of your Constitutional Rights."

Jason laughed louder. "Hey, what the hell—if it'll make you feel any better, go right ahead."

Lewis quoted the advice of rights from memory and had Jason acknowledge that he understood them. He then said, "Now, did you just cover for Barrows or did you help him plan and commit the murders?"

"I've been a very loyal employee and a close friend for a very long time," he said as he moved to the front of the desk. "Of course, I knew what he was doing. But I sure as hell wasn't gonna ruin a good thing and turn him in. Hell, I earn a very substantial salary for what a lotta people consider being a flunky. You know, I bet I'm the only million-dollar-a-year chauffeur in the world. Naturally, most of that is cash paid under the table."

"That's very bad, Jason. The IRS is really gonna be pissed off when they find out that you've been cheating on your taxes."

"Too bad you won't be around to tell them about it," he said, squaring his stance and raising the pistol with a two-handed grip, sighting along the barrel at a spot directly in the center of Lewis' chest.

Jason flinched when he heard the cold, spine-chilling sound of a shell being racked into the chamber of a shotgun. The distinct clack, clack is like no other sound in the world, especially when it comes from only a few feet away. "Drop the gun, asshole," the deep voice said from behind him.

"Where'd you come from?" the million-dollar man said as he closed his eyes and let the pistol slip from his hands and drop to the floor.

"Your boss' little toy room behind the bookshelf. You know, he has some real nice equipment in there. In fact, Captain Thomas and I took the liberty of playing with some of his toys and we made a great videotape of you and J.D. talking out here."

"Shit," he mumbled and shook his head.

"Now, park your ass behind that desk and tell me where Tiffany is," Lewis said, pushing Jason backward. "And whatever you do, don't fuck with me. If you do, I'll make sure the word reaches whatever prison you go to that you're a police informer."

"She's at Brampton Hills Estates. It's 30 White Lake Drive."

"Zachary's there too, right?"

"Yeah. He's there."

"I think I'll just have your helicopter pilot fly me there. It'll be a lot faster than driving."

Grayson put handcuffs on Jason and led him to the sofa. "Sit down there and don't get antsy."

Lewis walked quickly to the desk and looked into the open drawer. "Damn, will you look at this." He gave a whistle. "Pictures. Rope. Bottles of Night Heat perfume. And what's this?" he said, pulling a thick brown leather covered journal from the bottom of the drawer. He looked quickly through the book, rapidly scanning the pages. "Jesus. Barrows kept a diary about the killings. It looks like everything's here, even some out of state murders. This is un-fuckin'-believable. Wait till we drop this on the world."

"J.D., I bet Barrows is expecting a call from our boy here, telling him all's well," John Henry said. "Maybe you'd better get on that chopper and get outta here."

"Yeah. I know," he said, the sick feeling coming back.

Jason grinned. "You know, it's probably already too late. By now your hot piece of ass is a cold, wet corpse."

J.D. turned and sprinted from the room. Down the corridor and out the front door he raced, heading straight to the still waiting helicopter. "Let's go," he said to the startled pilot.

"Who're you?"

"Police," he said, showing his badge. "Now get this fuckin' thing in the air and take me back to where you picked up Dantely."

"Yeah. Sure."

J.D. felt the fist of anxiety slam him in the stomach once more and wondered if he'd survive the flight without heaving his guts out. *Tiffany can't be dead*, he thought. *Not now. Not after all of this. She has to be alive. I need her.*

Forty

J.D. stared out of the chopper, his thoughts in chaos as he tried to piece together a plan to save the life of the woman who'd grown to mean so much to him. He toyed with the idea of calling ahead to the state police and asking for their help, but it was his uncertainty about Zachary's state of mind that kept him from calling. Strangers acting to defuse the situation might send him into a rage and that could mean the end of Tiffany's life.

He realized the textbook answer to his problem was to step aside and let somebody without personal ties to the case handle it. But in this particular instance, he thought it might be far wiser to ignore the handbook.

Zachary was beginning to glance anxiously at the clock on the wall as his angry pacing slowed to a crawl. His outburst stopped as abruptly as it started and Tiffany's concern for her safety was growing with each nervous twitch of his head toward the antique clock.

She thought the old clock had suddenly become a stopwatch, its turning hands timing a race between life and death. She needed a distraction and she needed it now. She hoped something would slow the hands of the clock, but for some reason making love was the only topic that came to mind. "Zachary, why'd you stop making love to me? Did I do something to drive you away from me?"

"Huh? Oh, uh—no."

"Tell me, please. Why'd you stop?"

"Why the hell do you wanna know?" he said, staring at her.

"Call it a woman's need to know. God knows I've suffered through many sleepless nights trying to find the answer and try as I might, I couldn't find one."

"Don't worry, it was nothing you did," he said, hoping she wouldn't continue to press him on the subject.

"That's not very comforting." She looked at him, trying to see inside him. " I think I deserve a little more than that for a reply. Even if you don't care to admit it, I was a loving wife for many, many years."

"Well, maybe I'm not in the mood to discuss my position," he snapped.

"I'm certainly not ready to go to my grave without some type of explanation."

"All right, Goddamn it!" he shouted. He returned to his rapid pacing, momentarily forgetting the clock on the wall. "After my degrading at the hands of Elizabeth Ames, I lost it. I couldn't perform with you. I was impotent. Now, is that what you wanted to hear? That I couldn't get it up?"

"No," she replied, sneaking a look at the clock. "But there were things that you could've done. There're counselors—"

"No. No. None of that shit for me. I worked it all out on my own."

"You mean you took it out on someone else," she said, anger creeping into her voice. "Was that the only way you could obtain sexual satisfaction? Hurt somebody?"

"Yes," he said with a harsh laugh.

"Did you rape me just to hurt me?"

He flashed a cruel smile. "No, Tiffany. Not just hurt you. I wanted you to know I was still the man of the house. And I balled you with that fuckin' cop downstairs. That was pure satisfaction. It was real power. I stuck my dick where he wanted his and he couldn't do a damn thing about it."

"And that's the only way you could get back at me—hurt me. You had to show me how powerful you were by taking me by force. That's why you raped the others, to show them you were boss. That's the only way you could do it."

"Yeah. It was the only way after my castration by the Ames whore. I dominated those bitches. I crushed them. I was the one with all the power, not them."

"Why didn't you squash Elizabeth Ames like you did the others?"

"I wanted to, believe me. Oh, I wanted to," he said, fire filling his eyes. "But I couldn't get to the fuckin' slut. I tried. Damn, I tried. But I think she knew I wanted to choke the life out of her."

"There had to be another way to solve your problems. If you'd only asked me, I would've done anything to help you."

"I guess that's why you've been fuckin' that young cop. So you could help me. If you wanted to help me so damn much, why were you in his bed?"

"Damn you, Zachary. How can you throw that in my face? You left me alone in bed for seven years. Do you know what it's like being ignored physically? To do without the warmth and affection of making love?"

"I gave you other things."

"My God," she cried. "Do you think diamonds and gold can take the place of being held and driven wild with passion?"

"So you decided to cheat on me."

"Cheat on you! I was a loyal, loving wife and you just abandoned me. Left me alone in that bed night after night, wondering what I'd done wrong. Asking myself where I'd gone wrong. I wanted you. I needed you. I even tried to seduce you and you turned away from me and I didn't know why. For seven years I lived through hell, wanting to feel a man pressed against me. To have a man take me in his arms and make love to me. To have my needs satisfied."

"So this young stud comes along, winks at you and you just peel your panties off and say, 'fuck me,' is that it?" His glare was unforgiving. "You had no right to do that. To embarrass me in front of everyone."

"That's what this is all about," she said, springing to her feet and pointing a finger at him. "Not that I made love with another man. I don't think you care about that at all. It's the embarrassment factor. The almighty Zachary Barrows lost his wife to another man and everybody knows. Well, just remember this, it was you who made the announcement to the whole world."

"You made me look like a fool," he hissed, slapping her hand down and throwing her to the floor.

"I didn't call the press conference."

He raised his hand to slap her and noticed the clock. He lowered his hand and said, "You think you're pretty damn smart, don't you?"

"What do you mean?"

"Get up, you bitch," he yelled, grabbing her by the wrist and jerking her violently to her feet. "I know what you're doing. You're just trying to buy some time. Well, my dear, your time has just about run out. Jason should've called by now to tell me he'd taken care of everything. Since he hasn't called, I can only assume he ran into your boyfriend and there's trouble ahead."

"If that's true, do you think killing me's going to solve your other problems?"

"Not at all, my darling. But it'll keep you from your lover's arms. No, I'm afraid Mr. Lewis won't have you around to screw silly and show off to his friends."

"He's not like that. He's not like you. I'm not some prize he holds up for display in public. To him I'm not a piece of meat. He doesn't flaunt—"

"Shut up, you tramp." His open hand caught her fully on the left side of the face, the force to the blow causing her head to snap sharply to the right. "Don't say another fuckin' word."

Tiffany tried to hold back the tears of pain caused by the powerful slap, while she fought to break free of his grasp. Her struggle, though, was in vain. Zachary's anger only seemed to double his strength.

"It's time for you to have that terrible accident," he growled, pulling her to her feet and dragging her across the room toward the door.

"Where am I going to have this horrible accident?"

"About a mile up that path behind our house is a very steep drop into the lake. It's well over a hundred feet down to the water. Maybe 150 feet. If you're lucky, you'll be dead before you hit the water." He turned around and dragged her out the door toward the hiking trail.

Tiffany wasn't going to stroll willingly up the path and be thrown to her death. She took every opportunity to drop to the ground, drag her feet or tug in the opposite direction. Her efforts were rewarded early on as it took several minutes to reach the path, a trip that would normally take only a minute or two.

When they reached the path, Zachary dragged a large red and white barricade labeled Trail Closed across the entrance. "I believe that'll discourage anyone from interrupting our journey."

Tiffany fought against him with every ounce of strength she could find. Both of them were avid fitness buffs, although she did more aerobic workouts than he. If she couldn't overpower him, maybe she could wear him down through sheer endurance.

They'd covered a small part of the journey when Zachary began to show signs of the struggle. Beads of perspiration formed on his brow and were trickling along his temples and down his face. "If I have to carry you up there," he panted, "you're going. Do you understand, bitch?"

"I damn well won't go of my own free will."

He shoved her to the ground, grabbed the front of her blouse and furiously ripped it open. Buttons tore away and spilled over the ground, looking like tiny blue dots against the rich brown soil. He ripped the fabric in half and dropped to his knees beside the path and pinned her arms behind her. Using one half of the ragged blouse he tightly bound her wrists and with the other he tied her ankles.

"So, we'll have to do this the hard way," he said, getting to his feet and standing over her.

The helicopter landed in a clearing about a half-mile from the house. Lewis quickly got out and cautiously approached the cabin. He studied the front of the house from behind a large pine tree and noticed the front door standing open. He darted from behind the tree and raced quickly toward the porch. He dropped low and listened for signs that someone was in the house, but there was no noise from inside.

He looked around the outside of the house and almost immediately his keen eyes picked up the telltale markings in the neatly manicured dark green grass. He followed the tracks to the back of the house, where the signs were even more obvious. Someone was being dragged across the grass. The broken blades of grass and the turned up pieces of soil led him to the path blocked by the sign reading Trail Closed. "Bullshit. I ain't buyin it," he muttered.

As he stepped around the barricade, he felt a greater sense of urgency. The evidence on the ground in front of him clearly pointed out that the struggle was becoming more and more violent. He knew Tiffany was leaving the clues behind for him as she fought with her husband and tried to keep him from killing her.

He pulled his boots and socks off and started running barefooted along the hiking trail, looking over the path in front of him for more evidence. Small rocks and twigs that dotted the path had little effect on his heavily callused feet, their jabs were more a nuisance than painful.

He paused briefly when he came upon the small blue buttons scattered around on the ground. He plucked one from the dirt and noticed the tattered material clinging to the pale threads. To his left the leaves had been turned up, their dewy underbelly now exposed to the light.

He dropped the button and bolted up the trail. His pace quickened with each stride, while his eyes continued to search ahead of him and left to right, looking for Tiffany and Zachary. It was the eyes of the hunter that saw the shimmering reflection through the trees on his right. A quick glance and he knew he was approaching a lake and suddenly Jason's comment about Tiffany being a wet corpse became crystal clear. Now he wondered if he was already too late.

Zachary continued to carry Tiffany over his right shoulder and saw that his goal was finally in sight. He pushed hard to make the last few steps and dropped to his knees when he reached the top. He lowered Tiffany to the ground and remained on his hands and knees, breathing heavily. The climb up to the top in itself wasn't that hard for anyone who was in relatively good physical condition. But making the climb while carrying Tiffany, who fought him almost every step of the way, only made it harder.

"What now?" she said cynically. "You can't throw me in the lake with my hands and feet tied and expect everybody to believe it was an accident." She talked with a purpose, hoping to trick him into freeing her earlier than he wanted. If he untied her, she could fight him, or run when or if an opportunity presented itself. "Come on. Hurry. What's it gonna be? You can't wait all day."

"I'll take care of everything," he puffed.

"Oh, yes, I forgot. The brilliant businessman has a plan for every event. Bribery. Blackmail. Murder."

"That's right," he snarled, pushing himself to an upright position beside her. His eyes narrowed and he growled through clenched teeth, "I have a plan for you, Tiffany. I won't be fooled by your taunts. I know what you want. You want me to untie you so you can try to get away. Sorry. You won't escape."

He moved to straddle her, but she dug her feet into the ground and pushed, scooting backward to avoid him. He rapidly overtook her, pouncing like an angry bear on top of her and throwing her down to the dirt path. Fear rushed over her as he pinned her shoulders to the ground and glared at her with hate-filled eyes.

"Maybe I should fuck you one last time," he said, his face seemingly contorting into a hideous mask as his hands inched toward her throat. "Wouldn't you like to have one last fuck before you die?"

"Not with you," she cried.

For a few seconds his powerful hands actually caressed her neck almost lovingly. Then without warning the revolting monster tightened his grip on her throat and a smile creased his face. She fought to raise her body from the ground and throw him off of her, but he only increased the pressure on his death grip. She thrashed around beneath him, her lungs screaming for precious air that suddenly wouldn't come to them. She tried to scream, but there was no sound.

Suddenly, a blurred, dark figure appeared from nowhere and harsh words floated on the wind. The grisly monster above her sagged and she felt a distant sensation of being crushed and then the mass hurtled through space and was gone. The steel jawed wrench that had clasped her throat opened and cherished oxygen rushed into her lungs.

She coughed and tried to sit up while her heart pounded against her chest. She blinked to clear her watery eyes while she struggled to a sitting position.

She began to tremble and tears filled her eyes as she saw J.D. throw Zachary to the ground and put the handcuffs on his wrists.

After checking the handcuffs to make sure they were secure, Lewis rushed to her side. "Tiffany. Tiffany, are you okay?" he said, pulling her to him. He brushed her hair back and reached to untie her restraints. "Are you okay? God, please be okay."

She nodded her head and sobbed as he untied her. She tried to talk, but was too badly shaken. She shook her head again, fell into his arms and cried. Her nightmare was over.

He held her for a moment and then let go long enough to take off his black tee shirt. He gently eased the shirt over her head and helped her push her arms through the sleeves as she continued to cry. "It's okay," he whispered. "He can't hurt you now."

Several minutes went by before he got up and helped her to her feet. She felt weak and her legs seemed as though they were refusing to support her. Lewis held her and softly brushed his hand through her hair until she was able to stand without his help.

"Do you think you can walk down the hill?"

"Yes," she said, her voice a faint whisper.

He left her and walked to where Zachary was still lying face down in the brush. He guided him from a prone to a kneeling position and finally to his feet. He moved back a few steps to create his personal safety zone before facing the former king of the business world. "Mr. Barrows, at this time I'm gonna advise you of your constitutional rights. I sure as hell don't want somebody accusing me of improprieties in this case."

"Don't worry," Barrows said, slowly shaking his head. "I won't accuse you of any wrongdoing. I think you beat me fair and square."

"Well, I still have to advise you of your rights," he said, pulling a small card from his wallet and reading the Miranda rights to Barrows. As he tucked the card away he said, "Do you understand your rights?"

"Yes. I understand them. But I'll only talk to you."

"What do you mean?"

"I'll talk to you," Barrows said meekly. "I'll tell you everything."

"What? Why would you wanna do that?" he said, shaking his head and trying to understand exactly what Zachary Barrows was saying to him.

"Lewis, I knew from the moment I met you that you'd be a formidable opponent. And even knowing it, I very foolishly underestimated you. I don't like you. Make no mistake about that. But I damn sure respect you and I won't deal with any man I don't hold in high esteem."

He nodded. "Sir, in that case, I'd very much like to talk to you when we get back to Huntley Manor."

They walked in silence down the trail with Zachary leading the way. By the time they reached the bottom of the hill, state police cars were pulling into the driveway and a police helicopter circled overhead.

Lewis was told that Captain Thomas had asked the state police to help in the arrest of Barrows. But seeing that they were a little late for that, they offered to take him to Huntley Manor. Lewis welcomed their help and turned Barrows over to two troopers who walked him to the helicopter for the trip home.

When the last state police car left, J.D. and Tiffany walked toward the cabin. Even though the cabin was just a short distance away, it seemed liked a very long walk Just inside the door, Tiffany gave him a weak smile as she removed his tee shirt and handed it to him.

She went to the bedroom to get a new blouse and stood in the doorway fastening the buttons while she looked across the room at J.D. "God, I really need time for all of this to sink in."

"Yeah. I guess you do."

"I...I'm—Hell, I don't know what I am right now," she said, her voice still a harsh rasp. "Shocked? Stunned? I don't know."

"Yeah. I know how you feel," he said, taking a few steps toward her. "Believe me, I was surprised too."

"You didn't suspect him at all?"

"Not at first. Not until I started looking over every little detail."

"When were you sure?"

"When I found out that Ester Wentworth-Fox was his grandmother. Damn, that was like somebody smacking me between the eyes with a two by four. After that everything just sort of fell into place. But Ezra really sealed it."

"God, I almost forgot about him. Is he okay?"

"Oh, yes. He's definitely getting better."

"How did Ezra seal it?"

"It's a long story," he said, crossing the room and touching her cheek. "Why don't I explain it to you on the way home."

"On one condition."

"Name it."

"I think I need a good stiff drink. I have an unopened bottle of 25-year-old Macallan I've been saving for the right moment. You know, I think this is it."

He smiled. "Okay. I'll drive. You drink."

"You have to drive the Rolls."

"I can handle it."

She packed a bottle of spring water into a small cooler with ice and picked up the bottle of scotch. She glanced around the cabin and remembered happier times there. Days that now seemed like they were from another era. She nodded her head and said softly, "I'm ready to go now."

She sipped her Macallan straight and listened to a tale, which by its very nature seemed like it should belong to someone else. But she'd been unwittingly cast as an intricate player. The unsuspecting wife and near perfect alibi. Sadly, the saga remained incomplete. There were other chapters waiting to be released.

They were only minutes from the mansion when he ended what amounted to most of the story. She wondered what the unfinished part of the story would reveal about the man she once loved and what, if any, effect it would have on her life and the relationship with the man seated beside her.

Forty-one

The gathering outside the gates at 21 Huntley Manor Road looked like a Hollywood extravaganza. Television and newspaper reporters mingled with dozens of well-dressed nearby neighbors and hundreds of others who crossed the bridge to witness the homecoming of Tiffany Barrows. Three uniformed police officers raised their arms and waved their hands to part the sea of humanity to let the Rolls Royce pass under the archway. Inside the gate Lewis gunned the engine and sped up the hill away from the curious eyes and intrusive cameras.

He stopped under the canopy at the entrance to the mansion as the double doors swung open to greet them. John Henry and Captain Thomas escorted them into the foyer where Rose Anna and Lolita waited. Hugs and handshakes topped the agenda, with a few tears of joy mixed in to complete the welcome home.

Although Lewis wanted to stay there with Tiffany, he knew other very important issues needed his immediate attention. Zachary Barrows had said he was willing to talk with him, and the smart decision was to act before he changed his mind or an attorney stepped in and advised him against it.

Rose Anna immediately acted as a self-appointed guardian for Tiffany. She flitted around like a mother hen hovering over a nest of young hatchlings, but took time to walk Lewis to the door. "Please hurry back."

"I'll do my best," he said. "And listen, please don't let any of those other so-called best friends lurking outside the gate in here to hound her. She's been through enough and doesn't need to sit here and answer a thousand questions from them."

"Gee, all they want is a little juicy gossip."

"Screw 'em. Let 'em suffer."

He opened the holding cell and escorted Barrows to an interview room on the second floor. The room was empty except for a large wooden table and two chairs that sat in the middle of the room. Three of the walls were a faded shade of beige while the fourth was a mirror running corner to corner.

He informed Barrows of his constitutional rights again and had him sign the form acknowledging he was aware of his rights provided by the Miranda Decision. When the formalities were finished, Zachary Barrows agreed to a taped interview. "I certainly have a lot to tell you. I hope you have plenty of tapes."

"Well, we can always send out for more."

Barrows smiled. "Yeah. I guess we could."

The session lasted over five hours and several tapes were needed to document the secret life of Zachary Barrows. When the recorder was finally turned off, Barrows stood up and offered his hand to Lewis as if he was giving a final signal of surrender. "If there's anything else you want to know, you know where to find me."

"Yes, sir."

Barrows laughed. "Always the polite son-of-a-bitch. I like that."

Lewis took him back to the cell and walked to Captain Thomas' office. "Christ, did you hear all of that?"

"Damn near every word of it," Thomas said.

"Man, the shrinks are gonna have a ball with this one. Can you believe it? If my math's correct, Barrows is good for 26 murders."

"Listen, you've had a damn long day. Don't try and sort all of this out right now," Thomas said, sliding his chair back and getting to his feet. "Print up charging documents for one of the killings and I'll have Adams and his buddies take care of the processing and bail review."

Lewis smiled. "I bet they'll just love that."

"Fuck 'em. Let 'em eat a little crow."

"Thank you, sir."

"I'll wait for you," Thomas said, refilling his coffee cup. "We might as well walk out together and wave to the press."

"There's only one thing I'd like to wave to the press, but I'd better not."

Reporters and television camera crews swarmed around the front entrance of the police station like a pack of jackals. The story of the decade was in the making and each of them wanted a share of the glory as one who reported it.

Thomas and Lewis walked out into the gathering and immediately the questions began. "Is it true Zachary Barrows is under arrest for multiple murders?"

"Mr. Barrows has been charged with one count of homicide at this time," Thomas said. "The investigation is on-going and if it's determined additional charges are warranted, they'll be filed at that time."

"Captain, can you tell us which murder he's been charged with?"

"Yes. He's been charged with the murder of Gary Wilson."

"But Wilson's death was ruled a suicide by the medical examiner."

"At the time it was reported to the press that his death was a suicide. It was released like that at the request of Detective Jefferson Lewis in order to give him enough time to complete his investigation and not tip the killer he was on to him."

"Detective Lewis, what can you tell us about your investigation?"

"I have no comment at this time," he said coldly. "It's like Captain Thomas said, the investigation's continuing and if it's deemed that additional charges are appropriate, they'll be filed at that time."

"Detective, would you care to comment on your relationship with Mrs. Barrows?"

"I believe Mr. Zachary Barrows provided you with a most eloquent description of our relationship during a press conference he arranged," Lewis said, giving a picture of perfect self-control. "Or would you be happier if I gave it to you in much simpler terms? Would you like it a lot better if I stood here and told you we've been fuckin' each other's eyes out? Is that what you'd like?" His calm reply was like a tidal wave, first drawing them out from their shelters and then slamming them to the ground.

"Damn, they didn't expect that answer," Thomas said, ushering him through the stunned crowd and across the parking lot. "That's the only time I can recall any of them not having a follow-up question."

"Shit. I wonder how much trouble I'll be in for that remark?"

"I wouldn't worry about it. They had it coming. Anyway, they'll forget it in a few days."

"Oh, by the way, Captain, I've gotta tell you what happened when I went to get the search warrant signed."

"If you're referring to Judge O'Boyle, I already know. John Henry filled me in while we were waiting for you to get back. I've notified Chief Greenberg and he's taking the necessary steps in that regard, which will probably include criminal charges."

"Good," he said, turning to unlock his car. "It's about time somebody did something about that prick. He damn near cost Tiffany her life."

Thomas walked over and extended his hand to him. As they shook hands he said, "I want to commend you on a job well done. It took courage to stick by your convictions when everybody, including me, doubted you. If you gave up and walked away, God only knows how many other innocent women would've died."

"Thanks. And, just in case you didn't know, I don't give up easily."

"I always knew that," Thomas said, nodding. "That's why I fought so damn hard to get you in the Bureau."

He opened the car door and paused. "I'll turn over every rock and crawl under every leaf if it's necessary and if I step on a few toes along the way—so be it."

Thomas laughed. "Hell, the way things were going in my life, I'm surprised you didn't take a look at me."

"You never know, Captain, maybe I did," he said, sliding in behind the wheel of his car. As he eased the car from the parking space he nodded, saying, "And, if I had, at least I would've proved your innocence."

Thomas laughed. "Thanks. I'm sure you would've."

When he got back to the mansion he gave John Henry a brief rundown of Barrows' confession. But he still faced the difficult task of telling Tiffany that her husband was a serial killer.

Although Tiffany offered John Henry the comfort and convenience of staying the night in the mansion, he declined. He'd learned a great deal while J.D. was out of the house about the relationship she shared with him. And, in light of everything that had happened that day, he felt that having time to themselves was the best prescription. But he did agree to stick around town for a few days.

Everyone took John Henry's leaving as their cue to leave as well. It was obvious from Tiffany's anxious glances that she had a great deal on her mind and their being there was keeping her from clearing the air.

As soon as the large doors closed behind the last friend, she turned to J.D. and said, "Let's hunt down that bottle of scotch and go to the library. Or should I say your former office?"

Just inside the library door he took her in his arms and kissed her. When their lips finally parted, he said, "At least we don't have to worry about being filmed this time."

"Where's the camera?"

"In the bookcase over there," he said, pointing over his shoulder. "The bound book in the center is where the spying eye is hidden. Of course, that's how he knew everything I was doing. He was able to get my password to the computer and could access every report. What wasn't in writing he heard in our conversations or overheard when I talked to someone on the phone. That's why I was beginning to feel like the killer was always a step ahead of me."

"God, it's still so hard to believe."

"Yeah. I know."

"How many women did he murder?"

"Twenty-five," he answered, taking a deep breath. "And he and Jason killed Gary Wilson and tried to make it look like suicide. He told me that Jason wrote the note on his personal computer which, by the way, was the same computer used to write the letters to the victims."

"You mean Jason was in on it all along?"

"Yeah. In fact, Jason loyal employee that he was, helped set up a lot of the alibis. All the killings here took place while Zachary was out of town on business—or so it seemed. If you stop and think about it, Jason and Zachary are almost identical in height, weight and build. When Zachary popped his cork and started killing the women around here they started driving out of their way to use another airport when they left town. Jason would leave under your husband's name and Zachary would follow on a later flight after murdering one of his victims. On the later fight he used the name Jason Dantley."

"Very clever," she said, shaking her head. "But how did he convince Madeline and the others to let him get so close to them?"

"He was no fool. He told them he had a very confidential business deal to offer. He said it was so hush hush he had to talk to them in complete secrecy. Nobody, not even their husbands, were to be informed. Hell, he even went so far as to walk into their house with a portfolio under his arm."

"And the tidying up?"

"That came from Mrs. Wentworth-Fox. She was obsessed with neatness. She'd punish him if spilled a drop of soup or milk. She was a real tyrant. She disciplined him, one way or another, almost every day and forced him to keep everything in its exact place. I missed it at first, but I remembered seeing him arrange and rearrange papers on his desk until they were exactly like he wanted them. His knife and fork had to be just so on the table."

"My God, you're right. I remember from the time we first began dating that Zachary seemed almost consumed with cleanliness and neatness."

"Neatness wasn't the only thing he picked up from Granny Ester," he said, pouring a scotch. "I'm certain that's were the warning letter developed too. She'd warn him ahead of time about his next punishment and where it was to take place and a lot of times she'd do it in a note. Eventually she stopped the note writing and he stopped sending warning letters. A pattern of behavior learned in childhood."

"The black rope knotted on the right side of the throat," she said, taking a sip from her glass, "was that because of his grandmother's fixation with black silk scarves?"

"Probably. Of course, I don't know whether or not he was killing her every time he knotted the rope around somebody's throat, or if he was just killing another successful businesswoman. That's for the shrinks to figure out."

"What do you think will happen to him?"

"I don't know," he said, shaking his head. "It's too early to tell. I'm sure there'll be insanity claims and Christ knows how many motions'll be filed before the courts. Hell, this could go on for years."

She took a sip of her drink, causally eyeing him over the rim of the glass. A lifetime seemed to have passed in only a few days. So much had happened. So many ugly things that needed to be erased. Zachary's brutal penetration of her body, an act that she'd conceal from J.D. It was over and nothing could be done to change it, therefore she didn't think it was necessary to hurt him with it. But she thought that making love to J.D. with an animal-like ferocity would be the only way for her to chase away the demons left behind by all she'd been through.

Tiffany got up from the sofa, walked to the desk and put her glass down. A fire was beginning to burn in her eyes as she looked at him. It was an inferno the likes of which he'd never seen before. Her hands moved deliberately to the top of her blouse and, after a brief moment of hesitation, she ripped it open. Buttons tore away and showered into the air like hailstones as she hurriedly took off her bra. The hailstones fell silently to the car carpet as her breasts sprang free of their restraint. "Take me," she whispered. "Take me here. Take me now, Cowboy."

Clothes pulled off in a hurry landed in a devil-may-care heap. Boots with high-heeled shoes. Jeans with a skirt and a tee shirt fell with a blouse and became entangled with a bra.

Their bodies clashed in a passionate attack and quickly joined one to the other in a fiery embrace. There was an urgent savagery in their joining, fueled by days apart and her need to chase away the ugly demons that tried to devour her very soul. The savage battering lasted longer than they expected and when it exploded they collapsed in a pool of passion's sweet, pungent perspiration. Their slippery bodies remained meshed in love's tight grip as they breathed deeply, savoring the intimate but violent road back to sanity.

Forty-two

The arrest of Zachary Barrows sent shock waves rippling through the community. A man who, although ruthless in the business world, stood as a pillar of generosity and strength among the every day citizens. His contributions to worthy causes and charitable organizations caused blind eyes to be turned to his business dealings. Days later when he was charged with the vicious killings of his neighbors and friends, people were even more shocked. And when the total picture of what he'd done came into focus, reporters telling the story were clearly stunned.

Though Zachary captured the top headlines, Lewis and Tiffany were not spared from stinging barbs of criticism. Stories filled with phrases such as adulterous liaison, lust-filled nights, lascivious deeds and scandalous, erotic seduction were aired just as often and were talked about again privately.

Lewis was said to be a poor boy from the wrong side of the tracks and his pursuit of Tiffany was motivated purely by greed. It was his preoccupation with money that caused his failure to properly investigate the stalker murders reports said.

The searing comments about J.D. and Tiffany stopped abruptly when a local reporter stood up and defended them. The longtime journalist jumped into the fire with both feet. Her cutting editorial reminded other veteran reporters and citizens alike that Detective J.D. Lewis was, in fact, the man responsible for solving the crimes. Her brash in your face and refresh your memory reports sent seasoned newscasters scurrying for cover.

While newsmen and women backpedaled, she said, "If the fires of love were kindled by the meeting of Detective J.D. Lewis and Tiffany Barrows, remember, their introduction was not by chance. They were brought together by design. A devious, clever scheme by a murderer who sought to conceal his deeds by casting his own wife and the man assigned to protect her as his alibi. Detective Jefferson Lewis didn't go to the Barrows residence with the seduction of Tiffany Barrows in mind. He went there for the sole purpose of carrying out his assigned duties. The notion that his intent was to seduce

Mrs. Barrows exists only in the narrow minds of those who thrive on such trash and those who report it."

Even with a new ally standing firmly in his corner, J.D. Lewis was still troubled by growing thoughts of uncertainty. He continued to go around with Tiffany in a world where he believed he not only didn't belong, but also was unwelcome. Suspicious glances and accusing glares were more often what he got instead of pleasant smiles and greetings with open arms.

Publicly, Tiffany gave the appearance that the nasty words and scornful looks didn't bother her. Privately, however, she was beginning to show signs that all of it was beginning to get to her. At times she seemed listless, often excusing herself half way through a meal to go lie down and rest. Always a physical fitness enthusiast, she now dreaded the thought of going to the spa.

Lewis noticed her uncharacteristic behavior and saw the dark clouds that had once been over the horizon coming closer. It was time to break the chains that were pulling her down. After dinner, a meal she barely touched, he suggested that they take a walk and enjoy the evening breeze. She walked beside him in silence over the freshly mowed grass and felt the tension filled air that surrounded them.

"Tiffany," he said after many long minutes of agonizing silence, "I think it's time for me to leave."

"I don't want you to go," she said as the words she feared most, but had expected were coming, rang in her ears. "I want you to stay. You know that, don't you?"

"Yes. Yes, I do. But you know I can't stay."

"No, I don't know that. Why? Why can't you stay?"

"God, Tiffany, I don't belong here," he said. "I'm destroying your life. I'm driving your friends away."

"Pardon me, Cowboy, but to put it in terms that I know you understand, that's pure bullshit. My true friends are the ones, like Rose Anna, who stood by me when all of this blew up. I'm not the one who committed murder. It was Zachary. I don't have a thing to be ashamed of. I shared my bed with you. That's certainly not a crime deserving of the death penalty or life in prison. If it was, 90 percent of my so-called friends would be dead or off somewhere serving time."

"Please try to understand," he said, turning to look at her. "This isn't my world. I don't fit in on this side of the bridge. Hell, you know I'm not comfortable here."

"You seem to be doing just fine to me."

"I know I go through the motions and put up a good front. So I'm a good actor. But believe me, I feel like an alien every time we walk into the country club. Christ, the first night I walked in there with you after Zachary's arrest, they tore me apart with their eyes. I don't like that. You've seen what I like. Where I fit in. You've been there."

"They'll accept you in time," she said, trying to force a smile. "They don't know you like I do. But when they get to know you, things'll be different."

"Jesus," he said, tossing his hands up, "I can't stand in front of those people and bow my head and beg them to like me or accept me. And I damn well won't kiss their asses just to win their seal of approval."

"Let's forget them. What about us?"

"We're fine. Or we were. Things have been very tense between us for the past few days. I—"

"Think of what we've just gone through," she cried. "Think about what I've been through." For a fleeting instant she thought about telling him that Zachary had raped her, but pushed the idea aside. "Think about what you've been through. My God, the press tore you apart and I'm sure some of your fellow officers did the same. I certainly think that's reason enough for a little tension to creep into our lives."

"Yeah. Okay. So that kind of tension'll go away. But I'm not too sure about the dirty looks and snide comments. There'll always be somebody willing to insinuate that Zachary was really the one who was screwed in all of this and we should be hung in the market place for what we did."

"You've already made up your mind, haven't you? No matter what I say, you're going to leave, right?"

"Tiffany, I have to leave," he said softly. "I can't stay."

"Then at least stay with me tonight," she said, swallowing hard and fighting back the tears.

"God, I know I shouldn't," he whispered. "That's only gonna make things that much more difficult in the morning, but I'll stay."

They slept little during the night. The time was spent embracing and kissing away the tears. Soft words were spoken with hopes of easing her pain, but he knew in his heart no words would chase away her agony.

By the time dawn's first light streamed through the shades, he wished he'd left last night. He felt his own hurt starting and realized it was something that would probably last a very long time. This time the pain would linger much longer than other heartaches. But then his luck with love was never good.

Very little was said as they walked to his car. Their steps were purposely slow, prolonging the inevitable. There was no way to say a painless goodbye. Cheerful words would be a lie.

They shared one last kiss before he turned and walked away. His final steps to the car were quick and he didn't dare look back. He was afraid that if he looked back, he'd give in and stay. If he went back now the wounds would only be deeper with the next goodbye.

As his car sped up and disappeared over the crest of the hill, her tears fell freely and she sobbed, "Damn it, Cowboy, it's not supposed to end like this. Westerns are supposed to have happy endings."

Forty-three

By noon Lewis was at his desk, rummaging through the endless mound of paper and praying that work would make him forget that he'd just walked out of many a man's dream world. He got a few thumbs-up gestures and a pat or two on the back from some officers who'd gained a new respect for him. Adams, Wallace and Hargrove kept their distance, but Grayson openly praised him.

Tiffany cried a lot during the first days of his absence, but when Ezra made an unannounced return from his hospital stay, her life brightened considerably. Nobody could be around Ezra for very long and not be affected by his broad, infectious grin and keen wisdom. The old man truly could infect an entire roomful of people with his exuberance and wit.

He could see the sorrow within her eyes and hear the sadness in her voice when they talked. He patiently waited for the right time before he took the step from butler to love's counselor. And when the moment presented itself, he moved with the swiftness of a bird riding the wind and spoke as softly as a warm summer breeze. "Miss Tiffany, I can see you're deeply troubled."

"Oh, God, yes I am, Ezra. I think broken-hearted is more like it."

"Ah, things didn't go well between you and Mr. Lewis."

"I thought they were fine. Then all of a sudden they just fell apart."

"Why don't we just sit here at the table for a little while and you can tell me all about it, Miss Tiffany."

"You know, I'd like that, Ezra," she said, twirling the spoon in tiny circles in her cup of coffee. "That is, if you don't mind."

"Oh, no, Miss Tiffany. I don't mind at all."

"You know, J.D. put a new spark in my life. For the first time in years I felt alive. I was happy. Oh, I know the lovemaking behind Zachary's back was, by our moral standards, wrong. But the man I once dearly loved had already betrayed me. For seven long years I had no love life. Then by a stroke of fate J.D. Lewis walked into my life. Things changed almost immediately. It was crazy, but it was like he was the man I'd been waiting for."

"Well, Miss Tiffany, sometimes when you least expect it, a spark of mysterious magic just appears. Then you just have to wait for all the sparks to come together and make a ragin' fire. Once the fire's lit, everything else just kinda falls into place."

"I thought all the right sparks and the fire was there. Then he turns around and tells me he has to leave. He can't stay here on this side of the bridge he says. I don't understand that reasoning at all."

"Mr. Lewis is a proud man. He's got lots of pride for a man so young. I don't think he wants people to believe he loves you just for your money. He—"

"Do you think he loves me?"

"He sure does. Just as much as you love him."

"How did you know that?" she said, dropping the spoon to the table.

"Oh, that's easy, Miss Tiffany. I know how to read all the signs. I've had lots of practice."

"If I'm so much in love with him, why am I so miserable?"

"You can take my word for it, he's just as miserable as you. Maybe more."

"Then how do I get a man back who says he doesn't belong over here on this side of the bridge?"

Ezra's grin grew broader and brighter. "You know, Miss Tiffany, there's one nice thing 'bout a bridge—it can be crossed from either side."

Moisture formed in her eyes, turning an already lovely shade of blue, deeper. She began to laugh, then cry, and soon an odd combination of laughter and sobs mixed. "Thank you, Ezra. Thank you so much. That was a lovely thing you did and it's oh so beautiful and makes so much sense."

"You're quite welcome."

Detective Jefferson Daniel Lewis had barely completed the last sentence of his report on the Society Stalker murders when Captain Thomas dropped a fresh corpse in his lap. "This just came in. A convicted child molester was just found dead in his car about a block from his apartment. Smells a little like an execution to me. Sorry. Looks like you're it."

Sometime later as he stood looking over the crime scene, Doctor Sidney Wexler peeled off his latex gloves while walking toward him. "So, you caught this one too, huh? In a nutshell, I think you've got another live one on your hands. This was an execution, pure and simple. Double tap to the head at close range. I'm guessing a small caliber gun. Probably a twenty-two."

"Well, Doc, see you tomorrow for the autopsy."

Lewis stepped into his apartment, pushed the door shut behind him and shuffled aimlessly across the floor. *Another murder's the last thing I need right now*, he thought. *I'm tired. Worn out.* True, he was tired. But it was more than the tracking down of a killer that had taken its toll on him. It was losing the woman he loved that really caused him to have sleepless nights.

He cursed himself as he opened the refrigerator door and took an icy bottle of beer from the top shelf. He twisted off the cap and tossed it on the counter as he stared at the telephone, fighting the impulse to call Tiffany. It seemed like years had passed since he heard her voice, or felt her near. He only had to pick up the phone and push the numbers to ease the pain. But he stubbornly refused to take that step.

He raised the bottle to his lips and gulped down the frosty gold liquid, hoping it would drown his sorrow. Then again if he drank enough of it, it would certainly numb his pain. Of course, in the morning another pain would join with his heartache to make his life even more miserable. Then, aspirin washed down with coffee would take the place of his regular breakfast menu. All in all, it didn't seem like a good idea.

While thinking over his options there was a gentle tapping at his door. He trudged to door with beer in hand, wondering what kind of fool would dare invade his private moments of self-pity. He angrily jerked the door open and suddenly found his heart in his throat. The lovely, beautiful woman who haunted his dreams night and day stared at him with a look of determination in her eyes. "Wha…what are you doing here?" he said.

"Since you were too damn stubborn to come to me, I decided to cross the bridge and come to you."

"Why?"

"I took the advice of a wonderful, perceptive man."

"Ezra, right?"

"Yes."

"And what did he tell you?" he said, trying to hide his smile.

"First, that we loved each other. Then, that a bridge could be crossed from either side."

"Ezra's a very smart man," he said, his smile turning to a broad grin. "His advice, well, it's always good."

"That's why I took it. Look, Cowboy, maybe you think you don't fit in on my side of the bridge, but I know I fit in over here. I already have."

"Yeah. You have."

"So," she said, putting her hands on her hips, "are you gonna invite me in and make love to me? Or do you intend to leave me out here until winter?"

"I'll get your bags."

She gave him barely enough time to close the door before jumping into his arms.

"This is as far as I can make it without you."

"I didn't think I'd get this far."

As they laughed and kissed and talked about making up for past heartaches, a wise old man settled down in an antiquated rocking chair outside the house on Huntley Manor Road. A smile of satisfaction began to crease his lips as once again, Ezra, the mystical wizard, had concocted a magical potion.

Ezra Dawkins was as cunning as a spider weaving its web to snare an unsuspecting prey. With well-chosen words he'd captured the lonely woman and sent her on her way to find happiness. His job, for the time being at least, was finished. He rocked back in his chair, his smile broadening until he wore a grin so big it seemed to add another brilliant star to the dark night sky.

~~~~~

Printed in the United Kingdom
by Lightning Source UK Ltd.
124772UK00003B/67/A

In the hazy mist of happiness, storm clouds of uncertainty were already forming over the horizon. He was worried. He remembered that he'd told Rose Anna that he was unlucky in love. Now he wondered if his luck would run out again.